Beneath
The
Secrets

By

Alan J. Brown

ISBN 0-9720137-4-1

Acknowledgements:

Thanks to the Suders, cover models.
Adam Gilbert's photography.
Editing Mary Kay Peirce and John Nebeker.
Cover design by Sarah B. Seiter.
Deirdra A. Peirce (wonder woman coordinator).

Published by

Quick & Easy Publishing
P. O. Box 971411
Orem, Utah 84097
1-801-623-1597
nebekerjohnrc@msn.co

This book is dedicated to:

Bonnie and Josh
Without you two, this book, along with many other
aspects of my life, would never have been
completed.
I love you very much. Thank you.

Also, to my parents and extended family.
Your support has been wonderful and truly
appreciated.

And finally, to Doug. Thanks for the insight and
direction.

Chapter One

Cameron Bird stared down at the ground as he walked away from his friend's house. The sun scorched his arms and his feet were already worn out. Even worse, he hated the fact that he was leaving his friends like this, but he wasn't in the mood to party. He hadn't meant to be rude, although he was sure that was how he had come across. It was too bad, too. He liked Marcus Layton and Sandy McKell. The last thing he wanted was to make them mad.

The night had started off innocently enough, but as soon as Cam worked his way through the living room and into the kitchen, he figured that coming had been a mistake. After declining a beer, he knew he had blown the entire evening.

"You know you need it!" Marcus taunted, knowing that was all it was going to take to get Cam to join the party. That was all it ever took. No one in the world could control Cam, no one except Marcus. Marcus waited for a response and even picked up an extra beer off the oval kitchen table.

Cam bit his tongue nervously and tried to find a way to say no. Surely there was more to life than cold beer and parties. Marcus was right, though. He did need it, and this dependency was beginning to show more and more as his life went on. Because of alcohol, he was without a girlfriend—again; he was depressed, and he was skipping work more and more (a seven dollar per hour sales job at a local bookstore). He tried not to acknowledge these problems, but drinking was controlling his entire life.

Still, partying was his way of having fun. It had been for twelve of the twenty-five years he'd been alive. That was his way of enjoying himself. It was also how he was coping with the boredom the world was offering him. Lately, however, he found himself worried that his entire life was pointless. He was heading in the wrong direction. With nowhere else to go, however, he just continued traveling along that path.

"I don't know. I'm not really in the mood," Cam half-lied. The familiar kitchen seemed to embrace the faint scent of stale coffee and alcohol. It was a combination he was used to, and even enjoyed.

Marcus laughed out loud and lifted his can into the air. "It's a miracle! Cameron Bird isn't in the mood to drink!" Marcus stood up from behind the table and took two steps towards Cam. "And exactly what are you in the mood for, Cameron? What else is there in life?" Marcus mimicked Cam as if he had read Cam's very thoughts.

Cam smiled. He didn't really want to be left out of the game of quarters. He slowly held out his hand. "Fine, maybe one or two beers," he said and took the silver can from Marcus. It was cold and fit in his hand perfectly.

"Yea," Marcus said and laughed in victory. "One, or two, or twenty."

Marcus was a good friend, at least as far as Cam was concerned. Over the past few years, Cam had even learned to respect Marcus. Although he was a party animal, Marcus never let it get in the way of what was important. Cam admired that. If it needed to be done, Marcus always found a way to do it. Most obvious, was the fact that he had worked for Mr. Simmons construction business for six years. He seldom missed work; not even for a hangover.

Cam half laughed at Marcus and sat down in the empty seat next to Sandy McKell, Marcus' girlfriend of two years—someone Cam really cared for. To his right, sat a nice looking girl he had never met. The idea of a strange face in this house was not extraordinary. It was a party house. The fact that this girl was sitting at the table meant nothing to Cam—at least not until Marcus went out of his way to introduce her.

"Cam, this is Heather. Heather—Cam." Marcus turned his attention back to Cam, and as if Heather had just disappeared, he added one more thought. "Kinda' cute, ain't she?"

Cam wasn't sure if he was supposed to answer the question or just sit there and feel embarrassed. He could tell his face was turning bright red, which probably meant that the latter was the only response he would be able to offer. Yes, she was cute. Her blue eyes stood out prominently. She was skinny, blonde, and it looked as if she had intentionally accentuated her curvaceous body. He chose to keep these thoughts to himself.

Cam looked around the kitchen, mostly to hide his face. It was clean, other than a few beer cans sitting on the counter by the sink. One of the bulbs in the fixture above his head was burned out leaving the entire room dimmer than it really should be. It had been this way for quite some time, but at that moment, it seemed to stand out in Cam's mind. In reality, the entire kitchen was very bland. It was basically a drinking room. Once in a while, Marcus and Sandy actually used the room to eat in, but only when they couldn't afford to eat out. They never seemed to have money, but they ate out a lot.

"It's your turn, Marcus." Sandy's high-pitched voice broke the silence. Her words sounded guarded, but Cam was focused internally and barely even noticed.

The warmth in Cam's face didn't subside until he had consumed a few more swallows of what was once again serving as his safety net. He found it very easy to hide behind the feelings that the first few drinks produced. He certainly concealed himself there far too often.

For a while, Cam gave in to the fact that he needed a drink—whether he wanted it or not. Just like his friends, he had to drink. It was the only way to feel completely comfortable, especially if he was being set up with Heather—and it was obvious that he was.

As they drank, they listened to the loud pounding of rock and roll music. The sound came from everywhere. Marcus had installed surround sound speakers on almost every wall in the house. Each speaker had its own personal mute button— just in case someone needed a little peace and quiet, but this was seldom the case.

Marcus and Sandy did their best to get Cam and Heather together. In the end, however it all came down to the fact that Cam's mind wouldn't cooperate. As much as he tried to change the fact, he simply didn't want to be here.

He finally decided to make his break, although standing up to Marcus was not something

8

he was used to doing. "I gotta get going," Cam said. "Before I can't see straight enough to walk home."

"Why are you acting like this?" Marcus asked, knowing that a few beers was not going to make Cam unable to walk. His voice was heated and he snapped the words out much louder than necessary.

Marcus was showing his temper, and Cam hated it when that side of him came out. Why was he acting like this? Unfortunately, this attitude seemed to be showing up more often as of late. He used to be much more laid back and easy going. Now he just seemed uptight all the time.

"I just don't feel like partying tonight, okay?" Cam said.

It was obviously not okay. Marcus was mad. "What's the matter with you, man?" Marcus cussed and stood up. He used his tall muscular body to intimidate Cam. "You've been acting like a jerk since you got here. What's up with you?"

Cam looked at Heather and quickly decided that he wasn't going to find any help from her. He turned to Sandy, but she just stared back at him with a blank look in her eyes. Cam wasn't sure what that meant, but she, too, was acting strange. It wasn't as if she was going to defend Cam against Marcus. She would never do that, but she would oftentimes find something to cut through the tension and set things back to normal. Right now, she just stared at Cam.

"Nothing's up," Cam finally said, not daring to look Marcus directly in the eye. "I told you. I'm just not really in the mood to party. I guess I need to just go home and take it easy for a while."

"Why would you want to do that? It's party night," Marcus said—as if every night wasn't party night. Marcus calmed himself down and returned to his chair. "You know…do whatever you want, but it's pretty rude. We invited Heather over to meet you and this isn't exactly the kind of guy she was expecting. You're making me look bad."

"Sorry." Cam half-heartedly apologized to Marcus and then turned his attention to Heather. Again, he couldn't help but realize that she was very cute, but his thoughts took him in a different direction.

This isn't how you should be living you're life. There is something else waiting for you, but if you keep living like this, you're going to be in the wrong spot at the wrong time—as usual.

Although it felt very strange, Cam couldn't help but believe what he was thinking. He wanted to be in the right place if something good was in store for him. He definitely wasn't happy with the way things were going now, and if there was something better waiting around the corner, he needed to be in the right spot.

He shifted in his chair so he could focus completely on Heather. "I'm sorry. I really think it would be better if I leave."

Heather nodded and gave him a half-smile, although her disappointment was evident. She was almost pouting when she spoke. "Whatever. It's probably your loss."

Her assertiveness didn't surprise Cam at all. In fact, it almost made him laugh. Instead, he chose to be nice. "Yeah, you're probably right, but I'll just have to lose this time. It really has been nice meeting you," he said.

Without another word, Cam walked to the front door and turned the knob. He couldn't help but notice how slimy it felt. Was this because of the way he was acting? He didn't know the answer, but by the time he stepped out onto the porch and felt the rays of sunshine on his face, he knew he had done the right thing…at least this time.

Still, he felt bad that he had left his friends like that. Marcus was definitely mad. The anger wouldn't last long, though. Marcus would call him tomorrow and tell him that they would be partying again, probably at five, and that he had another girl waiting to meet him. That was just the kind of guy Marcus was. He was controlling, and he could get mean and rude, but he was persistent and he was a friend.

Cam's legs suddenly felt as if they were going to give out on him. The sun was now doing more than hitting his arms. It was sapping his energy. Still, he was glad that he had decided to walk to Marcus' house. Driving would be a bad idea right now. He slowed his pace and after a few more seconds, he stopped altogether. The six-pack he had consumed was really beginning to affect him. It wasn't just making him feel inebriated, though. It was also making him depressed. This was certainly not the effect that he had been hoping for.

Again, his tormenting mind bombarded him. *This is not the life you should be living.*

Of course it wasn't. The party life of drinkers leads to a life of anger and loneliness. It was going to leave him feeling as if his life was unimportant. He understood this, but what else was there for him? His parents had died when he was a teenager. All of his friends partied. He knew nothing else. Life just didn't have much to offer him?

Besides, Cam thought. It wasn't as if he completely disliked his life. He had a place to live. He didn't make much money, but he didn't need a lot of money to live like this. He had girls, although he and his girlfriend Angel had just broken up. Still, he could find someone easily enough.

Anyone could find that kind of girl.

He wasn't sure where that thought had come from, but Cam decided to argue with himself. "No! Not just anyone could get someone like that!" Cam waited for the voice inside his head to counter, but nothing came, and he shook his head at his own stupidity. Yeah, that's it, he thought. Argue with yourself.

It took several minutes for him to feel ready to resume his walk. The first few steps felt wobbly and almost out of control. He maintained a slow, steady pace, now forcing himself to focus on his legs. He wasn't feeling any pain, but suddenly his auto-pilot wasn't working quite right.

He rounded Culver Corner, and suddenly knew where he was heading. Until now, he had just been moving his tired, abused body with no real destination in mind. With the turning of this corner, he knew there was only one place he could end up. It wasn't exactly the kind of place he would normally hang out, but this wasn't exactly the most normal day in his life either. In fact, since the nagging in his head had begun about two months ago, no day seemed completely normal, which only left him more concerned and added to his sadness.

He crested the hill and the road veered to the right. He followed it, now walking down the center of the right hand lane—no longer worried about the cars coming up behind him. There wouldn't be many, and they could go around if they wanted to get past. Cam knew that this attitude was just one more step towards a bad mood, but he didn't care. He wasn't going to step up on the sidewalk and alter what felt like the natural course of life.

Ahead of him, a chain linked fence surrounded a large park and miniature golf course. The fence was nearly eight feet high; certainly tall enough to keep the non-payers out. A large rock path wound its way around the perimeter of the fence, adding a sharp textured look to the entire area. Once inside the park, you could putt on either of the two eighteen hole courses, shop at the small gift shop or the Snack Shack, or eat hamburgers just outside the small red trailer, which had been made into a makeshift deli. There was a small playground for kids towards the back of the park.

Cam noticed that the parking lot was full of vehicles and people walking around. Cam wasn't sure if it was normal for the park to have such a large crowd, but he guessed that it was.

A squealing noise caught his attention, and his eyes focused on a small white pickup truck that was pulling out of the parking lot. Whoever was behind the wheel of that vehicle obviously didn't care about the ten miles-per-hour speed limit. They were going at least forty, maybe more. The truck made its way around the two winding corners and was now coming straight towards him, still speeding, and obviously not concerned for Cam's safety—or their own for that matter. He apparently had no intentions of scooting around a drunk guy walking down the road. It would be more enjoyable to play games with him.

Cam moved to the right slightly, but did not step up onto the sidewalk. He was determined to force the driver, which he could now see was a teenage boy showing off for his friends, to move into his own lane. It didn't work. When the boy laid on the horn and continued on a straight path towards him, Cam realized they were playing a game that no one was going to win. The truck moved over even further into Cam's lane. Cam stepped up on the curb, stopped, and waited the two seconds for the truck to pass. He thought about showing the driver exactly what he thought about his stupidity, but decided to just stare him down.

He waited until the vehicle disappeared over the hill before turning away. As soon as he took two steps, he wished he had at least shouted something at the kid. Next time he would, he promised and continued to walk.

By the time he reached the main entrance to the park, Cam was ready for another drink. Actually, he had been ready as soon as he left Marcus' house (more proof that it wasn't necessarily the drinking part that made him want to leave). Until this very moment, he had been able to keep the thought deep inside of his mind. Now, the thought was beginning to surface.

What choice did he have, though? There were no beer stands around. There was a bar on the north side of town, but that would be a very long walk. If he had his truck, that was exactly where he would have gone. On foot, that option was out.

"Hey, Cam."

The words took him by surprise. He certainly didn't think he would see anyone he knew at the miniature golf park. He looked through the fence and saw a girl looking at him. He recognized her, but couldn't decide who she was, or why he would know her.

Obviously not worried about holding up the golf game she was involved in, the girl made her way off the putting green, down the hill along the small path, and onto the grass next to the fence. Feeling obliged to acknowledge her, Cam made his way towards the fence.

"Hi, Cam." The girl said through the links in the fence.

She had short blonde hair, but it grew darker towards the scalp. Her blue mascara was quite thick, forcing Cam to look into her dark eyes. She wore white shorts—obviously trying to show off as much of her legs as possible, a gray cut off T-shirt, and sandals.

"Hello," Cam said, trying not to let her know that he had no clue who she was.

The girl saw right through him. "You don't remember me?" She paused, but not long enough for him to answer. "I'm Chris. I was with Angel the day you guys met."

"Right, Chris." He remembered, but only a few minor details. "You cut your hair. Wasn't it long back then? He made it sound as if it had been years, but it had actually been less than six months.

"Yeah."

"How are ya'?" he asked.

Chris leaned up against the fence, apparently trying to look as sexy as she could. "I'm doing good," she said. "But I hear you and Angel broke up. What a shame."

Chris was obviously not unhappy about the break up, but Cam played along. "Yeah. We were just too different," he said. "We fought too much."

Instead of at least pretending to feel sorry for Cam's misfortunes, Chris smiled. "I know what you mean. I just ended things with my boyfriend, too—same reason, pretty much."

Cam knew that she was hitting on him. If he was interested, all he had to do was ask her to leave the park with him and she would have ditched her friends without the slightest hesitation. It would be that easy, and any other time, he may have done just that. Right now, however, he wasn't in the mood for that, either.

What a day! First he didn't want to party. He had blown off one cute girl at Marcus' house, and now he was about to reject another one.

"So what are you doing?" Chris asked.

"Just wandering—thinking. You know, just letting things filter out of my brain."

"Would you like some company?" she asked.

"No. I'm okay," he said, still amazed that he was telling her no. Just in case the thoughts of wanting a new life left him alone soon, he wanted to leave this option open. He finished his thoughts on a more positive note. "Maybe some other time, though." Speaking through the chain links was beginning to make him feel nauseated.

Chris' face fell slightly lower. "Sure," she said and moved a few inches away from the fence. "I work at Emily's Gas and Go outside town, towards Oak City. Come in sometime. Maybe we could—."

Her words were interrupted by the high-pitched sound of another girl. The sound came from the top of the hill where Chris had first called out to him. "Are you playing or trying to hook up?" the voice asked.

Cam glanced up. The girl turned away and went back to her game. She looked more like a street walker than a golfer, but Cam kept this thought to himself.

"I better go," Chris said. "Stop by sometime, okay?"

It wasn't much of a question. She sounded more desperate than anything. Cam figured that she just needed someone to help her forget whoever it was that she had just broken up with. Cam had no intentions of being a buffer for anyone.

"Maybe I will," he said. The tone of his voice should have told her that he had no intentions of showing up. It should have, but he wasn't sure if she was going to catch on.

"See ya'," she said and walked back to her friends with a quick smile and a wave. As soon as she reached the green, she retrieved her putter from her friend and took her turn hitting the ball. Cam figured that she had forgotten about him already and he turned away.

He could now hear screams coming from many of the children scattered throughout the park. One little girl's piercing screams seemed to grind at his nerves for a moment, but he quickly pushed it away. He also pushed away the smell of burning hamburger. It was making him sick.

Cam thought about playing a round of golf, but he quickly changed his mind. His legs wouldn't let him, even if he were in the mood. Instead, realizing how much he needed to sit down, he spotted a small bench and moved towards it. It was in the perfect spot, back away from the main stream of people, but close enough to disguise the fact that he was trying to hide from the world.

As soon as he sat down, however, his mind began to wander again. *When are you going to start taking control of your life? When are you going to grow up?*

If the thoughts would have stopped after the first question, Cam wouldn't have argued. He wasn't in charge of his life. Outside forces controlled him. Marcus controlled him. More than that, however, alcohol controlled him. Even now, after resisting the party scene, it was controlling him. He needed a drink, and before long, he was sure he would do whatever it took to get one.

If that was the only question posed to him he would have nodded and let the thought drift away. The second question just wasn't fair. Growing up was something he had been forced to do a lot earlier than most people. After his parent's death, which occurred when Cam was seventeen, he had taken care of himself—as if he hadn't done so when his parents were alive.

"I am grown up. This is grown up," he said this aloud, but not loud enough that anyone would actually hear him. "I think I've done just fine in the growing up department."

He had no intentions of actually contemplating his answer. He refused to look that deep into his past. As far as he was concerned, there was nothing else he could do that would help him grow up.

"Besides," this time he whispered, "why should I grow up anymore?"

Not expecting a response, he was a little surprised when his head concocted an answer and laid it out for him as plain and simple as possible.

You need a wife, kids, and a little happiness.

He was surprised at his thoughts, but it was true—sort of. He did want a wife and kids. He wasn't ready for that right now, but someday he wanted a family. Happiness, on the other hand, was a different story. If getting drunk and playing around with alternate states of mind wasn't making him happy, then happiness was probably overrated.

He actually believed that. He had been drinking for so long that his entire way of thinking had become that clouded. It didn't even seem odd to him. Drinking was the only way for him to have fun.

Or was it? Was there something else?

Cam looked up into the sky. The sun was rapidly descending. It would be gone within an hour or so. With a long walk ahead of him, he thought about heading for home. Instead, he lowered his head and allowed his mind to drift. There was nothing for him at home. I'll get there when I get there, he thought.

Chapter Two

Julie stepped out of her rented home and into the hot summer sun. She pulled her hair away from her sunburned, sticky neck and wished she felt comfortable in miniskirts or tank tops like most of the world. She barely dared to wear shorts. Maybe she was going a little overboard, but why give the world the wrong impression? Why should she risk ruining her image.

Besides, it could be worse. The thought came to her as she stepped off the porch and headed towards the sidewalk. *I could be back in Texas. Then I'd really be hot.*

That was an odd statement, or it would have been three years ago. Julie grew up in Austin, Texas, but she never felt like she completely fit in, although she never really understood why. Maybe she just wasn't a big city girl. Still, until she went on her mission and expanded her little world, Texas was where she planned to live forever.

Now, she couldn't see herself living anywhere but Utah. She figured that this was all a part of the Lord's plan. Actually, she trusted that her entire life was part of His plan, just like she had trusted Him when she was told she was going to serve her mission in Utah. At the time, this had seemed like such an oxymoron. "Everyone there is already LDS," she had been told by just about everyone she talked to. "There's no one left to convert." It was very confusing.

Several months later, after helping convert more than a dozen people to the church, she knew why she had been called to Utah. This was where she had been needed. Being here had also given her a real sense of importance. Now, that feeling of importance had grown into a true sense of belonging.

Besides her own personal growth, and the people she had helped convert, that year and a half had opened her eyes to a different world. It helped her to see that there was more to the world than good old Austin, Texas. Halfway through her mission, Julie knew that Pine Hills was where she wanted to live. The majestic mountains rose high in the air like angels watching over her. The streams and lakes seemed to wash most of her cares and worries away.

When she reached the sidewalk, Julie turned to her left and saw Mrs. Stevenson. She was sitting on the porch beside her front door, as she did every Saturday afternoon.

"Hello, Ms. Haws," Mrs. Stevenson called. "How is everything?"

"Good afternoon, Sister Stevenson," Julie returned the greeting. "Everything is perfect," she said and continued to walk. A few seconds later, she glanced down at her watch. It was just after one o'clock. She turned right on Main Street and headed away from the only stop light in Pine Hills. The light marked Center and Main, the exact center of town.

Julie realized that she had just lied to Sister Stevenson. For the most part, things were going well in her life. She felt good about what she had

21

accomplished, and up until this morning, she was sure about the future as well, but she was not feeling perfect as she had said.

This morning, something that had bothered Julie for a long time—but that she thought had gone away forever—decided to resurface. There was no reason for it to come back, but it had. It had started the moment she woke up.

There is no one for you.

Those words had haunted her throughout most of her latter teenage years. She heard them first from the mouth of her own friend, and over time, they turned spine-chillingly real. It wasn't until her mission that she finally was able to cope with this. It gave her hope for the future. That was important, because she desperately wanted to get married and have a family. This strong desire was the reason that the fear had become so prominent.

Apparently these words were embedded more deeply than she had thought, because they were bothering her again today. The whole morning had just been very difficult. She woke up feeling tight and edgy, and no matter how hard she tried, she couldn't keep the words from creeping back into her head.

After several hours of being bombarded by the feelings, Julie knew what she had to do. When she was younger, she found that people were a natural antidote to this problem. That was what she needed today. She wasn't sure where to go, but she had to end up where there were lots of people. She had no desire to talk or to mingle, but she desperately needed to watch and listen. Somewhere in Pine Hills was the temporary cure to her problem.

She slowly approached the fork in the road which split Main Street into Knolls Hill Drive, the ritzy part of town. They didn't really have that much more money up there, but for some reason, they did what they could to make others believe they did.

Julie quickly chose left and stayed on Main Street. The heart of town was behind her now. Everything was desolate. The stores were empty, and very few shoppers roamed the streets. This wasn't all that odd. There weren't that many people in Pine Hills. It didn't help her with her troubles, though.

Suddenly she remembered where everyone had gone, and her heart fluttered. She had hit the biggest jackpot in Pine Hill's history. She rounded the corner and saw what she desperately needed: large crowds gathered together, hundreds—maybe thousands—of people all in one place. This was the meeting place; at least it was for three days when the carnival was in town.

To anyone who lived here for any length of time, this was the strangest time of the year. For three hundred and sixty two days, people in Pine Hills seemed to stick to their own business. They didn't pry unless there was a need, and they certainly didn't stop on the streets to speak to strangers.

But for these three days, the third Thursday, Friday, and Saturday in June each year, everyone turned into what seemed like outgoing aliens. Suddenly it was time to catch up on all the gossip. This was the one time when it seemed safe to let your guard down, venture out for something other than groceries, and even strut your stuff a little.

It was this usual "keep to yourself" attitude, combined with an occasional outpouring of people, that had helped Julie decide Pine Hills was the perfect place for her. There was just enough variety to keep busy, and still enough space and freedom to practice her religion, and to really be herself, without the peering eyes of others.

Julie began passing people, and her ears instinctively honed in on their conversations. It was a gift. It was also a thorn in her side. There were times—so many times that she hated to remember—when she had to excuse herself because she'd been caught eavesdropping. It was embarrassing at the time, but it wasn't enough to make her stop listening. She wasn't really prying. She didn't even care what they were saying. She seldom remembered their actual words, but listening helped her.

"Are we going to the rodeo?" a man in a cowboy hat and boots asked as Julie walked by. He was staring at the well dressed lady standing beside him. Julie figured it was his girlfriend. He probably wouldn't have asked if she were his wife. "We're not gonna be late this time. Let's get goin'," he would probably say if a wedding ceremony had already taken place. This man even seemed generally interested in the young lady's reply. Julie was being cynical and she knew it. She thought about stopping, just to hear her answer, but it really didn't matter, and she walked past.

Ahead, she could see the lights of the Fun Time Carnival sign marking the entrance to the rides and games (Scumville, U.S.A as it was oftentimes referred because of the weird people who showed up, especially at night). That would be where the vast majority of people would be hanging out, and that was where she wanted to be, right in the center of everything. She was in no hurry though, and she slowed her pace allowing her eyes to search the area.

Two groups of people caught her attention almost simultaneously. They were both on her side of the street. Besides that, she could see nothing that the two groups had in common.

The first group, a few feet away, was a nice, large family—mom, dad, and their five kids. The second group looked more like a gang of punk kids, long hair, black T-shirts, torn Levi's, and cigarettes in their hand. They looked more like grease monkeys than a gang, Julie thought and she almost laughed. She quickly looked away from them and focused her attention on the family.

The youngest girl, dressed in a cute pink dress, held a bag of cotton candy tightly in her hand. She was nestled comfortably in her dad's arms. Before long, she began squirming and finally leaned forward. "Want some, Daddy?" the little girl asked. She held her sticky finger, with a dab of cotton candy hanging off the end, next to her dad's lips. He opened his mouth and allowed his daughter to stick her fingers in his mouth. He gave her a big smile and thanked her.

One of the boys—he looked to be about seven or eight—moved closer to his sister. "I want some, but I'll get it myself. Your fingers are gross!"

When he moved his hand towards the bag, the girl pulled it away. She was obviously old enough to know how to start a family feud. "Forget it Bradley—you had yours!"

"I did not, you brat. Did you see me with cotton candy. No, you didn't!"

Although she struck Julie as a pushover, certainly not the take charge type, the mother

25

handled the situation perfectly. "Brad, you had a drink. That's what you wanted." The mother looked away from her son, expecting the episode to be over, and it was.

Julie passed the family, impressed by what she had seen. She immediately focused on the main gate, hoping she could block out the gang from her mind.

Not that she felt too threatened—at least not physically. This place was too small to have full-fledged, mean-spirited gangs. Austin had real gangs. Salt Lake, twenty miles up the road might have real gangs, but not Pine Hills. These guys weren't going to shoot anyone like the gangs in big cities might do. They were harmless, although they looked like the type who would say something to her. They would certainly try to make her uncomfortable.

She could live with that. It might even help her. In fact, she was feeling better already. The tormenting words in her head were disappearing, though not entirely. Maybe they would never leave her entirely, but at least she wasn't close to tears as she had been earlier.

Another fifteen steps and she would be passing right in front of the group of kids. She thought about veering off to the side, even crossing the street, but that would only get them going. She had to be tough. She had to show them that she wasn't afraid or intimidated. It wouldn't be hard to hide her fear. She wasn't afraid of them, but she could definitely be intimidated and easily embarrassed if they wanted to push it.

The first thing she heard come out of their mouths was a cussword. She half expected this, and instead of letting it bother her, she just smiled and braced herself mentally for the onslaught that was sure to follow.

"I don't think they're comin' man," the boy closest to her said. He had a tattoo on his right forearm. It was a black cross sitting in a puddle of blood. He's too young for a tattoo, Julie thought. Then again, she didn't think anyone should have tattoos. Especially not ones that looked like that.

"They'll be here," another kid said. Just as he did, he looked up and caught Julie looking at him. He smiled at her, turned away, and finished his thought. "They said they'd be here, didn't they?"

"Well, they're late," the tattooed kid said.

"They're women, dude," a third boy added his thoughts. Julie now guessed that they were all about sixteen or seventeen. "They're going to be late for the rest of their lives."

Julie couldn't help but smile. If anyone saw her, they didn't acknowledge it. She was right in front of them now, as close as she would ever get. If she could make it through the next ten seconds, she would be safe. Her back would be to them forever.

She wasn't sure why, but she slowed down even more. Her need to know seemed to be getting in the way of her intelligence. Her body said speed up, but she still wanted to hear what they had to say.

Or did she? The next words out of their mouths were going to be derogatory and pointed directly at her, but it was a chance that she was willing to take (or that she forced herself to take).

"Oh, man. Check out that chick!"

Julie turned to them knowing that five sets of eyes were going to be boring into her as if she were a trophy deer.

27

But they weren't looking at her. They were staring at someone else—someone on the other side of the small metal fence that did very little to keep anyone in or out, but at least marked the boundaries of the carnival.

Two thoughts flooded Julie's mind. The first one was *whew, I got through it without a problem.* Her second thought, which suddenly seemed much more important to her—and much more puzzling—took her a little out of character. *What do they see in her that they don't see in me? Am I not appealing? Am I that ordinary and plain?*

It wasn't the fact that she was having these thoughts that bothered her. She was really upset that they had actually ignored her, just to talk about someone else…someone Julie decided wasn't all that cute. Sure, the girl was thin and curvy, but that was all she had. Julie had something to offer too. Maybe not what they really wanted, but it really hurt her to think that they hadn't even taken the time to look.

All of a sudden, Julie was no longer interested in what the people around her had to say. All of the conversations seemed to blend together in a jumbled mess. The entire carnival seemed to fade as Julie began to think backwards. This time she relived the moment when her friend had spoken those horrible words to her.

"Why did he say 'no'?" Sharon had asked just after Chance had turned down Julie's invitation to the dance. "I'm beginning to wonder if you're destined to be alone, Julie. Maybe there is no one for you."

That was all there had been to it. Julie realized at the time that Sharon had been joking, but it scarred her for a long time…maybe even forever.

As she stood among the people at the carnival, their conversations still inaudible, Julie also visualized the day that President Vance had helped her solve the problem. He taught her something that had helped the chilling words fade for a very long time.

"God has a plan for you, Julie. I'm sure you don't see it right now. None of us really knows what that plan is, but I assure you that somewhere, sometime, if it's in the plans, you will find someone. Remember, God controls the future. Right now, you need to focus on your mission. That's what's important right now."

After that, Julie had been able to get the problem under control. She placed her trust in her Heavenly Father. If there was someone for her, then he would take care of that. This worked for a long time.

Unfortunately, these teenagers, who would probably stare at just about anyone, had decided that she wasn't worth staring at. Instead, they chose to stare at an underweight blonde lady on the other side of the park. This did not help Julie's confidence at all. It did, however, add weight to her problem, just when she thought she was getting a handle on it—again.

Julie turned around. Unfortunately, her mind was still on the boys, and she forgot to look where she was going. She felt her body crash into something, and for a moment, she thought she had hit a pole. Hot flashes rushed through her face.

It wasn't a pole. It was worse. It was a person—someone who was now looking at her as if she were the clumsiest, strangest person in the world.

"I'm sorry," she said and reached out to him. She wasn't sure where she had hit him, but right now, her right elbow hurt. She rubbed it, and waited for his answer.

"It's fine. I'm fine. Are you okay?"

Julie did her best to keep their eyes from making full contact. She stared more at the top of his head, which was what he had been rubbing. Somehow, her elbow had hit his head. "I'm sorry."

"It's no problem, really." He wondered if he should walk away immediately, or introduce himself. He gave in. "Cam," he said and stuck out his hand.

Julie shook the man's hand. "Julie. Julie Haws."

A short moment of silence passed between them, making them both feel uncomfortable. Cam broke the silence just before Julie was going to. "I better get going," he said. "Are you sure you're okay?"

"Fine, thanks."

Julie watched the man walk away, and immediately her mind went back to the kids. Why was it that the only men who pay any attention are the ones I run into.

Suddenly, she realized what she was doing. Why am I acting like this? she thought. I should be grateful that they ignored me. I'm acting stupid and desperate.

As she spoke to herself, the gang moved towards the young girl. They didn't say anything to her though, and eventually the girl disappeared in the crowd and the boys turned their attention back on themselves.

There is no one for you.

"Go away!" she said.

She felt her face turn red as soon as the words came out of her mouth. Had she said it aloud? The words were supposed to be spoken under her breath, but because she still wasn't quite feeling herself, she wasn't sure if they had stayed there. She quickly looked around hoping that no one had heard, and almost sighed when no one seemed to be looking at her strangely.

As quickly as she could, Julie made her way through the crowd of people that had gathered by the entrance to the carnival.

There is no one for--.

This time, before the words had completely formed, she fought back, although she made sure she only thought the words. Heavenly father will take care of that part of my life for me. It's my job to do what's right. It was almost the same words she had thought after talking with President Vance.

The moment she finished thinking this, she felt a change. The voice was gone. The fear was still there, but it had taken its spot in the far reaches of her mind. Julie had no idea how long the words would stay gone, but it didn't matter. She knew how to fight it off...even when it got really bad.

Suddenly, all of the conversations that were being carried on around her became clear and more focussed. Again, she realized that there were people everywhere: kids, teenagers, and adults. There were lovers holding hands, walking and talking with their arms swinging lovingly back and forth. There were plenty of single people as well. Some of them were looking around—for someone or something. Others were just milling around having a good time. There was popcorn, cotton candy, and the sweet smell of barbecued hamburgers. She could even smell the relish, although she figured she was just making that up.

As she had done before, Julie focused on the people. She heard every word that was spoken, each one was clear and distinct. Each person was telling a story or revealing information about themselves; or more often revealing information about others—by way of gossip. Not wanting to hear the gossip, Julie tried to make the distinction as early as possible.

The entire scene around her was incredible. She needed this, and the more she heard, the clearer the world around her seemed to get. Once again, people were healing her.

For an hour, she walked and listened. She seldom spoke, other than to say "hello", until she heard her name being called. She didn't respond at first, but after hearing it a second time, she turned towards the sound.

Two girls were walking towards her. "Julie," the girl on the right, Tina Orwell, called for a third time. She waved and skirted around several people until she was standing right in front of Julie. "How's it going?" Tina asked.

A giant weeping willow tree extended from the sky and almost touched Tina's big hair. The top of the tree was more than a hundred feet tall, and seemed to dwarf everything else in the park, even the tallest rides. It was one of the oldest living objects in the entire city.

"Good," Julie answered. This time she didn't feel as if she had lied. She did feel good. If nothing else, she felt a whole lot better than she had when she left her house. "What are you guys doing?"

"I'm trying to find someone who will go on the Tilt-a-Whirl with me. Karen's too chicken. You want to go?"

"Not me," Julie said and patted her stomach. "I don't think my stomach could take it."

"Well how about a movie?" Karen Stubacker changed the subject. Julie had spoken to her once before, at stake conference, and it had only taken a few minutes for Julie to realize that Karen was one of the most spiritual ladies she had ever met. She had been so articulate, and so intelligent, that Julie had left that evening wondering if Karen had spend her entire life studying the LDS religion on a very deep level.

Right now, Karen was dressed as if she were ready to play. This was quite a change for her. Although she felt quite comfortable dressed casually, she usually wore dresses. She wanted the world to see her as a professional. That was the image she wanted to cultivate. Even more drastic, for her, was her hair. She always had her hair pulled up neatly. Now, her hair was down, very straight but still nice. She wore a red shirt with an American flag on the front and back, blue Jeans, and Tennis shoes.

Tina filled in a little more information so that Julie could answer Karen's question. "Yeah, we're going to see *The Other Side Of Heaven* tonight. It starts at seven-ten. Why don't you join us?"

Julie's first inclination was to turn down their offer. She wasn't exactly the movie type. She had heard great reviews about the show from a couple of people, however, and had actually thought about renting it when it came out on video.

Apparently she was taking too long, because Karen broke in. "Come on. You'll like it. It's a great show."

There was no real reason for her to say no, and Julie finally accepted. "I'll have to meet you there. I have to run up to work and grab something," she said and nodded. "I'll be there around quarter 'till."

"Perfect," Tina agreed. She reached out and grabbed Julie's arm and leaned in close, as if she were going to tell her a secret. When she spoke, however, it wasn't with a whisper. Everyone around could hear her. It must not have mattered. "Tom Harding asked me out," she said. The corners of her lips rose. "We're going to dinner tomorrow."

Tom was Tina's new next door neighbor. He was a very nice looking man. Even more impressive, he was an older man at that—five years older than Tina. He was also well on his way to a degree in psychiatry. That made him marriage material, and Tina was not shy about admitting this, unless he was around.

"Congratulations," Julie said. Tina deserved to find someone good to date, and Tom would be perfect for her. It certainly couldn't be any worse than her past two relationships. That had been painful.

A semi-uncomfortable silence followed, and Tina used the opportunity to continue on her quest. "I have to find someone to go on this ride with me, so we better go. We'll see you tonight."

Tina and Karen walked away, but not until Julie promised to be at the theatre by six forty-five.

Fifteen minutes later, Julie decided to make her way home. She felt much more relaxed and rejuvenated than before. In fact, she felt as if she were back to her usual, positive self, and that was all that she had set out to do.

Chapter Three

The movie ended, and Julie and her friends left the theatre two with tears streaming down their faces. The critics were right. *The Other Side Of Heaven* had been very good, and quite touching. The ending left all three girls contemplating their own roles in the building up of the church. Although only Julie had gone on a mission, Karen and Tina were doing their best to fellowship the world as well, through their examples and uplifting actions.

They entered the lobby, and were about to walk outside when Tina stopped them. "Hold on. I have to get some popcorn."

"I thought you didn't want anything. You didn't want to get fat," Karen reminded, although she was joking.

"Well, now I want some." Tina walked to the back of the line, and Karen and Julie joined her, though they had no intentions of getting anything.

The line moved slowly, giving them time to discuss the movie and their lives. Every time Tina looked at Julie, she noticed that Julie's eyes were drifting. After seeing what Julie was looking at, she couldn't resist pushing the issue.

"Don't just check the guy out. Go say hi."

Julie shook her head. "I'm not checking him out," she said. "I sort of already ran into him earlier today."

"Well go run into him again. You want to. You haven't taken your eyes off him. Don't be a chicken. He's cute. Just go for it."

Julie refused to admit it, but she had been staring. He was sitting on the small bench next to the video games. It was obvious that something was wrong by the way he sat, though she had no idea what. He was hunched over. His face was pale, and he looked either sad or upset. More importantly, he looked as if he were deep in thought. Julie admitted to herself that she was intrigued, but she wouldn't say so to Tina. "I don't think so," she said and then retracted a bit. "He looks like he wants to be alone."

Tina shook her head. "You don't know what he wants. If you don't go talk to him, I'm going to go talk to him for you." She turned away from Julie and scooted forward in the line.

Tina would probably do it, and the fear of being embarrassed was enough to persuade Julie to take action. She moved away from the line slowly, watching him, but not directly, just in case he looked up.

The man strongly resembled the steeple on top of the Salt Lake Temple. Even sitting down, slightly hunched over, there was no hiding his tall, lanky frame. His chin was well defined, almost distracting from the rest of his face. He looked very masculine, though maybe not exactly grown up. She tried to remember his name, but couldn't.

The longer she looked, the more she realized that the masculinity was probably more of an early aging problem. Her uncle Finley had this problem, and she wondered if this man had the same one— alcohol. That would not be good, because she really didn't want to approach a drinking man and strike up a conversation.

Still, she was definitely feeling a physical attraction to him, and this kept her moving, hoping he wasn't drunk. Until she knew the man's story, she wouldn't judge him. She turned to her friends, but they only stared at her, watching to see if she would actually approach the man. Both Tina and Karen looked poised to force her to keep going if it became necessary.

Suddenly, Julie stopped. What was she doing? What if it wasn't safe? Wasn't approaching strangers a very stupid thing to do?

It wasn't stupid. Maybe a bit haphazard, but not stupid. She had spent eighteen months approaching strangers. Some of *them* could have been dangerous. It hadn't stopped her then, and she resolved not to let it stop her now. She knew it was a bit different. In the mission field, she was being led by the spirit. Right now, she was being led by her desire to talk to this cute guy again.

Her body teetered for a few more seconds before once again continuing her walk towards him. She moved cautiously, trying to gauge his temperament. His eyes were glazed over, but he didn't look like he had been drinking. She had seen plenty of drunk people. She had even helped convert two alcoholics to the church. This man was not drunk—at least not right now. He hadn't been earlier either. At least not that she could tell.

"Hello," she half whispered as soon as she was close enough to him. He didn't look at her, and Julie could tell that he was lost in thought. Suddenly, she remembered his name. "Hello, Cam," she repeated, this time a little louder.

Cam sat up straight, obviously trying to hide the fact that he had been moping, and answered her. "Hi—how ya' doing?" The sadness in his voice was quite apparent.

Julie closed the gap between them to a comfortable five feet and stopped. "I'm doing great." She hesitated and then finished her thought. "How's your head?"

"It's fine." His words were very bland. He reached out and shook her hand again.

It was short and almost completely void of emotion. *He isn't too interested in talking to you. If he really wanted company, he would show a little interest.* Julie wished her mind would stop tormenting her. It was time to focus. If this was going to turn out like she wanted, she had to pay attention. Then something dawned on her. She wasn't exactly sure how she wanted this to turn out. Was she actually going to ask him out, or was she just going to chat for a few minutes and say goodbye?

"Are you from around here?" Cam asked politely, trying to stay engaged in this conversation.

"Sort of. I've been in Utah for about three years. I've only lived in Pine Hills for a year though."

"Really! I haven't seen you before and I'm sure I would have noticed you." He quickly checked her out with his darting eyes.

He sounded a little fake, but at least he was showing interest now. Julie thanked him for the compliment in her own shy way. She smiled.

"I keep out of the limelight." Julie shifted her weight from her right foot to her left. "I like people, but only from an observer's standpoint. I don't particularly like to stand out."

"Then why are you here now, approaching someone you don't even know?"

It was a genuine question, and she couldn't answer it. The truth would sound very forward. She wasn't opposed to taking the lead if the situation arose, but not usually with men. *You're cute, and you look like you could use some cheering up.* That is what she wanted to say, but she didn't.

"To tell you the truth, I'm not sure. I guess I just saw you sitting here and just--. Well, I just felt like saying hello."

Cam nodded, checking her out again, but trying not to let her know he was doing it. That would be deemed impolite by someone like her. He could just sense that in her. Although he wasn't sure why, he wanted to show her that he had some manners. He hadn't seen her before today, and although it was strange that they were meeting again this evening, the odds were that he wasn't going to see her again, but why not make a good impression, if that was possible in his current unhappy state of mind.

Still, it was necessary to check her out, so he hid it. She was cute…in a conservative way. Her white pants and yellow blouse showed off what little tan she had. She was slender, not model-like, which was a good thing. Cam never had been too choosy, but she would definitely rank near the top of the list in the women he had dated category.

"What movie you going to see?" Cam asked.

"Actually, we just got out."

Cam looked around, apparently trying to find out who she was with. "We?" he asked.

"Me and a couple of my friends. We saw *The Other Side of Heaven.*"

"Haven't heard of it," Cam admitted.

Julie shifted her weight from one foot to the other. "It's new. It wasn't too bad. What are you going to see?"

"I'm meeting someone." Actually, he was meeting Angel, his ex-girlfriend. They were going to see a movie and then talk. Had he decided to have a couple of beers before coming, it may have worked that way. Now, sober, he knew it wouldn't. He had ended their relationship a couple of weeks ago, and as long as he was sober, he knew that was the best thing that he could have done. He was just waiting for her right now so that he could tell her, again, that they weren't getting together anymore. After that, he had planned on leaving—alone.

Cam decided not to tell her the story, for obvious reasons. "I don't think he's going to show up though. He was supposed to be here ten minutes ago." It was a lie, but why tell her he was waiting for a girl. He quickly changed the subject. "So what, it's girls night out?"

Julie had seen through him. She wasn't sure why he had lied, but figured that it was because he didn't want to tell her that he was meeting a lady, just in case this conversation went somewhere. "We were just looking for a little excitement, you know. That's what Saturday nights are for, right?"

"Funny. You don't look like the type of lady who goes out looking for excitement." He was probing. It was important for him to know just what kind of person she was, lady or girl. There was a huge difference, and his approach would be different depending on which one she was.

Julie was more than happy to answer the question, yet it had almost sounded as if he was putting her down. She wasn't boring. At least she didn't think of herself as boring. The thoughts of this afternoons mental struggles popped in, and she forced them back. "I like excitement, as long as it's decent excitement."

Cam smiled, looked up at her, and then pulled back, emotionally, a little more. He bent over and looked away from her.

"Is something wrong?" The brazenness of her question made him look back up at her. She immediately wondered if she had just blown everything.

"No," he said. "Everything's fine. I've just had a long, entirely too exciting, week."

He had said that intentionally just to emphasize their differences. Julie caught on, realizing that he definitely didn't want her to pry. She disregarded this, however, and pushed him forward a little more. "How exciting is *too* exciting?"

This time when Cam looked up at her, she saw something else: maybe the truth—at least in part. Cam knew she was seeing right through him, but he wasn't sure if he wanted to go into the truth, especially with someone he didn't know.

"I'm sorry," Julie quickly said and had to fight back the heat that was threatening to pulse through her face. "I shouldn't have asked that." She shook her head and looked away from him. She looked at her friends, who were almost to the counter now. Hearing his voice, however, forced her to focus on Cam once again.

"It doesn't really matter," he said. "I don't know why I would tell you this, but if you really want to know, have a seat." Cam slid over on the bench until he was sitting on the very edge.

See, he's not interested. If he thought you were cute, he would have barely given you enough room to sit down.

She pushed her thoughts away and sat down on the bench. She turned her legs towards him. Out of the corner of her eye, she saw Tina. She was placing her order. Karen was standing next to her, looking at something on the counter.

Instead of speaking, she looked at him, and then she looked through him. She could see the sunlight beginning to fade. She pictured the sun just about to set over West Mountain. Within an hour it would be dark. Through the glass, she could see a few white clouds trying to make their way over the horizon in the east.

Surprisingly, Cam actually spoke first, again, forcing her to focus on him. He didn't want to wait for her to question him. "I don't know you…and maybe I shouldn't even say this, but I guess that deep down I want to talk to someone. I'd probably be safer telling you than someone I know."

Julie was a little surprised. Guy's don't just open up like this. She figured it had something to do with a girlfriend problem, something she had very little expertise in. Whatever he said, she was content to listen and to talk if that was what he wanted. It didn't matter where the conversation went. She just had a desire to sit next to him. She nodded, but didn't say anything.

"I think I'm an alcoholic."

That was the last thing that she expected him to say. That was going to ruin everything. She couldn't date an alcoholic. Maybe he was wrong. Maybe he wasn't an alcoholic. Didn't alcoholic's deny this problem to the very end? As bad as this was, Julie wondered if there was more. He definitely wasn't drunk now. His breath didn't smell like it, and he was in complete control of himself. She needed more, and she got more. In fact, she got exactly what she needed.

"I party too much, and I hate it. At least I think I hate it. Something just isn't right. I feel like I'm missing something—something that could explain my life." He tried to gauge her initial response but couldn't. "A little too much for you, huh?"

Things had definitely grown more intense. She felt like a weight had just been placed on her shoulders, as if she was expected to help now. Fortunately, she wanted to explore a little further. But what was she going to say? She had no experience in this field. She had never partied. She had never taken drugs, and had only tried drinking once. How was she going to approach this?

"What do you mean you *think* you hate it?" To her, the words sounded raspy and unrehearsed. She wondered if he was going to laugh at her or just blow her off as an unqualified idiot.

To Cam, however, her words had a relaxing effect. For a second, he wondered if this was due to the fact that he was a bit desperate. It didn't take long for him to realize that it was more than that. She was different. He could sense that, and it helped him feel better.

He tapped his head and suddenly realized that he had formed his hand into the shape of a pistol. He quickly pulled his hand down. He wasn't suicidal and he didn't carry a gun. He didn't want her to think he was that far gone.

"I'm a little messed up—you know—in the head. I've just partied way too much."

"So stop partying."

It was so matter-of-fact. Unfortunately for Cam, the world no longer spun along such simple planes. Now it was more like the ocean, tossing and turning, tearing at him and slowly forcing everything down into its deepest, darkest depths.

"It just doesn't work that way!"

"Why not?" Julie shook her head. "Are you really that addicted?"

Cam didn't want to answer her. Why did this woman feel like she could ask a question like that? So what if he had started the conversation. It didn't give her the right to delve into his personal life…not that deep and personal anyway.

"Obviously a touchy subject, huh?" Julie slid her body another two inches away from Cam. She didn't want to crowd him, and now that she seemed to have done just that, in a mental way, she had to be careful.

"No I'm--!" His voice was harsher than it should have been and he immediately lowered the tone and reversed his answer. "Yeah. I guess I am. It's just that--."

She waited for him to finish, but it became clear that he wasn't going to. She decided not to push him. Instead, she changed the subject entirely. "What do you do for fun, other than drink?" she asked.

Cam shook his head. He looked around at the many people who were milling around the lobby. "I like to golf and fish, but I don't do either one too often. I guess I don't do much of anything."

"Unless you're drunk…right?" Julie was reaching, and although she didn't pause, she wondered if she should back off. She wouldn't, but she thought about it. "Is being drunk fun?"

It was a trick question, but he figured he would answer it anyway. He would do it because it was something he had been contemplating over the past few months. He had asked himself that question, and others that were very similar, many times. "I used too think that," he said and looked at her.

"But now drinking isn't fun?"

"It's still fun," He didn't sound to convincing, even to himself. She wasn't going to buy that answer, and he didn't give her a chance to come back at him. "Where are you from? You have an accent."

"Texas, but no one's ever mentioned my accent. I thought it was gone."

"You definitely have an accent."

Julie forced the conversation back to Cam. "You said something in your life didn't feel right. What do you mean?"

This time, Cam had no idea how to answer her. He realized that alcohol was his major problem, but something else had certainly been bothering him. His life didn't have any meaning, and to look to the future wasn't something he really felt comfortable doing—mostly because he didn't see a future. He couldn't admit this to her, but he was beginning to feel as if he was failing at the game of life.

After a little thought, he decided to keep it simple. "I just think there is more to life than partying, but I don't know what it would be."

Hearing this made her heart flutter. She had heard those very words before. He was searching for the truth. He was looking for something that would direct him, or even give him a real reason to go on in life.

Julie's thoughts were interrupted. Tina and Karen, each carrying a small bag of popcorn and a box of licorice, were approaching. Although Julie wasn't ready to go, she couldn't just ditch her friends. She had her own car, but that would be rude. Then again, leaving Cam right now would be rude as well.

Tina solved the problem. "We're going to take off, Julie. I never did get to go on that ride, so Karen's going to go on it with me. You guys could meet us there if you want to."

Julie didn't feel like going to the carnival, but she left it open just in case. "Maybe," she said. "Thanks for inviting me to the show. I'll catch up with you either later tonight, or tomorrow."

Tina and Karen left, but only after Tina gave Julie the 'good choice—he's cute', look. As soon as her friends walked out the door, Julie stood up and moved two steps away from Cam. She turned her head around and looked at him. "Want to go for a walk?"

She was fairly forward, and Cam liked that. He looked at her and smiled. He quickly glanced at Julie, this time not hiding the fact that he was doing it.

Finally, he shifted his body and began to stand up. Julie offered her hand. Cam accepted it and allowed her to pull him up. He felt something strange. He wasn't sure what it was, or why he was feeling that way, but at the touch of her hand, his heart actually stopped for a split second. It was as obvious to him as her accent had been.

"Where we going?" Cam asked and followed her out the door.

"To see the ducks."

"The ducks?" The left side of his mouth lifted in a half disgusted smile. "Why the ducks?"

"I like ducks."

Why would you like ducks? Ducks are stupid. Ducks swim and fly. How intelligent is that? He thought it, but he never said it aloud. There was no reason to. If she liked ducks, then they would see the ducks...but where were there any ducks around here?

Julie led him to the other side of the complex. They followed the narrow sidewalk that skirted the perimeter of the theatre. As they walked, Julie listened to the world around her. Two seagulls made loud screaming sounds, upset that no one would allow them to swoop down and pick up the food that was being left behind. A light breeze rustled the tops of the tall trees, but did nothing to cool things off. Just as it had at the carnival, the smell of popcorn drifted through the air.

As they rounded the bend, now on the East side of the complex, Julie stepped off the sidewalk and cut across the street. Cam followed, even looked out in front of him, but there were no ducks.

"Maybe the ducks flew north for the summer?" he said. It sounded stupid and he flinched at his own uneducated comment.

She looked at him but said nothing.

They turned right once they hit the sidewalk, and it looked as if they were leaving the entire plaza. She picked up the pace and veered off the road. She led him though the weeds and then finally stopped.

Under the large Welcome to Pine Hills Theaters was a small pond that was hidden from the road by all of the weeds and large rocks. When the entire complex was complete, Cam figured that it would be some fountain with water shooting up high into the air. Right now, however, it just looked like a dirty pool of water.

Just as she had said, there were ducks. Three of them were drifting lazily in the water, and five others were lounging beside it, catching the last rays of light on their backs.

Without warning, Julie resumed their conversation, as if it hadn't been interrupted in the first place. "If you don't want to drink, but you know you are an alcoholic, then what are you going to do about it?"

Cam could not remember meeting anyone who had such a hold on him when she spoke. She was blatantly in his business…and he was allowing it. But why? The only answer he could come up with was, *you like the attention…especially from someone as cute as she is!*

That was the truth, but as usual, he disregarded it because it was not the answer that best suited his needs. It made him feel like he was less of a man. It made him feel needy, not needed, and right now that is not what he wanted to feel.

Before answering her question, he moved five feet away from her. One of the ducks stared at him, but it didn't even ruffle a feather. This was its home and it wasn't going to move for anyone.

Finally, Cam turned around, looked at her, and answered with the only words he could come up with. "I've thought about that. Believe me. But the only answer that I can come up with is…I'm not going to do anything about it. I can't. I'm not the type of guy who can just change the way things are. I can't just go off in a totally different direction. I'll always be looking over my shoulder."

"At what? What are you going to see if you look back?" This time Julie's words were a little more adamant. In fact, they were almost demanding. She was trying to break him down, to make him open him up a little more, and she could see that it was going to take a little pushing.

Cam shook his head. "I don't know."

She intentionally took a deep breath before asking her next question. "What do you see when you look back now?"

"I'm not looking back now. There's nothing to look back at. My past is pretty boring and worthless."

"And you figure that you'll look back later and see it as something different. Maybe it will seem really glorious later?"

Under any other circumstance, her words would have caused him to tear into her, at least verbally. He would never have stood for being toyed with like this. He was a man, and men were not supposed to be berated like this.

Then again, he already knew she wasn't ordinary. She was just the type who would say something like that to a man. For some reason, he couldn't find it in him to fight with her.

Still, there was no answer to her question. He thought about it, even paced back and forth for a short time hoping that something would come to him, but nothing did. There was a good reason for that. She was right. This life would never be glamorous or fun…in a reality-based sense of the word anyway.

Even after a full minute, Julie continued to watch him. She stared at him, determined to force him to answer the question.

"If I really think about it--," Cam stopped. There was nowhere to go. He had really thought about it and he was blank.

Julie nodded once, hoping that he would continue, but he didn't. She finally broke down and posed an entirely different question to him.

"Would you like help? Maybe I could help you get over the need...or whatever it is?"

"And what are you going to do?" He almost laughed at her. A quick snort escaped. "Are you just going mix some magic potion or something...or maybe you're just going to say abracadabra and whammo—I'm healed."

"Maybe," Julie said. She looked deep into his eyes, and even though he was several feet away, she felt the distance close immediately. At least it did in her mind.

"I'm serious. How are you going to help me?" Cam pulled his eyes away from her gaze as if he had been hypnotized and had finally broken free of the spell.

But while their eyes were still locked, just before he turned away, Julie saw something. It only lasted for a second, but she definitely saw it...and it bothered her. It caused a slight doubt to sweep over her. Is this really what you want to be doing? She wished she could understand what she had just seen. If she had to quantify it, she would say it was a mix of fear, anger, torment, and mental abuse (self-inflicted), all wrapped up into one not-so-neat package.

She turned away from him entirely, hoping that the image would quickly fade, but it didn't. In fact, it intensified. She wondered if it was a look that she was going to harbor deep inside of her mind for a very long time.

She knew that helping him wasn't something she was going to want to do on her own. First of all, she wasn't a missionary any more. Second, and probably more important, if things worked out, and Cam stopped partying and found religion, she wanted to pursue a relationship with him—even if they only ended up as friends. She knew the odds were against much more than that, but just in case, she wanted the missionaries to do the converting. She would be there for him, and help where she could; that is, if Cam even wanted help. He hadn't actually agreed to that yet.

"I'm LDS," she said.

Cam interrupted her, but the words that came out were not what she had expected him to say. "I figured that."

That was probably the most important thing he had said all night, at least as far as she was concerned. He knew she was religious, and he was still talking to her. That meant that it was possible that he might open up to the prospect of religion. She decided to go for it.

"Do you know anything about the Church of Jesus Christ of Latter Day Saints?"

Cam shook his head. "Only that they're more of a cult than a religion."

Hearing those words hurt. They were not a cult. Why did people think that? As harsh as his words had sounded, she realized that it was coming from someone who just didn't understand. He was basing his views on what he had heard or seen in the past. She downplayed it, but still tried to resolve this myth. "It's not a cult, Cam. It's a Christian faith. We believe in Christ, and in faith. Our principles go a little beyond some of the other denominations, but only because it's important to the world." She hesitated to give him a chance to respond, but he didn't and she continued. "We have missionaries—men and women who teach the truth to anyone who wants to listen. They can help you. I'll help you, too. If you want to hear what they have to say, I can arrange it."

"And you think that religion is all it will take to get over a problem like this?"

He was mocking her, but she didn't even hesitate. "It will help. You're still going to have to do the work, though. That's where I can help. Really, you ought to seriously think about it."

Cam didn't quite know what to say. He had never been interested in religion, any religion, but he had to admit that he was now feeling a bit interested. Or was it that he was interested in Julie? He admitted this was probably the real reason.

Just to help him make his choice, she tried to get him to commit—something she tried to do while in the mission field. "Why don't we come over tomorrow night and you can just hear what they have to say. You can decide what you want to do from there."

Cam hesitated and then nodded his head. "Fine. Anytime tomorrow night would be fine."

Julie's heart fluttered again. "I'll have to check with the missionaries, but why don't we plan on around seven?" Cam told her the address, and Julie stored it in her mind.

It was beginning to get dark, and not wanting to be out with a stranger too late, she ended the conversation there. "I better get going. I have to call them before it gets too late. I'll see you tomorrow, okay?"

"Sure."

Julie turned and began walking away. After a few steps, she stopped and turned back to him. "It was nice meeting you, Cam."

"You to," Cam said. "And thanks for listening to my sob story."

"My pleasure."

Julie turned around and walked to her car. Her thoughts, as she drove away, were more in the form of a prayer. She wanted to help him. She wanted him to help himself. She also wanted to see him succeed because she really wanted to see him again. There were definitely sparks between them. Unfortunately, what happened from here rested on his shoulders. It depended on his willingness to overcome the problems that he was facing so that she could date him. That was the only way it would work, because she would never go back on her promise to only be with an LDS man.

Chapter Four

Not having a couple of beers before Julie and her friends arrived proved to be very difficult. There was a six pack in the refrigerator, and it seemed to be calling out to him all evening long. At one point, Cam even thought he was going to have to dump the beer out or give in to the temptations.

As hard as it had been, however, one thought had kept him from drinking. He didn't want Julie to see him acting stupid. If he was drunk when they came over, there was a good chance that he would make a fool of himself. That would be enough to force Julie to run the other way forever, and that was not what he wanted.

Since meeting her last night, Cam had thought about Julie quite a bit. He had spent the entire evening debating whether or not he should have told her as much as he had. By the time he woke up this morning, however, he had given in to the fact that it was too late to worry about it. He focused the rest of his energy on getting ready to see her again.

This was a knew sensation for Cam. He was usually more superficial than this—going strictly for the looks, and on the fact that they partied. Julie didn't fit this mold at all. Just the idea of her being a religious person would have ordinarily been enough to turn him off. If all she had going for her were her looks, Cam would have ended their conversation after saying hello. Cute girls just weren't that hard to find. Julie was different. Actually, he had finally concluded that she was a lady. She had depth, intelligence, morals, and seemed to conduct herself in a mature, lady-like way. Although he wasn't exactly a moralistic man, he was impressed by the fact that she was. Not only did she have morals, she stuck to them, and was willing to share them with him. She had even offered to help him, based on her beliefs and morals. That was impressive.

If nothing else, she was intriguing, and as he sat on the couch waiting for a knock on the door, Cam pictured her in his mind. She certainly had a strange hold on him. He wouldn't admit that to anyone but himself, but it was true. It was this hold that had him sitting here right now. He was sure that this meeting with the missionaries was going to turn out to be a waste of time. Nothing that they could say would help him quit drinking. It was going to take more than religion to do that, but at least he would be able to see Julie again. That was what was important to him. If nothing else came out of this, he hoped to get a date.

The doorbell rang and startled Cam. He quickly stood up from the couch, hesitated at the bottom of the steps, and then ascended them slowly. For a moment, he thought about coming up with an excuse, a reason why he wasn't able to sit here and listen to missionaries tell him how bad his life was. Nothing came to him so he forced himself to open the door.

Julie greeted Cam as soon as she could see him. "Hi," she said and extended her arm towards him. Cam shook her hand, and Julie immediately introduced the two men standing next to her. "This is Elder Cummings," she said and pointed to the man on her left. She then looked at the other man. "And this is Elder Jacobson. They are missionaries from the Church of Jesus Christ of Latter Day Saints."

Cam wondered if he was supposed to introduce himself. Instead, he invited them in and stepped to the side as they shuffled by him, first the men and then Julie. Cam shut the door and took a long look at Julie as they all moved down the stairs.

She was wearing a long blue dress with a white shirt underneath, the collar perfectly pressed. Her brownish-blonde hair was pulled into a braid and extended down to the middle of her back. She had a dark mole on the back of her neck—just right of center. Cam stood in the entry way for a moment and marveled at how beautiful she really was. She was simply stunning, and the more he saw of her, the more incredible-looking she became.

They moved into the living room, and the missionaries sat down on the couch as soon as Cam offered. Julie sat down in the glider rocker, also at Cam's request. Cam excused himself to the kitchen to get another chair.

With Cam no longer in the room, Julie took in the ambience of the apartment. This was not what she had expected. She figured that there would be beer bottles laying everywhere, dirty clothes laying in the corner, and a baseball game playing on the television.

Instead, she saw a clean, well-decorated living room. This was not how a drinking bachelor lived, was it? He probably spent all morning cleaning, she thought. This was a good sign. He had manners, and was at least interested enough to clean up for them. On the other hand, she thought, maybe he was just a clean person. She also realized that he appeared to be sober—another plus.

Two pictures caught her attention. One of them, on the wall above the television set, directly in front of the Elders, was of spirals and lines moving in and out of an empty vase. It meant nothing to Julie, but to someone who drank, it probably looked cool. The other picture, which was across from where she was sitting, said a bit more about Cam. It was of a naked woman standing in the middle of a small pond. She was facing the other direction, so all Julie could see was her back. The bottom half of her body was under water, barely hiding what it needed to. To Julie, this could only mean one thing. Cam didn't have as much respect for women as she would hope.

Cam reentered the room and Julie focused on him instead of the picture. He still looked lanky, as if that was going to change overnight, but at the same time, he looked strong. He was wearing shorts that hung down almost to his knees, a nice plain gray T-shirt, and high-top tennis shoes. His eyes were small and gray. She also noticed his hands. They, too, were small but well-groomed.

Cam sat down in his chair forming a complete circle. "Okay," he said, getting right to business. "What do we do now?"

Julie thought about speaking, but instead, she yielded to the missionaries who went to right to work.

"Cam," Elder Cummings took the lead. "What do you know about the Church of Jesus Christ of Latter Day Saints?"

"You know, sir," Cam said, (he admittedly didn't know much). "I really only know what Julie told me last night."

Julie had already told the missionaries about the previous nights conversation, and Elder Cummings was ready for this answer. He immediately delved deeper. "Ms. Haws told us that you have been wondering about the purpose of your life. Can you tell us more about that?"

Can I really do this, Cam thought? It was one thing to open up to Julie. She hadn't seemed all that threatening. He really had no desire to tell his life story to a couple of people determined to change him into a religious man. He decided to answer their questions with nothing more than simple generalities.

"I just don't see much purpose," Cam said.

"What if we could show you what the purpose to your life is? Would you be willing to listen to what we have to say?"

Cam shrugged his shoulder. He wasn't sure how to answer. It sounded like a leading question, one that was going to trap him in a place he didn't necessarily want to be.

"I guess what I'm asking, Cam, is are you willing to open your heart to what we have to say long enough to hear our message?" Elder Cummings sat perfectly still. "If you do, I can promise you that you will see a purpose to your life."

Again, Cam felt like he was being trapped, but oddly enough, he didn't feel as if he was being pressured. These men, as weird as Cam thought they seemed, were trustworthy. Cam really felt that. At least Elder Cummings was. The other man hadn't even spoken, although he was certainly fidgety. Even now, Elder Jacobson was shuffling around in his seat constantly. "I can't say I will believe what you have to say," Cam said and watched Elder Jacobson sit back and cross his arms. "But I'll listen."

Cam saw Julie smile, and he silently thought how much more beautiful she was than he had first thought—especially with her lips curled up in a smile. She had perfect lips, and a perfect face as well.

Apparently, that was what the missionaries wanted to hear. They both smiled and immediately went for their bags, in unison, as if they had been rehearsing for this very occasion. Each one of them pulled out two identical books. Elder Cummings handed one of his books to Julie, while Elder Jacobson stood up and approached Cam, extending one of the books out to him. It was obvious that Elder Cummings had been doing this for a while. He was so sure of himself, unlike his partner. Cam accepted the book and immediately read the title.

The Book Of Mormon.

Cam had heard of it, but had never actually seen one, at least not that he recognized. He certainly hadn't ever held one. Surprisingly, it felt like a normal book, but why wouldn't it. He wasn't sure, but somehow he thought it would feel different. Based on what he had heard, Cam had equated this book with the Bible, and even assumed that they were the same books—just with a different title. He waited, not willing to open the book without being instructed to do so.

"This is another testament of Christ, our Savior," Elder Jacobson finally spoke. He almost sounded as if he were learning as he went along. He was a rookie, Cam thought. Elder Jacobson continued, although he was trying too hard. "It goes along with the Bible. It proves, just like the

Bible does, that Christ came to earth, gained a body, and died, just as we are all doing right now."

Cam nodded showing that he understood, but he didn't say a word. He had no intentions of saying much throughout the rest of the meeting.

Elder Jacobson continued. "In this book, we learn all the principles that we believe in. It teaches us to have faith, to believe in Christ, and to pray. It also teaches us the necessity of the church, how we should treat each other, and what we can do as members of the church to make it back to our Heavenly Father after we die." Elder Jacobson pulled at his tie as he went on. He also continued to move around on the couch. "More importantly, for all of our sakes, it shows us the meaning of our lives. It shows us why we exist and how we should act. Believe me, Cam, if you understand these things," Elder Jacobson held the book in the air as he finished his thought, "your life suddenly takes on a special meaning—a special purpose."

Suddenly, Cam had something to say. It was going to sound confrontational, but he wanted to ask it anyway. He waited for Elder Jacobson to pause, and he asked his question. "Why is your church better than another church? Can't I go to any church and find these answers?"

Elder Cummings fielded the question. "Any religion is better than no religion at all. The difference between our church and the others will become clear later on, but to understand them, you have to know the basics. I promise you that if you let us teach you the gospel, you will know what the difference is—and you'll understand it. If we tell you now, you probably won't understand. At best, you would get confused."

Julie nodded her head. She didn't know these missionaries all that well, but after hearing Elder Cumming's answer, she immediately knew that they were perfectly capable of handling any situation. Not that she had ever doubted them, but he had taken a difficult question and answered it beautifully. It took a spiritual person—one very in tune with the spirit—to be able to deal with difficult questions so well.

Elder Jacobson went back to what he was saying. "Maybe the most important thing you can hear right now is that there really is a God, a Savior, Jesus Christ, and a Holy Ghost. They are three separate people working to help us make it back to Heaven. That's what we're here on earth for, to get a body, to learn as much as we can, and to progress spiritually, so that we are ready to return to our Father in Heaven."

Again, Cam nodded his head. It made sense—at least in a bizarre way. He had never really doubted that there was a God. He had just never taken the time to think about what that meant. If there was a God, then there had to be a purpose for his being a God. He didn't disbelieve this, but he wasn't sure to what extent he understood—or whether he would ever understand. At least he didn't think they were wrong—yet.

"Let me ask you something, Cam," Elder Cummings said and looked into Cam's eyes as if he were trying to focus on him so that he could get a true reading of the answer that Cam gave. "Why do you feel like you have no purpose in life?"

"Because I drink." Cam answered his question and looked right back at the man who had asked it. "I don't think I've ever really cared about the future, or about what happens after we die, if anything. I just feel like I'm stuck in a rut with nowhere to go but down, and I'm sure it's because I drink."

"And you're beginning to wonder if there is something else, right? Maybe something that you're not seeing, but that might be out there?" Elder Cummings leaned forward and rested his chin in his hands. He was really getting into the conversation.

"I've had this feeling that I should be living my life differently, yes."

"That is the spirit of the Lord talking to you."

Elder Cummings words were a bit too much for Cam. The Lord didn't talk to people, at least not to him. Cam refused to believe that. The Lord wouldn't waste his time. Why would he?

Cam leaned back in his chair. He wasn't sure if they noticed or not, but he was purposefully taking a more defensive posture. He was on the verge of starting an argument, or at least a debate about what they had just said.

Apparently, Elder Jacobson sensed something, because he jumped in with a question of his own. "Cam, do you believe in God?"

Cam wasn't sure what to say. Maybe he did, but obviously not like they did. He wasn't even sure if it was a belief. It was more like he figured there was a God, but he certainly didn't believe that God was going to talk to him.

He was about to answer, when he realized something. If he was to admit there was a God, and yet deny that God could talk to him, would that be a contradiction? Actually, if God existed, then he could talk to people. That just made sense. That would mean that he wasn't accepting the fact that

God was talking to him simply because he didn't want to hear what God had to say.

That was a bit deeper than he intended to go in the thinking department tonight. He hadn't figured that talking to the missionaries was going to be easy. He had even planned on discussing his own failures—to a degree—but he had no intentions of delving into something that seemed so weird, even though they made it sound so possible, and even normal.

"I don't know," Cam said. "Why do you believe in all of this?"

Cam figured that he had turned the tables on the missionaries. They would explain their reasoning, and they would probably sound very convincing. In the end, however, Cam would be able to tell them he wasn't interested and politely turn them down. It may cost him a chance to date Julie, who oddly enough hadn't said a word since the missionaries had started to talk, but he just wasn't ready for all of this.

"I have a testimony, Cam." Elder Jacobson relaxed and for the first time, he sat perfectly still. It was a subject that he was quite sure of—much more so than the other words he had spoken. "I have found out for myself that the church is true. That is what you have to do, if you really want to know the truth. You gain a testimony by learning as much as you can, by praying, and by asking Heavenly Father if it's true. I promise you that the Lord will make the truth known to you. That's how you can find out if that book is true, too. You pray and ask if it's true."

Cam half-heartedly accepted this answer. He was about to tell them that he just wasn't ready to buy all of this, when Julie finally spoke. She first asked the missionaries if she could add something, and after they nodded, she turned to Cam.

"I grew up in the church, Cam. I served a mission, just like these men are doing right now. During that time, I saw many people's lives change. Some of them changed so drastically that before we were done teaching them, and usually before they had been baptized, they knew, without a doubt, that God lived and that the church was true. They told me that they felt the change, first in here," Julie touched her heart with her open hand, "and then it grew to encompass their entire bodies—as well as their entire lives. Cam, I saw people who were much more fixed in their ways than you are turn their lives around. This happened differently for everyone I met, but one thing was constant in every case. They all said that changing was the hardest things they ever had to do, but that it was more than worth it. It will be worth it to you, too, if you only open your heart and hear what these Elders have to say."

Cam was speechless. Something about what Julie had just said made him think a little harder about turning these men away. Maybe this was his chance. How many times had he tried to quit drinking and partying? It was hard. Actually, it was more than hard. He felt like it was impossible. If others could do it, people in much more trouble than he was, then why couldn't he? Did he really want to blow this chance?. What if this was the last chance he would ever get?

He shook his head. Confusion was setting in, again. This was a feeling that he was getting very used to as of late. That familiar cloudy feeling sunk into his brain, and for a moment, he had no idea what to say.

"Maybe you should just think about what we've said for a couple of days, Cam."

Elder Cummings words helped to clear some of the clouds from Cam's mind. That was exactly what he needed—to think. If nothing else, he would be able to evaluate his own feelings without the pressure of coming up with an answer to difficult questions while people stared at him.

Still, Cam didn't verbalize his thoughts. He nodded his head, and Elder Cummings continued, "Thanks for letting us come, Cam. It really was nice to meet you." He stood up, but Elder Jacobson and Julie didn't follow suit. This seemed a bit odd to Cam, but he soon found out why. "I'd like you to keep that book, if that's okay. If you want a little help making your decision, maybe you could start by reading the testimonials at the beginning of the book. Maybe the Joseph Smith story will help you a bit, too."

Cam looked at the book in his hand. He had no clue whether he would read it or not, but he did agreed to keep the book.

"Can we leave you with a prayer, Cam?" Elder Cummings asked.

Cam knew that was why Julie and Elder Jacobson hadn't stood up. This wasn't over yet. They wanted more. They wanted to pray, but Cam wasn't even sure what a prayer was. He had seen people do it in the movies, or on television, but he had never taken part in one. There was no real reason to refuse the offer, unless they asked him to join in. Not only did he not know what to say, he really didn't want to. "Sure," Cam said and hoped that he wouldn't have to do anything.

Elder Cummings carefully moved to the floor, kneeling down on his knees. Elder Jacobson did the same. Julie stepped towards Cam, took his hand, and together they too knelt down on the floor.

Cam imitated everything that Julie did. He folded his arms in front of him, watched her for a moment, lowered his head, and then closed his eyes. From that point on, he just listened as Elder Cummings prayed. Cam heard every word that was said, most of it having to do with helping him to find the truth. While it felt a little awkward, it felt good to think that someone was trying to help him, even if it was by means that he was having a hard time comprehending. Elder Cummings finished and both of the Elders, as well as Julie, mumbled something that Cam did not quite comprehend.

Cam immediately opened his eyes but did not move, nor did anyone else for a short time. During that period, Cam felt something that he couldn't quite understand. It was a feeling, something that he couldn't describe, even to himself. It was soothing, and yet Cam had no idea why. It almost felt as if something was trying to break through the defenses he had built around himself.

Finally, after letting the sensations sink in, Elder Cummings stood up. Elder Jacobson followed suit. Julie and Cam stood up also.

"Thanks again, Cam." Elder Cummings took Cam's hand and shook it. Elder Jacobson did the same. "Can we come see you next Sunday?"

That was a bit pushy, but at least they were giving him plenty of time to think though. If he decided that he didn't want to hear anymore, he had plenty of time to think of a way to let them know. "That would be fine," Cam agreed.

"If you need to talk to us before then, you can call us anytime," Elder Jacobson added. "We'd be happy to talk to you whenever you want. If you'd feel more comfortable, just give Julie a call and she can get hold of us." Elder Jacobson handed his number to Cam.

Cam took the paper, and without another word, the two missionaries left. Julie stayed behind, but only for a second—long enough to give him her telephone number. She then stood on the porch looking at Cam. "I really do hope you read some of the book, Cam. It's interesting. Just like they said, it may help clear up some confusion."

"I will," Cam said and nodded. "Thanks."

"You're welcome," she said and started to turn around, but stopped. "Call me sometime. We can talk."

Cam nodded and watched as Julie walked to her car, got in, and drove away. He smiled, again thinking of how great she looked. He turned around and went back inside.

He began to fight with himself almost immediately. Do I drink a beer or read the book? It was a decision that was going to drive him crazy and he knew it.

Chapter Five

The phone rang in her ear for the fourth time, and Julie was about to hang up. She sighed, feeling half empty and yet grateful at the same time. She wasn't sure why she wanted to tell her mom about the man she had just met, she just did. Just before pulling the receiver from her ear, she heard a click and then "Hello."

The voice on the other end of the telephone line sounded raspy, almost out of control. Julie could tell that something was wrong. Was her mom sick, or had she been crying? "Are you all right, mom?"

"Hi, Julie." Mrs. Haws cleared her throat. "I'm just getting a little cold. It's nothing. How are you?"

It sounded like she had much more than a little cold, but Julie let it go. "I'm fine." Julie hesitated, and as soon as she did, her nerves stretched tighter. "I just called to talk to you—to see how you and dad are doing."

The short pause meant that Mrs. Haws doubted the honesty in Julie's comment. She had a way, just like most parents who are in tune with their children, of knowing when their kids are hiding something. She knew, but she chose not to pursue it. "We're doing good," Mrs. Haws said. "Your father's working non-stop, but when it's just the two of us, you know, what else is he supposed to do."

"Well, make him retire."

Mrs. Haws half snorted. "You know when that will happen. He'll be putting in fifty hours a week when he dies. I have no doubt about that."

As they spoke, Julie paced the house. By the time they finished talking about her father, Julie had straightened the living room. As she cleaned the kitchen, they spoke about Julie's work and about her old friends. Two of her high school friends were getting married, and another was dating Timothy Darrinton. Julie lived next to Timothy. He was the one person she figured would never allow himself to be tied down to one woman.

As Julie worked her way down the hall, Mrs. Haws decided that it was time for the truth. "Okay, Julie. What is it?"

"What?"

"You didn't call here to see how we are."

Julie pictured her mother standing in the parlor holding the phone against her right ear. Her left hand would be doubled up in a ball and resting uncomfortably against her hip.

"Why would you think that?" Julie was about to wait for an answer but knew it was pointless. She quickly moved on. "You're right. That isn't the only reason I called."

"What's his name?"

Why were parents so smart? Were they given this gift when they gave birth or was it something that they were born with and it just manifested itself after they had the baby? Julie wasn't sure what the answer was, but she hoped that she had the gift one day as well. It would come in handy.

"His name is Cam."

"Cam, what?"

Julie realized that she had no idea what his last name was. He hadn't offered that information, and she hadn't asked—even last night at his house. At the same time, she hadn't given him her last name either. "I'm not sure. I just met him."

"So," Mrs. Haws said. "Tell me about him."

Julie wondered where to start. This was the part that she had been dreading. Did she really have to tell her that he drank, but was seeing the missionaries. Actually, even that would be a lie. Cam hadn't said no, but he hadn't exactly shown much interest in the missionaries continuing their discussions either.

"He's cute. He's about my age and he's very smart." That was all that she offered.

Mrs. Haws wasn't satisfied. She began to fish for more. "What does he do?" she asked, and then quickly added "and where did you meet him."

Julie started with the last question, mostly because she knew the answer to that one. "I met him at the movies. He was there waiting for someone." She hesitated and then answered the other question. "I haven't the slightest idea what he does. Like I said, I just met him."

Mrs. Haws went deeper—probably too deep. "And when is the wedding?"

Julie knew her mother well enough to know that she was joking, but Julie decided to play the game, to give her mom a scare. "Next week. That's what I'm really calling you about. We're eloping to Vegas next Friday. If you want to see me get married, be there by Friday afternoon."

It had worked. Mrs. Haws was speechless. Her motherly instincts were failing her, at least for

71

the moment. She had no idea whether Julie was telling the truth or not. She prayed that she was kidding, but she just didn't know for sure.

"Julie," Mrs. Haws began, "you better be joking me."

Julie burst out laughing just as her mother was finishing her sentence. "I'm just kidding," she said and stifled the rest of her laughs. "I'm not marrying him. I haven't even gone out with him. I hope to see him someday, but I haven't yet. It just depends."

"On what."

Those words trapped Julie into the conversation she had hoped wouldn't have to be dealt with. Deep down inside, however, she knew that they would, and part of her wanted the truth to come out. She wanted to talk about it. She just wasn't sure if her mother was the right person to be talking to, but who else was there? She had few friends, none of whom she would actually want to discuss her personal life with.

"It just depends." Julie hesitated, and her mother said nothing. Finally, Julie went on, giving her mother the information she didn't really want to hear. "The missionaries are talking to him."

Again, there was a long, dreadful silence. Neither lady said anything. Julie was waiting for her mother to speak, but her mother wasn't ready. It took extra time for Mrs. Haws to gather her thoughts enough to comment.

"He's not a member of the church?"

"No."

"And you want to date him because--?"

Julie had no idea how to answer that question. She wasn't sure why. It certainly wasn't as bad as it sounded, but admittedly, to her mother, it sounded very bad. It wasn't as if she were going to dump her morals to date this guy. If he didn't change, then there would be no future for them. It would be very difficult to explain this to her, though.

"I just do, mom. He's cute. He has the potential of being a great guy. I can just see that in him." Julie wasn't sure how she even knew that, but she did. She was in the bedroom now. She adjusted the picture of the Savior, which sat on the dresser, so it directly faced the bed. Not that it was all that far off kilter, but she needed to busy her hands while she continued to explain her choice of men to her mother. "Besides, I already told you. We're not getting married. I promise you that we won't go out if he isn't willing to quit drinking and join the church." That was the best she could come up with, and she hoped it would be enough.

"That isn't all that comforting, Julie. You shouldn't be messing with guys like that. You never know what he could do." Mrs. Haws shook her head, knowing very well that her daughter was quite capable of taking care of herself, and that she wasn't going to listen to her mother's words of advice if she didn't want too.

"You don't know what he's capable of either, mother. Maybe he will surprise us both."

Julie walked out of the bedroom and headed back to the living room. The phone was cradled between her raised shoulder and her tilted head. Mrs. Haws continued to argue, and Julie knew that it was time to change the subject.

"Mom," she said and sat down on the edge of the couch. "We're not getting anywhere. Let's talk about something else."

73

A soft beeping sound echoed in Julie's ear. Someone else was trying to get through. Ordinarily, that was a sound she would disregard while talking long distance to her mother. Right now, it was a blessing. "Can you hold on, mom? I have another call."

Without waiting for a response, she pulled the receiver away from her ear and clicked the button allowing the second call to come through. "Hello," she said, fully expecting to tell whoever it was that she had to go. It was a nice break, a little time to settle herself down, but she didn't want to leave her mother on hold.

"Julie?" The man's voice was timid, almost inaudible. "Is Julie there?" the man repeated.

"This is Julie." She knew who it was, and she exhaled deeply, but silently.

"Hi," he said. "It's Cam."

"Oh, hi," she said, trying to sound a little surprised. "How are you." She almost forgot that her mother was on the other line. Before she did, she interrupted Cam. "Cam, can you hold on for a second." Again, she didn't wait for an answer. She transferred back to her mother. "Mom. I need to call you back later. I have to take this call."

"It's him, isn't it?" Mrs. Haws sounded annoyed, but she refused to argue about that as well. "Fine. Call me tomorrow. We're heading out for the rest of the day."

"I'll call you," Julie promised. "Get better." She said goodbye and then switched back to Cam, hoping that he hadn't hung up. "Hi. I'm back. Sorry, my mom was on the other line. I had to tell her I'd call her later."

"You could have just told me to call you later."

"I'd rather talk to you right now." Julie wasn't sure how high-schoolish she sounded, but she refused to worry about it. "So, how are you?"

"I'm fine," Cam said. He was sitting at the kitchen table. His back was sore from staying up all night long. "I was wondering if we could talk?"

"Sure." Julie tried to gauge what he meant but couldn't quite tell. Either he was curious about the church, or he had found a way to say that he wasn't interested.

Maybe he's interested in you.

She was surprised that she had even thought that, but yes, it was possible. Just the thought of that made her squirm in her seat a little. "Pick me up in an hour. I know where to go, unless you have something in mind already?"

"No, wherever you want to go will be fine. What's your address?" He pushed the *Book of Mormon* a little to the side and jotted the address down on a small piece of paper in front of him. "I'll be there in one hour."

A little less than an hour later, Cam pulled his black Toyota pickup truck into Julie's driveway. She was waiting for him on the porch dressed in nice fitting blue jeans, a white blouse, and tennis shoes. It was warm, around eighty degrees, and as far as he was concerned, anything but shorts and a T-shirt was over doing it, but she looked nice.

"Hi," Julie said as soon as she opened the truck door. She climbed in, looked at him, and hesitated. "Maybe I should drive." He looked drunk.

"I'm just tired," he said, knowing full well what she was thinking. "I haven't had a drink since before I met you at the theater. I haven't slept much

75

since then either. Really, I'm just fine." He waited for her to settle in, and as she directed, he headed for Piute Canyon.

Julie's curiosity got the better of her half way down the first block. "Why haven't you slept?"

He hesitated, as if confused about what to say, and then finally told her the whole truth. "I started reading your book as soon as you left and didn't put it down until this morning."

Julie figured it would take him two or three weeks to get started. That's just how it is with most people. They put things off as long as possible. While on her mission, Julie tried to set distinct deadlines and goals. It seemed to get people moving a little faster. It also gave her a way into her discussions. The missionaries had done the same with Cam, but she didn't think he would stick to it. This proved, even more, that Cam had greatness inside of him. She just hoped that he let it out someday.

"You really read all night?" she asked.

"Yeah. You sound amazed."

"I guess I am—a little bit. Actually, I'm impressed."

Cam understood her skepticism but was grateful for her positive words. He was also happy that she had been willing to talk to her. He was confused, and he certainly had a lot of questions. After spending his entire life shunning religion—all religion—he was finding the one Julie was involved in to be a bit intriguing. He decided to start asking the questions immediately.

"Was Nephi part of your church?"

Julie thought about the question for a moment before answering. "He lived the same teachings, but actually no…he wasn't. The LDS church wasn't restored until the late eighteen hundreds. This book took place in—."

"600 B.C." He interrupted her and was pleased with himself for having remembered the date. "So why do you follow what's in the book, if it has nothing to do with your religion?"

"It has a lot to do with our religion. Just like the Elders said last night. It's another Testament of Jesus Christ. We believe in Christ. We believe that this book was written for everyone on earth, so that we could have proof that Christ existed. We know that he is real, in part, because of this book. He shows himself to the people of Nephi, and we know that we will see him again some day."

Content with her answer, yet fully knowing that there was much more to it, no doubt more than he would ever be able to understand, he immediately bounced to the next question.

"There are parts in the book, just a few pages long, that's out of context, at least chronologically. "The Words of Mormon". Why is it like that?"

"How far did you get?" She was even more amazed. He really had read all night if he had read "The Words of Mormon".

"I'm only on page seventy five," he said, "but I thumbed through the rest of it."

She wasn't sure what was happening on page seventy five, but she estimated it to be somewhere in the middle of Second Nephi. "I'm even more than impressed," she said, and then answered his question. "These records were kept for hundreds of years. Mormon was the man who took all of the records and compiled them into the *Book Of Mormon*. He added his own words in certain spots to clarify things, or to add to what had already been said."

There was a moment of silence. He was finished questioning her for a moment, and this allowed her to ask him a question. "What do you think about it so far?"

He did not even hesitate. "It's interesting. I don't know how much of it I believe—I mean that was a long time ago, but it is fascinating enough that I want to keep reading. It's not boring like I expected it to be."

"Do you believe that dinosaurs roamed the earth?"

"That's a bit different, but yes, I do. They've found bones and stuff that prove they existed."

"They've found things that prove that this book is true, too. You just haven't heard of them yet." Julie looked out the front windshield and let him absorb what she had just said.

Cam began drifting off into his own little mental world. Julie sensed this and didn't say anything else. Cam was grateful for the break, because at that exact moment, he no longer wanted to talk. He wanted to think.

He began wondering where things in his life started down the wrong path. He wasn't a terrible person. He wasn't rude to people. In fact, he helped people when he could. He didn't go out of his way to do it, like some of the people he had read about in Julie's book, but he wasn't the kind of guy who would turn someone down if they needed something from him.

The more he thought about it, the more he realized that he had no idea when things began to go wrong for him. By the time he started drinking, he was already in trouble. Something had happened before then. Most likely, it was a choice he made earlier in his life that had sent his life spinning out of control. Alcohol and drugs just spun him faster.

He felt his mind wandering even more, and was about to delve into some of his past relationships, wondering if that was where things had gone wrong, but decided that he didn't want to go there. He forced his mind back to Julie. She was looking at him as if waiting for his return.

"Did you take the Elder's advice and pray about the book?" she asked as soon as she thought he was ready to hear it. It was a question that she wished she had waited to ask—not because she felt like it was the wrong thing to say, but it was poorly timed. Before he could answer, she had to direct him to where they were going. "Pull over right there!" she pointed.

The change caught Cam off guard. By the time he reacted, he had almost missed the turn. The tires slid in the gravel before finally catching. He pulled the truck onto a dirt road and slowed down. The road quickly turned into a small path. It looked more like a four-wheeler trail than a road.

As she suspected, Cam didn't answer her question. She let the subject drop, and when the road forked she had him go left. They were almost cutting their own trail now. At some point, there may have been a resemblance of a road here, but it was overgrown and non existent now. Cam began to wonder if Julie knew where she was going. Just as this thought formed in his mind, she told him to stop.

He pulled off to the side as much as possible, as if someone else was going to be on the road, and turned off the engine. A chipmunk scurried up a tree in front of the truck, and both Cam and Julie watched it until it disappeared. They walked together now, moving slowly along what looked like a game trail. The smell of dirt mixed with the clean air and Cam inhaled deeply. The fresh canyon air was rejuvenating. It was also a little cooler up here, but still too warm for pants. He took a quick look at Julie's legs and wished that she had worn shorts.

It took them two more minutes to reach their destination. Both of them were lost in their own thoughts and had very little to say. When they arrived, Julie didn't have to tell him. Cam knew this was where she had wanted to bring him.

A small creek, not quite small enough to jump across, wound its way lazily amidst hundreds of large quaking aspens. The water barely looked as if it were moving until it fell off the edge of a cliff and turned into a small, soothing waterfall. Cam took the lead now. He walked to the bottom of the hill and looked up. The water cascaded down the ten foot embankment splashing below as if trying to show off its force. From there, a soft mist drifted into the air and then fell back into the water. Forty yards further downstream, a family of beavers had been long at work. The water was backed up, forming a deep pool. *Nice place to build a house*, Cam thought with a touch of admiration.

Between the dam and the waterfall, the water was perfectly clear. It looked deceptively shallow, but Cam figured it was deep enough to swim in. He stared into the water for a long time, only looking back at Julie to see that she too was taking in the beauty around them.

This would be a nice place to party.

Cam shook his head. That was why this whole quitting thing was going to be so difficult. Too many things seemed to remind him of his habit. Everything seemed to reach out and slap him in the face and force him to remember what he was up against. Still, he had fully committed to quitting his bad habits at two o'clock this morning. It was the right thing to do. That was what he had wanted for a long time now. It just took a friend, and the book that the missionaries had given him, to push him in the right direction.

The water reminded him of the ocean described in the book. He could even smell the salty air. He pictured Nephi's family standing on the beach waiting to push off in their ships using nothing more than blind faith to guide them. That was exactly what Cam felt like he had done, pushed off using nothing more than blind faith. It worked for Nephi, and maybe it would work for him, too. He didn't have to cross an ocean, but before it was all over, Cam wondered if he may be wishing for the blue waters instead of the cold beer that he was going to have to battle.

With that thought, Cam turned to Julie and broke the silence. "I'm going to quit drinking and partying. I stopped last night."

"Why is that?" Julie asked, truly wondering what his answer was going to be.

"I want to. I hate the way my life is right now. I know things are the way they are because of the choices I've made, but I want to change that starting now—starting last night."

Julie smiled, moved closer to him, and suddenly had a strong desire to reach out to him. She wanted to touch his arms. She had a built in excuse. It would seem completely right. He needed

81

comforting. He needed to know that she was happy with his decision. That wasn't the reason she wanted to touch him, though. She liked him, although she knew that she shouldn't be having these thoughts. There was something about him that she liked, and as hard as she tried, she couldn't deny it.

Still, she fought off the urge to reach out to him. "I'll help you—if you still want me too. The missionaries will help you."

"I'll need it." He paused and then looked at her. "I'm not a strong-willed person." Cam turned away, bent down, and picked up a flat rock. He threw it sidearm and watched it skip across the water and up onto the bank on the other side.

"I'll bet you're stronger than you think. You just haven't had enough practice."

She made it sound as if he hadn't given much effort in life. The more he thought about it, the more he figured she was probably right. He hadn't tried very hard. If there was an easy way, that was the way he had always chosen—until now. This was not the easy way, no doubt about it.

"Will you answer the question now?" she asked, changing the subject so suddenly that he had no chance to know what she was really asking.

"What question?"

"Did you pray about the book?"

"No."

His answer was so straight forward that she shrunk back a little. Had he ever prayed? How could anyone make it this far in life without guidance from their Heavenly Father? It was something she couldn't even fathom. Then again, she had grown up knowing the truth. Cam hadn't had that luxury.

"Why not?" she asked.

It was an innocent question. He tried to come up with a gentle way to explain, but there wasn't an easy way. There was a blunt way though, and that was how he decided to answer her.

"Why pray to someone you don't believe in?" He stopped. That wasn't exactly the truth, not anymore anyway. He quickly changed the wording. "Or to someone you don't understand anyway."

She addressed the change. "So, now you do believe?" She didn't try to hide her hope.

"Maybe. I know it sounds weird, but like I said before, something is missing in my life. When I read your book, I couldn't help but wonder if this is what I needed. I guess it's possible that having a knowledge of a God would be beneficial." He shrugged his shoulders. He felt a little embarrassed, uncomfortable showing this much emotion, and he had to fight off the urge to turn around.

"It doesn't sound weird at all," she said. "I know exactly what you mean." This time she did reach out for him. She placed her hand on his arm, just below his elbow, and felt the warmth that his body was emitting. It almost felt unnatural…in a good way.

Cam looked straight ahead, directly into Julie's eyes. He wanted to look down just to see if she was really touching him, but he didn't dare. She might pull away, and that was the last thing he wanted. At the same time, he felt guilty. He couldn't have feelings for someone like Julie. No, he could have feelings for her, but she couldn't reciprocate. He wasn't worthy of a true lady. Still, he couldn't pull away.

"Do you want to pray?"

Julie's question caught Cam off guard. His body flinched, and he felt her pull back slightly. She didn't actually break contact, but for a brief second she came close. He thought about the question as if it could make or break his entire world. The more he pondered it, the more he wondered if it was something that he needed to do. If one choice had sent his world into a downward spiral years ago, then maybe one choice could start it back on the right path. This could be that choice.

He carefully weighed his options, knowing that she was going to give him all day to answer if he needed it. He could certainly buy a little more time if he just politely refused. It would give him time to re-evaluate everything just to see if this was the direction he wanted to head. On the other hand, he had probably over-evaluated himself already. He needed to make some very drastic changes, and this would qualify as a drastic step in the right direction.

He suddenly felt as if he were being given a second chance at life.   "Yes!" He blurted out. "If you'll show me how?"

Julie smiled, but for a long time that was all she could do. Just as she had been surprised at how much he had read, and about the questions he was asking, she was equally as shocked at his willingness to move forward. He was starting to believe, although she wasn't sure how deeply, but it was far more than she figured most people could have done in one day's time. Then again, the Lord works in mysterious ways. Why not in rapid ways as well?

The amazement, the joy, and the happiness combined and left Julie speechless. It took her a little extra time to regain control of her own emotions and thoughts. "Let's go over there," she finally said and nodded. She turned towards a large boulder but made sure she didn't let go of his arm. She was quite content with the feeling that his body was giving her. At the same time, she reminded herself that it was imperative that she move slowly. They could be friends right now—nothing more. She was content with that.

They moved to the rock and without hesitating, she knelt down. Just like he had done last night, he emulated her posture. Reluctantly, but reverently, she removed her hand from his arm and folded her arms.

"The most important thing to know is that we pray to Heavenly Father, but we are going to do it in Jesus' name. We use Jesus as the mediator—a go between—to God. I guess the only thing that you have to know is what you want to say to him."

"There isn't a set chant you do, or something like that?"

That wasn't the first time she had ever been asked that, and she didn't even flinch. "No. You say what you feel in your heart. If you feel like saying thank you for something that he's given you, say it. If you feel like asking for help, ask for it. Whatever you want to say, you can say. What you have to remember is that whatever you pray for he can give you, but you have to believe that he can, and will, give it to you. You may not always get it right off. It may be something you have to work for, but I guarantee you that if you have faith and perseverance, you'll get it when the time is right. Do you believe that?"

Cam paused. If there was a God, which at the very least, he was beginning to see as a possibility, then of course he could believe what she was telling him.

"I guess I believe it. I mean, I don't know for sure, but I could believe it."

"That's called faith; believing in something that you don't know for sure. It's the premise that the entire religion hinges on. You have to have faith."

Cam felt as if he were beginning to understand, though he also realized that it was only on a small scale. His confidence seemed to grow slightly with this realization. Of course there were things he wanted. There were also things that he had that he was grateful for. Yet, the more he realized, the more he was troubled. Was he able to say a prayer and actually talk about these things with someone sitting next to him? Weren't these things private?

As if she had read his mind, Julie gave him a way out. "Do you want me to actually say the prayer this time? You can do it later, when you're alone. I know this isn't the most comfortable thing in the world."

That was exactly what he wanted. For now, he wanted to keep his thoughts to himself. Then again, if he was praying to God, his thoughts weren't actually private, but that seemed different somehow.

Cam suddenly realized something else. To accept God, and to believe in Christ, meant realizing that he wasn't the only one who saw the secret things he had done in his own life. There was someone who could, and would, hold him accountable for every decision he had made.

The past was the past, however, and he had to get on with the future...his brighter, happier, more fulfilled life. It was time to take the plunge.

"That would be perfect." His words were very calm and yet very emphatic.

Julie sensed his confidence, and immediately pressed forward. "Okay, then let's do it."

Julie bowed her head and prayed. She kept it simple, thanking Heavenly Father for many things including the opportunity to teach the gospel to others. She asked for help in showing Cam the way to true happiness, and prayed that he would be able to quit partying. She also prayed that Cam would find out the truth about the *Book of Mormon,* but she also added 'if he asks to know the truth.' She closed, as always, "in the name of Jesus Christ. Amen."

When she finished, she looked at Cam. His eyes were still shut and for a brief second, Julie silently prayed for Cam. When he finally opened his eyes, he looked almost lost...or was he afraid? Julie wasn't sure, but she decided she didn't need to know.

"When someone finishes a prayer," she said. "Everyone says 'Amen'. It basically means that you are in agreement with what's been said."

"Amen," he said and nodded, realizing that was what everyone had said after the Elders prayed at his house.

After a few seconds of silence and pondering, they stood up and walked back to the waterfall. Julie stared into the water. From the corner of her eye she could see him. He stared at her for several seconds before looking into the sky. She looked up as well.

She was unsure why, but the memory of this morning's argument with her mother came back to her. Why would her mother begrudge her this happiness? Had she not spent the first nineteen years of her life being reminded by dear old mom that everyone is capable of being forgiven? How could she teach that but not live it?

The actual words of the argument began slipping into her conscious mind. As they did, Julie suddenly began to see things from her mother's perspective. It didn't take long for her to realize what her mother had been trying to tell her. It wasn't Cam that her mom was worried about. Of course she believed he could be forgiven. But what if he didn't want that. No one really knew. Cam was certainly in a position to cause real pain; even more so now. That is all her mom had been saying.

Julie vowed to call her mom as soon as she got home, just to clear things up. The last thing she wanted was to have her mother go through life worrying and afraid for her daughter. Julie could solve that problem, and she would. She promised not to allow her and Cam to become anything more than friends until the time was right. That would help.

A soft crackling sound came from behind her. She swung around so fast that her shoe caught on the ground and she almost tripped.

Cam was ten feet away from her, staring as if in a trance. He had wondered away while Julie was off in her own world. Julie could see the faint signs of wetness in his eyes. She didn't think he had actually cried, but he looked like he was very close. She slowly approached him, placed her hand on his arm again, but neither of them said a word. Cam reached up, took her hand in his, and together they walked back to the truck.

They drove home without saying a word. The silence was awkward, but out of respect, neither of them broke it until they reached Julie's driveway.

She wanted to ask him what he was thinking about, but she didn't. Whatever he was feeling had obviously hit him pretty hard. He was almost acting lost, or was it truly a trance? Whichever it was, she didn't want to ruin it with words. She had to say something, but she kept it brief.

"Call me, okay?" she said and climbed out of the truck. Before shutting the door, she looked at Cam and smiled. "Congratulations. You've already taken one of the hardest steps to feeling better."

Cam smiled but didn't say a word. He got in his car and drove home feeling quite mixed up. He even wondered if he was going to be able to walk into his house. His legs felt stiff, and he suddenly felt as if he had lost his energy. Although he wasn't exactly sure what had just happened to him, he definitely liked the feelings that it had produced. What he did know was that he needed some sleep.

Chapter Six

"Look at them," Julie said and glanced at the couple sitting at the table across from her and Cam. "You can tell they're on a first date."

"And how do you know that?" He looked at the couple and as far as he could tell, they could have been married for ten years and had five kids. They each looked about thirty five. She wasn't exactly cute, but neither was the man.

"No rings," she said starting her debate.

Cam looked at their fingers. He would have picked up on that one, he thought. "Maybe they're about to get married," he said, knowing that she was going to come up with something to refute his comment.

"They haven't touched their chips and salsa," she continued. "If they had been dating for a long time they would have downed them. They haven't eaten one chip—especially not with salsa on it."

He rebutted. "So that means that they both are planning to share a big long smooch later and don't want to have bad breath."

"Possibly," Julie said and chanced another look at the couple. They looked cute together. In fact, they looked perfect for each other. They were both dressed up, not for comfort but more to impress the other. "That or else they are sitting there hoping that they get a kiss after their big first date."

He was going to give in to her, but before he could say anything their waitress came around the corner, spoiling their little game—for the time being. She carefully balanced the large serving tray with her left hand while spreading the legs on the makeshift table in her right hand out on the floor. She served the food professionally, as if she had been doing it forever.

"I'm proud of you, Cam." Julie said as soon as they were alone again. "For letting the Elders come back, I mean." This had been their third meeting, and things were going wonderfully.

Cam smiled. "It's all a bit confusing," he said, "but it makes me feel good. That's enough to keep listening and learning."

Julie swirled her steak in A-1 sauce and lifted the bite to her mouth. Before eating it, she asked a question, one meant to make Cam think. "Elder Cummings asked you a question tonight, but you didn't get too deep. What really are your reservations about the church?" She then placed the meat in her mouth, planning to have a long pause before he answered.

He surprised her, however, with a much deeper, much more involved answer than he had given before, and he did so immediately. "I've been thinking about that since he asked me about it. I guess I'm just afraid—afraid that if I fully embrace the church, and fully admit that all of this is more than just a possibility, then I have to deal with the consequences of that decision."

Cam looked as Julie. She was chewing, and obviously not ready to comment, so he continued. "I mean, I've done a lot of bad things in my life. If

91

I have find out that the church really is true, and that there is a God, and a Savior, then I have a lot of work to do to repent for it. That was pretty much what the missionaries were saying I would have to do. I don't know if I can do that."

"Sure you can."

Julie's answer left Cam almost in a state of shock. Three simple words, and yet they made him glad that he wasn't swallowing at the time, for fear of choking. She really was in his corner. She was standing up for him like no one had ever done before. Not only that, but the confidence that she was showing in him was likely to give him strength as well. Maybe he could do this.

Deep in thought once again, they ate without saying a word. Julie picked at her food, but only actually swallowed a few more bites. She was more interested in the show going on at the other table.

"Look," Cam whispered. "Her leg."

Julie had already noticed that the woman was making her move and nodded at Cam. The woman slid her foot out and was almost touching her dates leg. That was not what amazed her the most, however. Cam was actually playing her game. He was actually getting into it.

"They're definitely first timers," Cam finally agreed.

Julie laughed and quickly hid her mouth behind her glass as she pretended to sip from her drink. It was impolite to stare, and worse to make up stories as they stared, but she couldn't help it. She was having fun.

Both Julie and Cam turned back to their food. Julie's steak now lay in a couple dozen bite-sized pieces. She noticed this and looked at Cam's plate to see how he was fairing. Not much better. *He's not eating because you're not eating.*

Just in case that was it, Julie stuck her fork into a piece of steak and put it into her mouth. Cam immediately followed suit. Again, they fell into silence, this time for at least five minutes.

"Bingo," Julie finally said. "She did it."

Cam's eyes moved to the other booth. The couple legs were resting against each other, and their meal had been picked through and left for the waste disposal. Now, with their first touch of the night, it was apparent that they were lost in the excitement. They had completely forgotten about eating. They were more interested in making their lingering touch last as long as possible.

"Which one's going to make the move with the hands?" Cam asked, talking as quietly as he could. He tried to conceal the fact that he was talking about the new off-camera stars.

"We'll never know," Julie said. The couple stood up just as Cam finished his question. They were leaving, and somehow Julie couldn't help but wish she could follow them just to find out how the story ended.

As if fishing for something that would fill in the empty void that the couple was leaving, Cam asked a question. "What do you do…for a living? Or what do you want to do?"

"I'm a paralegal. I work for Timothy Washburn and Jeremy Adams, in Salt Lake."

"You drive to Salt Lake every day?" It was only a thirty minute drive, but to Cam, that seemed like a long way to go every day. "Have you ever thought of moving up there?"

"I don't like Salt Lake. Well, I wouldn't want to live there anyway. It's too big for me. I like it here in Pine Hills."

"Is that what you want to do in the future—be a paralegal?" Cam asked.

Julie thought about the truth. This might not be the perfect time to tell him, but he was the one who had brought it up. "I hope to get married, in the temple of course, and raise a family. What I would really like to be is a stay-at-home mom."

Before he could respond, Julie posed a similar question to Cam. "What are you going to do with your new life?"

Cam began to fidget noticeably. His fingers twitched and he quickly laced them and pulled them under the table. He knew what he wanted to say. Writing was all he had really ever wanted to do, but how was he supposed to say that. Writing was a poor man's job, at least it is unless you get lucky, and lucky wasn't exactly how he would classify his life.

He decided to take the plunge anyway, just to see where it took him. "I write. I haven't exactly been published yet, but I plan to be."

Julie prejudged him immediately. "What do you write about?" She put down her fork, intent on listening to him.

Cam smiled and shook his head softly. "I'd really like to write a romance novel."

He said it with a straight face and although it took her a few seconds to come to grips with it, she knew he was serious. "Have you written a romance novel?"

"Actually, I haven't started a novel. I'm working on some poems and a bunch of short stories."

"Can I see them?"

He was prepared for this question. He had replayed this scenario in his mind several times, just in case anyone happened to ask him. "When I'm completely finished with something I feel is decent. No one gets to see anything until it's done."

"Fair enough, but you have to tell me when you finish something, okay?" She asked another question, one that surprised Cam. "I saw some books on your table at your house. Interesting selection. Can I read one of your horror stories? I've always said I want to try a book in every genre."

Cam shook his head and grinned. "Yeah. I'll pick the spookiest one I have. How's that?" He fully expected her to back away from the idea. She didn't seem like the type who would like a real good horror story.

Julie shrugged her shoulders, not really worried about something frightening her. Fear was nothing to be afraid of, just dealt with like everything else in life.

As the conversation began to drag, it became increasingly obvious that neither of them had any intention of eating anymore. It was a waste of good food, but appetites had to wait. Cam pushed his food away and slid his iced tea around the plate until it was directly in front of him. The water from the glass beaded on the table and left skid marks.

A small boy raced past heading for the bathroom, not bothering to look back to see if dad was still on his heels. He was, but he was losing ground quickly. Cam briefly remembered going out with his family when he was little. He probably took his dad on the very same chase some time. Mom and dad used to take him to dinner every other

Friday. Cam knew after a short time that it was a bribe so that he would watch himself while his parents disappeared every Saturday and got drunk. It didn't matter though. It was a meal, a really good meal.

Cam looked away and re-focused on Julie. She was sipping her sprite like it was fine wine.

Alcohol!

The thoughts of alcohol bombarded him. Suddenly, it was all he could think about. For a brief, but vision-filled moment, his mind wandered. When he snapped out of it, he was left with the lingering effects of the craving. He wanted a beer.

"Cam...Hello?"

Cam barely heard Julie, and when the waitress placed the bill on the corner of the table and walked away, he almost missed the act entirely. He wanted that beer, and it was more than a craving. All of a sudden, he wondered if he wanted a drink even more than he wanted to be here. One beer wasn't going to kill him. He could always say "oops, I blew it", and start over tomorrow. Besides, he had done quite well. It had been more than two weeks since he had had a single drink.

"Is everything okay?" Julie asked when she finally got his attention.

Cam took a deep breath and looked at Julie. "Yeah. I'm fine."

"You're wanting a drink, aren't you?"

He nodded. A sense of guilt rushed through him. He felt bad, but his mind refused to give him a break. *You can't quit. Just have a drink. Why torture yourself?* "I'm not sure if I can do this, Julie. It's driving me insane. I freak out about alcohol all day long, every day, and it doesn't seem to be getting any better."

"Sometimes you wonder what's really important to you, huh? It's like something is talking to you, tempting you. Maybe I don't know exactly what you're feeling, but I can tell you one thing. Those temptations are lies. They're coming from the devil. He wants you to fail, and he is doing everything he can to make you keep drinking. He knows he has you if he can keep you drinking. There will never be a better time to quit. No matter what he tells you, now is the time—no matter how hard it is—but it's your choice. You just have to decide you don't want to drink and say no. Don't allow the feelings to linger. Push them away."

"That sounds so simple, but it's not" Cam said sarcastically.

"It's not simple, I'm sure. But if anyone can do it, you can. You're tough enough to pull this off. Just make the decision."

Cam shook his head, very slowly at first but increasing until he looked like he was saying no. Julie watched him, wondering what "no" meant. Was he going to give in to the craving, or did no mean he wasn't going to take that drink?

Suddenly, she saw that look in his eyes again. It was bad...ugly bad, and she wanted to turn away. She hated that look.

"I'm not going to drink."

His words were quite contradictory to the look in his eyes. He appeared to be in so much pain, like the devil had possessed him, yet at the same time he was battling, fighting off the temptations—and he was winning.

"I don't need to drink to be happy"

This time Julie smiled. He was definitely a winner. She already knew this, which was why she agreed to go on a date. Cam was going to succeed.

She watched as the look in his eyes slowly returned to normal.

"You're right," she finally said. "You don't need a drink to be happy. Alcohol doesn't make anyone happy. You already know that."

Cam smiled, and she could see a transformation taking place inside his brain. His face was glowing, like he really believed that he was doing the right thing. He had more color in his face and he looked like he really understood what she was trying to explain to him. He was allowing it all to sink in.

"Why don't we get out of here," Julie suggested. After writing a check and leaving it on the table, he stood up and moved to Julie. He held her hand and helped her up. It felt a little awkward, but he did it anyway.

For Julie, it sent tingles up and down the back of her neck. That was what Prince Charming was supposed to do. Cam was not Prince Charming, not yet anyway, but he was certainly showing the signs.

Before leaving, Cam looked back at the table. Most of their food was still sitting on their plates. He couldn't help but think of the couple they had almost been making fun of earlier. He and Julie had done the exact same thing the other couple had done. It was almost a funny thought, but when he looked at the bowl of chips, he knew it was not a joke. The bowl was full, as was the saucer of salsa. He smiled and led Julie to the truck.

When he pulled into her driveway, he again began thinking about the couple in the restaurant. Had the guy kissed his date? Did he even try? Cam couldn't answer the question, but he did equate it to his own predicament. Was he supposed to try giving Julie a kiss? Was she going to tell him no? Before long, he began to wonder which mental problem was driving him more insane; the drinking or wondering how to end this evening.

They spoke on the way home about what the missionaries had taught him earlier in the evening—our relationship to God, how we should live our lives, and what we do when we mess things up. They also shared with each other, a little more about themselves, which proved to be a more difficult task. After stopping off at Cam's for the book he picked out for Julie, Stephen King's *Pet Cematary,* he drove straight to her house.

As soon as he pulled into Julie's driveway, Cam's mind took over and left him wondering how he should react at the close of this date.

Julie solved this problem, which took Cam by surprise; a reaction he figured he better get used to if he was to spend much time with her. She reached her hand out and placed it on top of Cam's. He was sure his hands felt rough and clammy, but she didn't give him much chance to think about it.

"Thanks for dinner," she said.

The soft feel of their hands touching felt good—to both of them. She leaned over and kissed him. It was a simple peck, but the energy that overtook both of them was powerful. Julie found herself having a hard time controlling the wonderful feelings that were rushing through her entire body. It was time to leave and she knew it.

She pulled away and clamored for the door handle, never taking her eyes off of Cam. She missed it the first time but grasped it on the second try. She quickly opened the door. "Can I see you Tuesday?" she said. "Maybe miniature golfing or something." Cam nodded. "I'll pick you up," she said and stepped out of the truck. She shut the door and turned around. When she did, it was all she could do to keep walking. She listened to the sound of the truck's engine as Cam backed away.

Chapter Seven

For another four weeks, Cam successfully battled his alcohol problem. Hearing the lessons from the missionaries helped, but still the desires would not go away. In fact, instead of becoming easier, the craving increased, both in frequency and intensity. He fell victim to these cravings exactly one month from the date of his first date with Julie.

Go for a drive—maybe to Julie's.

The feeling came suddenly, completely out of nowhere, as he sat watching a Utah Jazz game. He was alone, because Julie had to attend a work party. They had been spending quite a bit of time together, especially during the past two weeks. Cam used the fact that she wasn't home to ignore the warnings that his own mind was giving him…or was it the spirit he had been hearing so often? Whatever it was, he ignored the thought.

Twenty minutes later, there was a knock on the door, and Marcus and Sandy were standing on the porch when he opened the door. Marcus was holding a case of beer in his right hand, and an already opened can in the other.

"Let's party," Marcus said. He didn't give Cam time to say no. He stepped into the house, right past Cam, and walked straight downstairs.

Cam stepped to the side and allowed Sandy to enter as well, not really knowing what else to do. She looked at him, closed her eyes briefly as if she was ashamed of Marcus' behavior, and then moved down the stairs as well.

Cam tried to stop this sudden threat, but his words came out mixed, leaving plenty of doubt as to his conviction. "I don't party anymore, Marcus."

"Yeah, right. You party—just like the rest of us."

"I quit." This time, Cams words were direct and there was no way for anyone to misconstrue what he was trying to say.

Marcus moved closer to Cam. "What's with you, man? You're freakin' out on me. Why?" Marcus looked like a rabid wolf. "Are you tripped out on some drug that I don't know about? Cause if you are, give me some. We need to get back on the same wavelength—like old times. It's not good if some of us get left out of the loop if you know what I mean."

Marcus was talking like a drug addict, intentionally trying to sound like a stoner dude from the eighties. "So what's the deal, man. Are you going to share or what?"

"I'm not doing drugs." Cam defended himself. "I'm sober. I'm sick of being drunk all the time."

"You're full of it. You love it and you know it." Marcus looked down at the case of beer he was holding and stared at Cam. "There's nothing wrong with drinking with your friends, man. If it doesn't feel right, just keep it more under control. You don't have to get wasted. Just have a few beers. After that, if you want us to leave, we will. But if you want more, I'll spend the entire night handing them to you. Whatever you want okay?"

Cam wanted to say no. He desperately fought with himself. But it was a losing battle. He wished that Julie would show up, but that wasn't going to happen. She wasn't going to be home until after eleven, and she wasn't coming here first. He was stuck with Marcus, and he couldn't say no to Marcus. He never could, and he doubted if he would ever be able to.

"Fine."

That was all it took. One word. That was the end of what he figured could be a great relationship with a great lady, but he needed a drink. At least he did tonight. Maybe he could start again tomorrow, but tonight he couldn't let Marcus down—even if it meant letting himself down.

After putting the rest of the beer in the fridge, Marcus handed Cam one can and smiled. "That's better," he said and helped himself to the couch. "Come here." Marcus looked at Sandy and Cam couldn't help but wonder when she had become an object. That was exactly how Marcus had spoken to her. Was she really bowing to his wish when she walked obediently to the couch? Is that how it was now, or was he just seeing his friends from a step back? Maybe that's how it had always been all along, and he just hadn't been sober enough to see it.

Cam sat down in the chair and began sipping the beer. It was cold and tasted like cold spring water with a real strong kick. It didn't take long for him to slip back into the comfort level that he was so accustomed to. It was a relief, but at the same time there was something nagging at him. Despite this feeling, he continued to drink.

"So where have you been, Cam?" It was Sandy's turn to question him.

"I've just been busy. Actually, I've been seeing someone. You know how it is. You have to

103

give a new thing a chance to grow, to see where it ends up."

"And where is it going to end up?" Marcus asked condescendingly.

Before Cam could answer, Sandy asked another question, and Cam wondered if she was trying to protect him from something. "What's her name?" she asked and stared at him.

Cam was grateful for Sandy's question, because he wouldn't have been able to answer Marcus' question. He had no idea where the relationship was going to end up. At least he hadn't known until tonight, and he didn't want to come right out and admit that he was blowing off the entire relationship for a couple of beers—not to Marcus, anyway. That would prove to Marcus that he had won.

"Julie." Cam gave a simple, straightforward answer. One that couldn't lead to other questions.

"Well get her over here. I want to meet her." Marcus was dead serious, and if it weren't for a good excuse, he may have been able to talk Cam into it.

"If she wasn't out for the evening, she'd already be here," Cam said and shivered inwardly. The idea of Marcus and Julie together for any reason made Cam cringe.

"Fine, but I'm going to meet her, you got that," he said and pointed at Cam. He was playing with Cam's head, bothering him as much as possible without crossing the friendship line. "We'll have to party with her sometime!"

"She doesn't party." Cams words were very defensive.

"What do you mean she don't party? How much fun can a woman be if she don't party?"

"Excuse me!" Sandy said. "I--." Sandy stopped as if realizing that what she had to say would be absolutely stupid or inappropriate.

Marcus shot a look at her that made Cam take a mental step backwards. Why was he so controlling? Was she that afraid of him? "Stay out of it," he said. His words were hard for Cam to hear, and he wondered what it had felt like to Sandy.

Sandy smiled, but it was very false, as if she had been rehearsing that response for a very long time. "Sorry, hon," she said. Marcus turned away from her and Cam could see the relief in Sandy's eyes, as if she had just gotten away with something.

"So I guess we'll just have to change her," Marcus said. "We'll initiate her into the drinking club of America. We can make her fun...we have our ways." He tipped his beer into the air and toasted Cam, but Cam did not return the toast.

Marcus stood up and walked over to Cam. He towered over him, but Cam just watched, wondering what he was going to do...and almost looking forward to it. Marcus was very capable of making a party fun, and right now, Cam figured that was exactly what he needed.

"Drink your beer," Marcus said as if he were a drill sergeant. "Guzzle every drop. Hurry up."

Cam turned his head and looked at Sandy. She was smiling, knowing full well that the party was about to begin. He looked up at Marcus and smiled. The can was almost half empty, and he knew he could finish it off in seconds. With Marcus watching approvingly, nodding with each swallow, Cam downed the contents of the can and crushed in the sides as he pulled it away from his lips.

"Well," Cam said and handed Marcus the empty can, "aren't you getting me another beer?"

Marcus looked at Cam as he walked into the kitchen, almost tripping over his own feet. When he returned, he was still staring, and Cam wondered if he had been mentally watching him while he was gone. He was carrying three beers. He handed one to Cam, one to Sandy, and then popped the tab on his own.

"We race!" Marcus yelled, much louder than he needed to. It didn't matter though. Mr. Devost, Cam's neighbor, had moved out almost a month ago. The landlord didn't seem to be all that concerned about filling the vacancy, either. He had barely put up a for rent sign last weekend.

Downing beer as fast as he could was one of Cam's favorite pastimes. Marcus' challenge was one that Cam would not refuse. He was juiced now, primed and ready to down the entire can without stopping. He pulled the tab and lifted the can to his mouth. Both he and Marcus looked at Sandy, waiting for her to get ready as well. When she did, and before Marcus could take charge, Cam started them.

"Ready—Set--."

Before saying go, he began downing his beer. It went down so smooth, so natural, that he nearly forgot about his desire to quit drinking entirely. Cam finished first, of course, and again dented the sides of the can. He bent over and slammed the can onto the floor just as Marcus finished his beer. Sandy finished seconds later.

"What's the matter? You two still can't keep up?"

Marcus laughed. "Welcome back, man. Welcome back." Without a pause, he added, "I gotta' use your bathroom!"

"Use the one upstairs," Cam said. The toilet down here isn't working right."

Cam watched Marcus dart upstairs, skipping every other stair. Out of the corner of his eye, Cam saw Sandy flinch. Something had hurt her. She resituated herself on the couch, trying desperately not to show the pain. Cam pretended not to notice and half-looked away. Thinking that he couldn't see her, Sandy pulled up the bottom of her shorts to look at her leg.

A gigantic bruise, about the size of a softball, covered her right thigh. She wasn't athletic, but she wasn't usually the type who would fall over and hurt herself either. Even completely drunk she was smart enough to fall into someone's waiting arms or onto a soft bed. Cam knew exactly where that bruise had come from. It wasn't the size of a softball. It's the size of Marcus' fist, Cam thought.

He turned his head away, not wanting her to think that he had seen. At the first sign of movement, Sandy quickly pulled the cuff of her white shorts back into place and sat perfectly still.

When Marcus returned, he refueled everyone with another drink. Cam just stared at him as he did it, hiding his disgust. He suddenly had the urge to say something to Marcus. Why would he hit Sandy? She was decent, especially to Marcus. But Cam didn't say anything. He couldn't. If anything, it would only get Sandy in more trouble later on.

"You want to race again?"

"No." There was a hint of contempt in Cam's voice. If Marcus picked up on it he didn't bother to acknowledge it. "I'm just going to drink a couple more and then call it a night."

"You're feeling guilty aren't you?" Marcus asked. "You're a drinker, man. Don't change what you are, especially for some woman. Man, what kind of hold does she have on you? Be a man!"

Yea, real men beat up their girlfriends.

Cam almost let it slip out. "Just drink your beer," he said trying to sound like he was still kidding around.

For the next little while, the three of them drank, but the mood was more serious now, certainly not a party. Sandy seemed to slip more and more into the background. It just wasn't the same anymore, and the more Cam tried to make it seem as if it was, the more things seemed to feel wrong. More troubling, he couldn't get that bruise out of his mind. He wasn't sure if she had been doing it before, but every time Sandy moved, Cam could see the pain in her eyes. Even with the sedating effects of the alcohol, she wasn't able to hide it entirely.

Cam spent the rest of the time looking for a way to get them out of his house. What he really wanted to do was send Marcus away but keep Sandy here. He had a burning desire to ask her about Marcus. It would be hard, especially on her, but he needed to talk to her. He wanted to warn her. As if she needed to be warned. She had enough of a warning on her leg.

It was a thought that he regretted having. Although it did not actually affect anything, his thought seemed to set off a scenario of events; things that Cam wished he didn't have to witness, but he did. In fact, it was almost as if he were tied to his chair watching a very bad movie.

"Maybe we should go," Sandy said. "It's obvious that he doesn't want to party anymore."

It was an innocent statement. She hadn't meant anything rude by it, but apparently it had been the wrong time to say it.

As if by reaction alone, Marcus lifted his hand and swung it at her mouth. The back of his hand connected with the side of her cheek, and the combination of the blow and her trying to avoid it sent her head into the wall behind her. The sheet rock dented and Cam wondered if her head had dented as well.

She let out a stifled scream, but instead of reaching for the back of her head or her cheek, Sandy grabbed her leg. The quick movement had caused the bruise on her thigh to shoot excruciating pains down her leg.

Seeing her pain did not seem to effect Marcus at all. Cam could see the anger in his face. He wasn't sorry. If anything, he was steadying himself, daring her to say something else.

Finally, after staring at her for several seconds just to make sure she wasn't going to talk back, Marcus stood up. "I'm going upstairs."

Cam waited until Marcus had shut the door to the bathroom before saying anything. "How long has this been going on?" he finally asked.

She had no intentions of answering him. She turned her head and closed her eyes.

"You don't have to put up with this crap, Sandy." For a moment, he had no idea where to take the conversation. But as if someone had put the words into his mouth—and he couldn't help but wonder if they were Julie's words—he knew what to say. "Leave him. We can help you. Julie's an incredible person. We can get you help."

He wasn't sure why he believed that Julie would help. She probably wasn't even going to talk to him, let alone help another alcoholic woman. Deep down inside, though, he knew that she would be there if he and Sandy needed her.

Cam slumped back into the chair. The toilet flushed overhead, and he knew he was running out of time. "Leave him! Call me!"

Instead of addressing the problem, Sandy blurted out something that really forced Cam's blood to boil. "He's threatening to get your girlfriend—and you—if you don't stop acting like you're better than us. Be careful, Cam."

Cam didn't have time to respond. What would he say anyway? If she was telling the truth, and why would she lie, then maybe this was a desperate problem. Why else would she risk her well being, just to warn him of something Marcus had threatened?

Marcus came down the stairs as if nothing had happened at all. He went straight for the kitchen and returned with what Cam figured was the last three beers. Just as he had done all night long, he handed the first one to Cam, the second to Sandy, and kept the third one for himself.

"I'm sorry,"

These words slammed into Cam's brain and probably hurt as much as the bruise on Sandy's leg seemed to be hurting her. The words bothered him because they hadn't come from Marcus. They had come from Sandy.

What did she have to be sorry for, except being with a jerk? She hadn't done anything wrong. He was the one who should be apologizing.

Marcus still didn't say a word to her. Suddenly, Cam realized why she had said it. She was sedating him, hoping there wouldn't be any more abuse later.

Cam had no idea how long the torture had been going on, but he was sure that it had been happening for a long time. It had no doubt been happening when they were partying together (he said it as if it had been a long time ago). He had just been too stupid—or too drunk—to see the signs.

But now that there was a big sign on her thigh, and there would soon be one on her cheek and on the back of her head as well. Cam finally knew the truth, and he felt sorry for her. Sandy was a good person. She had definitely always been good to Marcus. She didn't deserve to be slapped around.

She's a junky.

The words that came from his own mind forced Cam to sit up straighter in his chair. Why would he think that? She's not a junky, he rebutted his own thought.

But was she? His mind began flipping images of the past into his conscious mind like a slide show. Each picture showed Sandy when she had been drunk or messed up on drugs. Of course there were times when she wasn't drunk or stoned, but the more he thought about it, the more he realized that it hadn't been all that often.

Another picture showed him just what she was like when she wasn't messed up, and the thought scared him.

"Come on, Marcus," Cam remembered Sandy saying once. "Just let me have some. You promised."

111

Marcus had made her beg, and she had done it without hesitation. Cam now wondered just how far she would have gone for a fix?

The more he thought about it, the more he realized the truth. Maybe she was a junky, and while seeing her for what she really was, something else scared him. He was a junky too! They all were.

How many times had he begged, in his own little way, for a drink or something to smoke. He was no better than she was. That scared him, but just as he thought it, he realized one obvious difference. He had help…or at least he used to have help. He had blown his chance, just like a typical junky, for a drink. If anything, he was worse than Sandy. She never had a chance.

Be her chance!

All of these thoughts rushed through Cam's mind in what felt like a fleeting second. Sandy's "I'm sorry" had barely come out of her mouth. In that small amount of time, however, Cam had made two important decisions. He was not going to be a junky any longer. With or without Julie's help (but he hoped it would be with it), he was going to stop drinking and partying—no more messing up. Secondly, he was going to help Sandy.

But how?

Marcus stood up and looked at Cam. "I hate it when things get out of control like this." He turned away from Cam and started up the stairs. "Let's go," he called to Sandy. He didn't wait for her like a gentleman. Instead, he walked out the front door, not even bothering to say another word to anyone.

Cam took the chance, and he knew exactly what to say.

"Leave him. I'll help you. I promise. I know some people who can help."

Sandy wanted to say something. That much was obvious, but she wouldn't allow herself to speak. It wasn't that bad with Marcus, she thought. It wasn't like she was getting beaten up *all* the time. It looked like it to Cam, and he probably deserved a better explanation than what he was getting, but not now. She had to get outside. Marcus was waiting, and she didn't want him to get any madder than he already was.

Cam watched as Sandy looked away from him and headed for the stairs. When she looked back at him, he could see the tears beginning to form in her almost colorless eyes. He wondered if all the will to live had been sucked out of her entirely.

"Be careful, Cam," she said.

She walked out the door, and other than the sounds of the car door shutting outside, and the drunken squeal of tires on the loose gravel, the rest of the world seemed to become blurry.

Chapter Eight

The loud rumbling of thunder shook the tiny store entitled "The Reading Barn." It put Cam on edge even more. It had been a terrible weather day from the moment he woke up. This, combined with the anger and depression that had plagued him all night long—not to mention the mass confusion of what he really wanted in life—had given him a headache. Two aspirin, more than an hour earlier, hadn't helped at all.

Work was the last thing that Cam wanted to do right now, but what choice did he have? The work had to be finished. Sometime tonight, probably right after work, he was going to have to call Julie, or stop by her house and tell her how he had blown everything. Knowing this was coming made focusing on his job even more difficult.

Still, he had to get something accomplished. There were stacks of books behind the counter that he needed to have put away before closing. They were the trade-ins, most of them in very good shape. The others were at least readable. It wouldn't take long to put them away, but he simply couldn't find the energy. All he was in the mood for was being lazy and feeling sorry for himself.

The lights flickered, and he finally got off the stool. There were candles in the storeroom, and just in case the power went out, he had to find them. Mrs. Collins was the only one with a key to the store, and if the power went off he would be locked in here alone. Ordinarily, this wouldn't have bothered him, but right now, he wasn't quite feeling up to it. It would give him an excuse to do nothing, but he didn't want to be alone in the dark.

Cam made his way down the center isle, peering at the books as he went. He didn't pay much attention to the titles, but the three books in the romance section that were crooked caught his eye. He straightened them, but didn't stop moving. That was as much work as he had completed all day, and his shift was two hours away from being finished.

The storeroom was small, well lit, and quite cluttered. Hundreds of torn books were sitting on the shelves and on the table in the center of the room, and had been for years. Sometimes, a few of them were fixed and added to the shelves in the store, but other torn books always seemed to take their place. Along the north wall, directly across from the door, were several unmarked boxes. That was where the candles were, but which box?

Starting with the top left box, Cam began shuffling through the items. He found a box of matches in the fourth box he opened, but the candles proved to be more elusive. It wasn't until the next to last box that he finally found what he was looking for.

As soon as he retrieved the two white candles, a buzzing sound pierced the store room. Cam jumped and almost dropped one of the candles. Someone had just walked into the store, but who would be out right now?

He had intended to walk back to the front of the building via one of the other two isles, just to give them a quick look over as he had the middle isle, but he didn't. With the candles and matches in hand, he quickly walked to the front of the store.

"Hi."

It was Julie. Cam's brain seemed to scramble instantly. Seeing her standing in the store made him realize how much he already cared for her. At the same time, it caused him pain—mental pain. He felt like running to her, holding her, feeling her soft hands in his. He also felt like shrinking into the back room and crawling under the table.

Julie looked very nice, as usual. She wore a long blue and white dress and a light jacket. Her hair was wind blown, but still in place. The strong smell of perfume drifted through the air and made Cam want to move closer. How did things get so messed up?

"Hi," he said and moved behind the cash register. He placed the candles on the counter between him and Julie, and looked up. "How was the party?"

Julie knew something was wrong. She didn't even have to look at him to tell. The air, as soon as their eyes had met, had grown thicker and now she could sense something. It was almost the same feeling she had the day they first met. She knew immediately that he had become drunk. Everything about this situation proved that.

"The party was fine." She looked at him and shrunk backwards—mentally. "I'm sorry," she said. "I should have called before I came over."

"No. It's fine." Cam lit the first candle, hoping that with that one small act he could change the mood. It didn't work. He put the matches down and looked back at Julie. "I'm glad you came."

"So--." Julie thought about questioning him, but decided a more subtle approach would be better. "I hear you sell books here."

Cam was amused at her attempt at humor, but he didn't laugh. What he wanted to do was to sneak back to the horror section and hide out with the rest of the butchers, because that was exactly what he had done to Julie. He had cut her up, destroying their relationship, and the trust that he had worked so hard to earn, in one night. It wasn't worth it.

"I'm looking for a good, clean, romance novel," Julie asked, still pretending as if she didn't know him. "You got anything like that here?"

Cam smiled and stepped out from behind the counter. He felt exposed, like an injured deer caught out in an open field. As he walked down the isle, he had to fight off the urge to look behind him. She wasn't after him, but it sure felt like it.

He focused on his goal: a good book. By the time he reached the correct shelf, he knew just the one. He reached for the book, but before he could grab it, the ringing of the bell startled him again, though not quite as bad.

Cam quickly pulled the book from the shelf and handed it to Julie. "I'll be right back," he said. Julie nodded and watched as he walked away from her. The smile on her face, which she had been using to mask her sadness, drifted away.

Although Cam was happy for the distraction, he wished that whoever had entered the store would have waited. Eventually, he was going to have to tell Julie the truth. She knew already. She was probably just waiting for confirmation. He had to tell her, but now it would have to wait.

"Can I help you," he said.

117

A tall man in a navy blue suit and black tie, contrasting perfectly with his white shirt, turned to Cam. A lady stood by his side; she too was dressed up as if they were going to a very important business meeting. The gentleman looked at Cam. "No, thank you. We're just looking."

"If you need something, just let me know. I'm back here with--." With who? Was Julie his girlfriend? Was she just a friend, or had he blown it entirely? Maybe they were about to become old acquaintances. "Another customer," Cam finished.

The man nodded and began walking around, browsing through the stack of books on the shelf just inside the door. The lady moved towards him slowly, reading the titles of books on the wall. Cam turned away from the couple and slowly made his way back to Julie, who was no longer in the romance section. She was searching the books against the west wall.

"There aren't any romance books here, ma'am. This is the western section."

Julie turned around and Cam noticed that she didn't have the book he had chosen for her. He decided that she had changed her mind, but he didn't figure that she would be a fan of the old wild-west. "May I make another suggestion?" he asked.

"No."

She sounded upset, or was it full blown anger? It was time to confess. There was no way of saying it that wouldn't make things horrible, so he just said it. "I got drunk last night. Well, not really drunk, but I did drink."

Julie looked at him. She had known that from the moment she had walked in. Hearing the words coming directly from Cam's mouth shouldn't have made it worse, but it did. What did this all mean? What was she supposed to do? Was she going to just forgive him? Could she? Was it even her place to forgive him?

"I couldn't say no," Cam continued. "Marcus and Sandy came over and I couldn't get rid of them."

Just as the words came out, another loud blast of thunder shook the store. Julie shuddered. The thunder only caused a small part of this. Cam's words told her what she figured she needed to know. If he couldn't say no, then he wasn't going to quit. That meant--. She didn't finish her thought.

Lightning slashed out of the sky. Neither of them could see it, but they knew. The lights flickered and the power went out. The shop went completely black, and for a moment, Cam stood still and wondered what to do.

He reached out to Julie and took her hand in his. She was cold. The truth had affected her more than he had even realized. He led her to the center isle, following the flickering of the candle. Before reaching the front, he met the man and lady.

"This way," Cam said and continued to walk up the isle. He had worked here for four years now. He didn't need light to know where to go. They reached the front of the store and Cam stood to the side, expecting the couple to leave, but they didn't.

"I'd like to get this book," the man said and placed a large paper back book on the counter.

Through the window, Cam could see that the sky was as black as he had ever seen it during the day. The streets of Pine Hills were deserted, and for good reason. It was about to rain.

Magically, his thoughts triggered another rumbling in the sky. It sounded as if it had began several miles away and had worked its way right up to the front door of his shop. It hadn't even begun to die down when the jolt of lightening exited the dark clouds and shot to the earth.

Seconds later, even before Cam could tell the man the bad news, the rains came, instantly pounding against the ground. "I can't get into the register." Cam finally said.

"Well how much is it?" the man asked. "I'll just leave the money and you could ring it in later."

Cam thought about it. One year ago, he would have followed company policy and told the man that he couldn't help him. It was different now. He was a manager. Not that anything had changed when he was put into this position. It was still just him and Mrs. Collins, but he decided right then that this gave him the authority to make changes to the policy if it were necessary.

"It's two-fifty," Cam said.

By the light of the candle, the man began pulling money from his pocket. He pulled out three dollars, stuck it in Cam's hand, and he and his wife headed for the door.

Cam watched them walk away until the door began to swing shut. Suddenly, it opened again. Before Cam could tell them that they were closed, he looked up and saw two men wearing black ski masks over their faces.

"Get back there," one man shouted at Cam as soon as they both entered the room. "Open that safe. Do it now."

Cam looked at Julie and then at each of the men. "I can't open it," Cam said, trying to seem under some self control. "The power's out."

There was just enough light to see one of the men reach behind his back. When his hands reappeared, the candlelight was bouncing off cold steel. The man had a gun, and it was now pointed directly at Cam.

"You better find a way to open that safe, boy. I don't want to see my friend here put a hole into that pretty lady over here, but if you don't do what you're told, that's exactly what he's going to do." The anger in his voice was almost matched by the anxiousness.

Cam cringed at the thought of Julie being hurt. The only thing worse would be his inability to open a cash register. He slid over and grabbed the sides of the metal box. He had no clue how to open it, but he would find a way. Even if he had to smash it on the ground.

"Hurry up!" the man yelled. "Open it."

Until now, the second man had been silent. Hearing his partner yelling, set his mouth in motion as well.

"Don't move!" He was yelling at Julie, who had started moving slowly towards the back of the store. It the second man hadn't been there, Julie would have been able to sneak away.

"Get over here," the man ordered.

Julie figured she had to do as she was told. Panic was beginning to set in. Julie felt her heart racing and her body was numb. She wasn't sure if she was going to be able to move anymore, but when she willed her legs to move, they took her in the direction they were supposed to. Apparently not fast enough, however, because the man closed in and reached for Julie's arm. Julie pulled away, which only made him angrier.

"I said get over here!" He reached up and grabbed a handful of Julie's hair.

"Leave her alone!" Cam said, trying to sound as if he had some control over the situation. "I'll get it open, but you leave her alone." The man let go of Julie's hair, but took hold of her arm. At least his words had forced him to calm down.

Julie stared at Cam. Her eyes were much more adjusted to the darkness, although the sheeting rain outside was pelting the window and it was still hard to make out any real details.

"Open it." The man took over now, waving the gun at Cam and at the cash register.

Cam tried to pry open the money drawer, all the while wishing for a generator. Better yet, he wished the power would just come back on.

At the same time, he couldn't help but wonder if he had heard that voice before. Was this someone he knew? And if so, why rob a store for such a small amount of cash? They had to know they weren't going to get much. The only answer was that it was drug money. People will do just about anything for drug money.

"Hurry up!"

The more the man yelled, the harder Cam pried, wiggled, and shook, but to no avail. All he could think of now was to throw it up in the air and hope it opened. The plug was next to the window and he pulled it from the power strip.

Before he could get his balance, the wind began howling and the rain slammed hard against the window. Cam jumped and so did the man holding Julie. He let go of Julie's arm, and Julie didn't waste the opportunity. She backed away from the man, but only a few steps.

"Get back," Cam said, speaking mostly to Julie. He really didn't care if the register landed on top of their assailants or not.

It was heavy, but Cam used all his strength to lift the metal machine over his head. At the peak, he stepped to the side and let the register fall. It smashed to the ground, and for a brief second, Cam worried. The door did not fly open as he had hoped. Instead, the explosion of change slamming around inside echoed through the dark room. It flipped up on the side, and then, finally, the drawer fell open.

One hundred dollars fell out. He knew that, because that's what he started with and there hadn't been a soul in here since then. Some of it was change, but most of it was ones, fives, and ten dollar bills. Even after the resister settled on the ground, change continued to clang to the bottom.

The man closest to Cam didn't waste another second. Why should he? The reason he had entered the store was now lying on the ground at his feet. He began gathering the money, and his partner reached for the candle, holding it beside his cohort. Within seconds, they had cleaned the till, and the floor, of every bill available.

"Now wasn't that easy?" the man who had been holding Julie said and stood up. "Now get in the back of the store."

The other guy stood up as well, his gun once again trained on Cam's head. He followed Cam and Julie into the back storeroom. Julie wasn't sure what was going to come next, but she had heard too many times of people being tied up in the back room and killed. She began to pray even more fervently than she had been so far.

"I'm shutting this door," he waved the gun warningly, "and don't either of you move for five minutes. You got it?" He didn't wait for an answer. "You come out before then, you die." He was now speaking coldly, but calmly.

That was plenty warning. The door shut and the room went jet black. Cam and Julie couldn't even see themselves.

A few seconds later, the bell to the front door rang. That meant that they were gone, but Cam and Julie refused to move. If the man wanted five minutes, fine. They could live with that if it meant their lives would be spared. Julie fought back the tears, as she had done during the entire robbery.

"I'm sorry," Cam said. His apology did nothing to hide the fact that he was afraid. Julie felt this in the tone of his voice and in the way the sound wavered. She reached out to him, and when he took her hand and pulled her close, she melted in his arms.

"Maybe we should say a prayer."

That was exactly what Julie was thinking, but it hadn't been Julie who had spoken. Cam had said it, and Julie's heart stopped—almost too long. Less than ten minutes before, she was almost sure that he was going to tell her it was over. He was going to say he couldn't quit drinking and that he wanted to stop hearing about the church entirely. She knew that was what he was going to say. Now, after the most traumatic thing they had experienced together, he wanted to pray?

"Do you want to say it?" she asked after a very brief hesitation.

The darkness closed in on him even more. He couldn't pray. He was too much of a mess-up. Actually, he had almost given up trying to quit drinking, which would have meant giving up on life. Suddenly, he was thinking of praying? He couldn't pray.

"I can't," he said. "I'm not capable of saying a prayer."

"Cam, do you believe there is a God?"

"Yes." That was the most definitive answer he had ever given when it came to religion. "I do," he added.

"Then you can pray. Will you pray for us?" Julie squeezed Cam's hand. "Please."

Something changed inside Cam's mind. A sense of calmness came over him, and he almost believed that he just might be able to do this. He could at least try. "Okay," he said. "But I have no idea what to say."

"Yes, you do. Cam, I have faith in you. You can do this, just like you can quit drinking and just like you can do anything else you want to do in life. You can. All you have to do is try."

All you have to do is try.

Her words echoed in his head just like the coins had done when the register slammed to the floor. The difference was these words were comforting. She said she had faith in him, and those words seemed to drive home the truth. She really did have faith in him, and if she had faith, then the least he could do was say a prayer.

"Okay, I will."

Together, being careful not to trip on anything, they made their way to the floor. Just like the other times, they bowed their heads and closed their eyes. They did not let go of each others hands, however. They both felt safer feeling each other's skin. Right now, it felt right.

Cam did not speak for several moments. He used the time to gather his strength and to remember everything that the missionaries had been teaching him. When he felt ready, he took a deep breath and began.

"Our Father in Heaven." Again, he paused, but then went on. At first, Cam thanked Heavenly Father for protecting them, and asked him to help them calm down. He also thanked him for sending Julie. At the very end of the prayer, Cam prayed for help. "I'm very sorry, both to you and to Julie, for failing. I will continue to learn of the gospel, but I need help in quitting. Please help me, and please help Julie not lose faith in me."

He closed the prayer and heard a faint 'amen' from Julie. She didn't say anything else— neither of them did. They stood up, walked out of the room, and up to the front of the store.

The candle was still sitting on the floor, as was the broken cash register. It didn't matter though. They were safe. That was what really mattered.

Julie gripped Cam's hand even tighter. "Thanks for saying the prayer," she said.

Cam didn't have to look to know that she was crying, and it made him even more upset that he had let her down.

"I better call the cops," Cam said, mostly to distract himself from the memory of his faults. He moved behind the counter, but never let go of Julie's hand. They just belonged together, and that was where they were going to stay.

Chapter Nine

Over the next few weeks, Cam didn't touch a single drink. In fact, he stayed away from the party scene entirely, which made it much easier. He avoided the wrong crowd, and spent most of his time with Julie—or with members of the church.

Julie changed as well. She stopped worrying about her future. She finally understood that she wasn't destined to be alone forever. She was just waiting for the right man. Even if she and Cam didn't work out, although she now prayed that it would, then someone else would come along. There was no telling how long it would take, but at least she was able to look forward now...thanks to Cam.

Even more important, Julie's need to watch other people, and to eavesdrop on their conversations was diminishing. She had Cam. In all the years of watching, listening, and eavesdropping, no one had ever been able to hold her spellbound like Cam could. She felt as if she were becoming more normal—or at least closer to what she perceived normal to be.

Cam found another job working with mentally handicapped children. He wasn't afraid of the job. If anything, his new employment was much more dangerous. He was threatened daily, by grown men who simply didn't know better. He quit the bookstore two weeks after being robbed, because he wanted more money. Deep down inside, he wondered if the fear of being robbed again pushed him forward even faster. Probably. He wanted to be more responsible, and that included supporting himself appropriately.

Between the job and the relationship that was blossoming with him and Julie, there wasn't time to party. This too made things easier. He still craved a drink quite often, but he used his three prong system to successfully fight it off each time. The first thing he would do was to say a prayer. He still felt a little awkward doing it, but it was becoming easier, and much more natural. Secondly, he reminded himself of the way Sandy had been treated. He pictured Marcus slapping her and the bruise on her leg. He didn't want to be a junky. Just as important, he didn't want to be viewed as a junky.

The third part of the equation was the cure-all. He thought of Julie. She was an incredible lady. He had never met anyone like her. Not that this was all that surprising. He had spent his time with other drunks and drug addicts. You can't meet decent people in the bars or sitting around a kitchen table trying to throw a quarter into a glass of beer.

He loved Julie. There was no doubt in his mind, and by August, he was ready to do just about anything to show his love. He wanted to prove to her that he was worthy, and that he would always fight to stay worthy of her love. Julie was giving him a way to show it today.

"You look nice," she said as she placed her hand on his shoulder. "You'll turn every girl's head in church."

"I don't want to turn any one's head but yours."

Julie blushed and blew him a kiss. "You've already turned mine," she said and winked at him.

"I'm not sure that I really feel comfortable going to church. I don't know enough about the church to be a part of it. At least not this much a part of it."

"Just sit with me, listen to what they have to say, and see what happens. We won't stay for the last hour. We'll just go to Sacrament Meeting and Sunday School. Then we'll leave. I promise."

She was making it sound easier than it was going to be. There had to be a catch. He just had no idea what that catch would be. This was completely new to him, and he was going to have to trust her. He did, but it still felt strange.

He picked up his suit coat and slipped it on. Julie's hand brushed his back and then fell to her side. "Ready," she said.

No he wasn't ready, but if it was time, what choice did he have? He was nervous, and even a bit afraid, mostly because he didn't know what to expect. He put his hand around her shoulders and then let it slide down until it rested comfortably on the small of her back. Julie led him to the door, and Cam couldn't help but feel as if he was being taken to a funeral. It felt so odd—his going to church— that it slowed down his entire world. He wanted to sit down on Julie's leather sofa until things felt more normal.

To make the world move even slower, Julie drove as if her car would break down if it made it all the way to third gear. She thought she was doing him a favor, giving him time to collect his thoughts and relax. Instead, Cam spent the entire ride stressing, wishing she would speed up, and wishing that the clock would speed up as well.

He rolled down the window, but it didn't help. The Weather Channel had promised another rainstorm, but so far it had held off.

Figuring he had to do something to distract his mind, he decided to question her. "What am I really supposed to do here? Should I really be asking questions? Am I going to have to chant and turn circles around some totem pole or what?" He knew that sounded absolutely ridiculous, but he asked it anyway.

Julie laughed at him, but only for a moment. She then took a serious tone causing Cam to worry. "No. There is nothing weird about going to church. It's peaceful. It's rejuvenating for the soul. It's a place for you to really get in touch with your feelings. Other than the temple, there is really no better place to get close to Heavenly Father than in church."

Cam pondered these words as they continued down the road. What did she really mean by rejuvenating the soul. It was probably something that he ought to know by now, but he didn't quite understand. Instead of asking, he just thought about it until they pulled into the large church parking lot. As they walked hand in hand up the sidewalk, he tried to picture what the inside of the church was going to look like. Again, he only had the visions he had seen in the movies and on the television as a guide. He pictured the gold statues, the candles, and hundreds of people walking to the front, kneeling, and saying their prayers.

When they walked through the front doors of the chapel, he knew that nothing he had seen, or planned to see, was true. Just like Julie had said, it was very peaceful and very serene. It couldn't be full of all of the oddities he had been picturing.

The white walls and the soft, light-colored carpeting blended into a soothing, relaxed atmosphere. Cam's nerves calmed considerably. As they walked down the long hall, however, one of his biggest fears instantly came true. He had been battling this fear since agreeing to come.

He knew quite a few of the people in church.

That wasn't surprising. Pine Hills was small. There were a lot of people he didn't know, simply because that hadn't been his kind of crowd. But now, he was staring straight into the eyes of the one person he really didn't want to see—Michael Stringer.

Not that Michael was the problem. Cam was the problem. How many times had he made fun of Michael (or was it geek, bonehead, straight-lace, or the million other names he had called him, some of which were down right crude)? Cam had been mean in school, and it had continued in the years after graduation. This rude behavior had happened a lot more than Cam wanted to count— especially now.

Michael looked at Cam and smiled. Cam could see the wheels turning inside Michael's head. It was time for revenge, and there was nothing Cam was going to be able to do about it. He was going to have to deal with it just as Michael had been forced to deal with it when Cam had been so willing to dish it out. He was in Michael's territory now.

The short overweight kid didn't waste a second. Why should he? He had a lot to make up for. He couldn't waste this easy opportunity?

He looked the same as always. His tie was too tight. His blue suit made him look like a book worm, and his eyes stared straight forward, never waning to either side.

Cam's body tightened as Michael neared the 'too close for comfort' zone. Julie felt the awkwardness and looked first at Cam and then at Michael. As if to ease the stress, she stepped towards Michael, almost in between them.

"Hi, Mike," she said, and held out her hand.

Michael shook her hand but barely took his eyes off of Cam, only adding to the tensions that was running through Cam's body. "Hello, sister Haws, how are you?" Michael asked.

"I'm doing great." She hesitated, realized that something was about to happen between the two men despite her involvement, and instinctively stepped back.

"Hello, Cam." Michael finally stopped moving.

Cam couldn't read Michael's thoughts or body language as well as he hoped. He immediately felt at an even greater disadvantage. "Hi," he said and waited for Michael to let him have it.

"Nice to see you here."

This time, Cam did see through the man's bland looks. Michael actually meant what he had said. There was no revenge in his words. There wasn't even the slightest hint of hatred or malice. He really was glad to see him here.

"Thank you," Cam said.

Michael smiled and looked at him, almost as if he sensed Cam's fears and thoughts. "I've always wished I could get you to come to church. I just never had the guts to ask. Thank goodness for awesome people like Julie."

Cam wanted to say something. He felt like apologizing to him, but the words wouldn't come. There was no doubting the need. It was

132

bombarding him like bricks on an old building tumbling down in an earthquake, but he couldn't say the words.

"Well, I better get going. Mom's waiting."

Cam couldn't believe how sincere Michael had been. He hadn't taken even a single pot shot at him. Even stranger, he had walked away as if Cam didn't owe him an apology. Cam knew the truth, however. He did owe Michael an apology. For that matter, he suddenly realized that he owed apologies to a lot of people.

Julie led Cam into the chapel leaving him to his own thoughts. For a moment, Cam wondered if she too was reading him. She was letting him fret? Why wasn't she helping him? If she said something, anything, he would probably forget about Michael—and about everyone else. But she walked quietly, found a place to sit, and didn't say a word. Cam didn't say anything either, though he was pleading inwardly for a distraction from his own guilt.

As Sacrament Meeting continued, the feelings of guilt continued to haunt Cam. Even when Julie did speak, the guilt didn't subside.

Finally, just as Sacrament Meeting was ending, as if the question were about to burst inside his head, Cam told her what he was feeling. As they walked to Sunday School, Julie explained the plan of forgiveness in greater detail. The missionaries had explained it, but she gave her own version of it. She reminded him of the steps involved in erasing the guilt, and the benefits of going through each step. She gave him the quick version.

As she spoke, a calming feeling came over Cam. The words she was telling him made perfect sense, and they began to soothe him. Somehow he knew that following through on the steps of forgiveness would bring him even greater pleasure and happiness than he had ever experienced. It would set him free.

He couldn't wait for church to be over. Not because he wanted to leave, but because he wanted to start the steps. He wanted to apologize to Michael. Not only that, but he had a burning desire to apologize to others...starting with Julie.

He decided not to even wait for a break in Sister Carling's voice to apologize to begin this process. He was only half listening to the lesson anyhow. He bent over, as if apologizing was the most natural thing in the world, and whispered in Julie's ear. "Thank you for helping me. I'm sorry I haven't trusted you more. I know I would be feeling a lot better about myself right now if I had opened my heart to you all the way. I will from now on."

Julie lifted her hand to her face, and it took Cam a few seconds to realize why. She was crying. Tears were streaming down her face as if she had just lost someone close to her. Had he hurt her, or were they tears of joy? Cam hoped for the latter. He hardly dared to look at her.

As the tears finally subsided, in stages just like her laughter had done earlier, she placed her hand on his. His skin was cold, and she wondered how long he had been fretting over the words he had just said. No matter how long it had been, she was sure they were words that she would never forget as long as she lived. They were touching, thoughtful, and full of proof. She was doing the right thing. That was important to her because she

134

was falling in love with Cam. Now she was going to be able to show it even more.

As soon as class let out, Julie stood up and hugged Cam. It was a short hug, but one that reminded Cam that he needed to say nice things to Julie more often.

Just as they were about to get into Julie's car, Cam spotted Michael walking out the door. His little sister was loping along right beside him. She was a short girl, and destined to be picked on just like Michael had been.

"I'll be right back," Cam said to Julie and walked away. He left the door wide open, but didn't intend to be long.

The short time that it took to reach Michael left him feeling different than he had two hours ago. He felt peaceful, as if he were being helped along. There was no doubt in his mind as to what he was going to say. He also knew he was going to be able to get the words out this time.

"Michael," Cam said as he got close. "Can I talk to you?"

Michael looked at him and then turned to his sister. "Marci, go get in the truck okay? I'll be right there."

Marci did as she was asked. Not wanting to make her wait on his account, Cam got right to the point.

"Michael. I just want to say I'm sorry for all of the crap I've put you through over the years. I know that doesn't make up for it. I mean, we both know I've done a lot of crappy things to you, but I am sorry."

That was it. That was all he intended to say. What happened next, surprised even him.

135

"I forgive you." Michael said and slightly turned away from Cam.

Michael was crying. What was it about these apologies? Why did it bring people to tears? Were they just overly sensitive people? Instead of wondering, he asked. "Why do you cry? Why do people cry when someone says I'm sorry?"

It was an odd question, one that Michael wasn't exactly ready to tackle. He had to think about it for a moment. Finally, he tried to answer. "Do you really want to know the truth to that question, Cam?"

"Yes," Cam answered. He shifted his weight and bit his lower lip.

"When you're a part of this religion, you don't hold things against other people. Instead, you pray for them. I've prayed many times that you wouldn't do the things you used to do to me. But they weren't answered until I changed my prayer. Instead of praying that you'd stop being mean, I started praying that you would find the truth. I prayed that you would find Jesus. Now you have. At least it seems as if you have. That makes me happy. The more you follow Jesus, the more you will make people cry. But trust me—they're good tears."

Cam had nothing else to say. He stood completely still in what was now a cloudy, cold, nearly rainy afternoon. He was completely stunned. Michael walked away, climbed into his truck, and pulled out of the parking lot. Cam noticed the smile on the Michael's face.

Julie didn't even ask what had taken place. She knew by the look on Cam's face that he was truly going through a remarkable change in his life.

They drove home talking and sharing more than they ever had before. Things were opening up between them, and both of them could sense just how right it felt.

Chapter Ten

The entire concept of the Church of Jesus
Christ of Latter Day Saints was beginning to guide
Cam's life in directions that he never would have
dreamed before. He felt good being around
religious people—especially Julie. He had a
burning desire to repent for everything he had done
in his life. Even more than this, he was finding out
there was a purpose to his life. It felt wonderful
knowing that there was something to look forward
to, and that if he repented, he could make it to
heaven again.

He could tell that this was another large step
in the process of turning his life around. He had a
long way to go. He recognized this, but he refused
to allow the hard road ahead get him down. Before
finding the truth, he would not have been able to
look to the future with such ambition and hope.
Now, not only did he look forward to the future, he
was making plans for it. He hoped that those plans
included Julie.

But he was not going to worry about the
future today. Today he was going to relax, clean
the apartment, and lounge. Although it was
Saturday, and Julie normally didn't have to work on
the weekend, she did today. It happened to be one
of those "you're needed in the office really bad"
days for her.

That left Cam alone, and although he would have loved to have her keeping him company, he fully intended to use the time to get caught up on things that he had neglected lately—sleep, cleaning, resting, and basically being lazy.

If Marcus comes over, kick him out.

Marcus had come over twice since the time he had talked Cam into drinking. Each time, Cam had a built-in excuse. After telling him the truth, that he wasn't going to drink anymore, Marcus just didn't seem all that interested in being friends. Each time, he disappeared into his own life, and Cam was happy not to be in that life—or at least in that style of life. Every time he was alone, now, Cam readied himself for the possibility of Marcus' return.

Cam stood straddling the invisible line that separated the kitchen and living room. Something was telling him to turn on the television and sit down. Another part of him was telling him to leave it off and get something accomplished.

He decided to do both.

After clicking on the television, setting it to the news, and turning up the volume so he could hear it in the kitchen, he went to work.

He started with the dishes. The warm water and soapy suds soothed his mind and helped him to relax even more. There weren't many dishes to wash, just the pans that wouldn't fit in the dishwasher from last nights spaghetti and the plate and fork that he had used for breakfast. By the time he had finished, he actually wished there were more dishes. He even thought about hand washing the dishes that he had put in the dishwasher last night, but changed his mind. That seemed to be bordering on neurotic behavior.

From the living room, the news continued with today's top stories. He wasn't sure exactly what they were talking about, other than the war in some other country featuring rival nations looking for peace. *What a way to go about it,* he thought. *Why don't you try actually being peaceful?*

Cam laughed out loud, pulled the plug, and watched the water swirl around until it disappeared down the drain. Even that was relaxing. He quickly equated it to his life. He had just finished washing the terrible stuff from his life and now all of his troubles had slipped down the drain where they would never be allowed to come back up.

Unless the drain backs up!

While that thought had the potential of bothering Cam, and maybe even forcing him back into minor depression, he brushed it away and was proud of himself for having been able to do so.

He grabbed the broom from the closet. Two more minutes and the kitchen would be complete. Then on to the living room and then his bedroom. After that--.

Actually, he had no idea what would come next, but it didn't matter. Whatever he did, he was confident that it wouldn't be hurting his life. Everything he used to do seemed to be one more step down the old ladder of guilt, depression, alcoholism, and anger. He wasn't doing that anymore. He was climbing back up.

After dumping what little dirt he had swept into the dustpan from the kitchen floor into the garbage, he moved into the living room. He looked around and sighed. There wasn't much to do in here either. It was already clean. Maybe a quick go-over with the vacuum and he'd be done.

"Coming up, local headlines including an update on last night's apparent suicide in Pine Hills."

Cam hadn't heard of anyone killing themselves, but he hadn't been worrying about the news until just now. A commercial came on just as he was plugging in the vacuum. He made it a point to keep watching the screen while he worked. Maybe it would show a picture or something.

It took a lot for Pine Hills to be mentioned in the news. The last time it had happened had been almost two years ago. A violent snow storm tore through the town leaving the entire city blanketed with five feet of snow, which fell in less than thirty-six hours. This was a total that the mountains were used to, but not down in the valley. Power was cut to just about everyone. Every time the plows tried to clear the roads they wound up stuck. It was complete gridlock for several days.

Cam worked himself out of the room—just as he had been taught to do—all the while hoping that this death wasn't one of those blame-it-on-God, type suicides. He tried to keep the vacuum lines on the carpet running the same direction. It just looked better that way, like he actually cared about details.

By the time he shut off the vacuum, the newscaster had already begun her story. Cam was a bit mad at himself for missing the first part, because that was when they would give the name.

"Police say that the lady intentionally overdosed on meth-amphetamines. The boyfriend found the body late last night."

The woman on the television spoke so blandly, without showing the least bit of concern, that Cam wondered if she was even human. She even does it with a smile on her face, Cam thought.

"According to one neighbor," the newscaster continued. "She had been taking drugs and drinking alcohol as long as she lived in the neighborhood, and had been going off the deep end for a very long time."

"Yeah," Cam said to the television, as if they would hear him. "The man probably killed her himself."

Maybe the newslady had partially read his mind, because her next comment followed his. "The police say there is nothing suspicious about her death and that it was clearly a suicide."

That was all. The lady didn't follow up the report by reissuing the name of the victim, as any good reporter would do. Instead, they switched topics to a more pressing matter: a transient found by the railroad tracks in Salt Lake City was now being charged with stealing food from a gas station.

Cam gritted his teeth. Who was the girl? He suddenly had a burning desire to find out. He quickly picked up the remote from off the couch and flipped through the channels until he reached another Salt Lake channel. It too was showing news, but they were talking about the weather.

"Whatever!" Cam said and tossed the remote back onto the couch. He walked upstairs leaving the set on just in case they went back to the story later on.

The bedroom took less time to clean than he expected as well. He pulled the covers up on the bed, leaving the bedspread folded at the foot. A pair of shorts and a shirt went into the laundry basket in the closet, and that was the end.

But what next!

He wasn't sure why, but all of a sudden, he didn't feel like lounging. *Do something,* his heart

142

was saying. That's why people commit suicide. They get complacent, lazy, and then depressed. They can't handle life because they aren't accomplishing anything.

There was so much truth in that thought, and he knew it first hand. Not that he had ever thought about committing suicide, but drinking all the time had made him complacent. He never wanted to do anything else. It was easy for him to see how things could spiral that far out of control for people.

At the bottom of the first flight of stairs, Cam actually reached for the door. He wasn't sure what he was going to do outside, but at least the sun would feel good. He would have opened the door, but the television was still on.

He turned, walked down the rest of the stairs, and entered the living room. It was only then that he realized that the story was on again. This channel had a male newscaster recanting almost the very same information as Channel Two had done, but it was only his voice. The picture on the screen had transfixed Cam's eyes. Several police officers were milling around the front yard of the victim's home. Cam suddenly had a strange sensation that he had been there, although he wasn't sure why he thought that. It wasn't actually showing the house, or anyone that lived there. Still, he had to wonder if he had been there.

"The twenty-three year old female victim was rushed to the hospital where she was pronounced dead—an intentional drug overdose."

A handsome, well-dressed gentleman came on the television. The story was over; or so Cam thought. He was about to yell at this station too, for not repeating the victim's name, but before he got the words out, he realized that they weren't finished with the story.

"Adam," the newsman said trying to catch the reporter on the scene before he tuned himself out. "Are you still there?"

"Yes."

The newsman turned away from the camera as if speaking directly to the other man, who was at least thirty miles away. "Do we know if she had any relatives in the area? When are they going to release the name of the victim?"

"We aren't sure, Bob. According to police, they are working on that information right now."

"And is there any suspicion of foul play here," Bob asked, obviously reverting back to his own reporting on-scene days.

"At first, police thought this was certain to be a murder case. But in fact, the girl's live-in boyfriend is being very cooperative with the police, although he had declined an interview with the media saying, and I quote 'This is all a bit too much to deal with right now'. But that's all the information I have right now, Bob."

"Thanks, Adam."

Well, that would explain why no one was giving out any names, Cam thought. Seeing that place, and wondering if he had actually been there, now had his interest peaked.

For a moment, he thought about driving around for a while. Pine Hills was small enough that he could probably find the house in no time. It wouldn't be hard to locate a house with police activity. He thought about it, but decided against running out the gas in his truck for no reason.

He sat back comfortably against the back of the couch, shifted his weight, and placed his right ankle on top of the left, legs out straight. He noticed two things. First, there was the bare spot on the wall. He had taken down the weird pictures. They no longer felt appropriate. The other thing he noticed was the *Book Of Mormon*. He stared at the book, and was about to pick it up and start reading when the television screen pulled his attention away.

"Coming up after the break—an update on the suicide in Pine Hills."

The news broke for a commercial. Not wanting to miss anything, he decided to leave the *Book Of Mormon* where it was. If he picked it up, there was a good chance that he would zone out, just as he had done the first time he had started reading it. He would miss the news. Not that this would be a bad thing. What he would read between the covers of the book would be far more interesting, and far better for him, than learning who was unable to hold out on life. Still, he watched each commercial intently.

He felt as if his eyes were attached to the television screen. As each commercial passed, his apprehension grew. There was no reason for it, but by the time the newscaster came back on, Cam's head felt ready to explode. If they didn't tell him who it was, he was going to have to go for that drive after all.

"We are getting a late update on that suicide in Pine Hills. We can now tell you that the twenty-three year old girl's name is Sandy McKell. It has been confirmed, by the coroners office, that Ms. McKell died of a drug overdose." The man paused as if getting some more information and then continued. "Marcus Layton, the lady's boyfriend has cooperated fully with the police. According to

145

officers, there is plenty of evidence that proves that this is nothing more than a suicide."

The rest of the newscast faded into the far reaches of Cam's mind. The shock of hearing Sandy's and Marcus' names, sent shock waves down his body. He was embraced by a strong sense of dreaming. He was sure he was awake, but he suddenly wanted to be asleep. He wanted to be able to say he was making all of this up. Because of this, he suddenly found it more difficult to decipher reality from the strange sensations that were threatening to take control of him.

So many thoughts rushed through his head one right after another. They came so fast that his head began to swim as if floating in liquid. Why would Sandy do that? Why would she take her own life when there was so much help available. Was Marcus making her life that bad, and if he was, why wasn't he being blamed for this?

So many questions and so few clear-cut answers.

"She's not really dead."

Cam said the words out loud. No one was going to hear him, and that was a very good thing because it was nothing more than denial. He knew that. The local media wouldn't get something wrong—not something that important. He knew that Sandy was dead, but right now he was finding it much easier to deny the truth than to admit that his friend was gone.

Even worse, was the one thought that seemed to be bombarding him. It started out as a sharp kick to the brain. *She didn't kill herself! Marcus did it!*

Although he wanted to deny that as well, the moment he thought the words, he had a very strong sense that he was right. He had thought this earlier, but he hadn't been serious then—not entirely, anyway. Then he remembered that Marcus had threatened to get him and Julie. Maybe Marcus found out that Sandy had warned Cam.

Marcus killed her!

The words rolled around in Cam's head like an unmanned ship at sea. There was no control and no life aboard. More importantly, there was only one place the ship could end up. It was heading for the bottom of the deep, cold ocean. That was exactly where his thoughts were going to take him as well—very deep and very cold.

Several more questions raced through his mind, but to him, they all seemed so mixed up and out of context that he couldn't make them fit into one nice coherent phrase that actually made sense.

Each time the questions started to erode, his mind filled the blank space with, *she didn't kill herself! Marcus killed her!*

This only led to more questions. Why would Marcus kill her? Did she try to leave? Was he that whacked out? If Marcus really did it, how could he get away with it? He was controlling, but he wasn't exactly smart.

Just more questions without answers.

Now, joining his already confused and almost depressed head, something else began to creep in. He couldn't get a strong hold on what it was, and he was quite sure that he wasn't ready for any more, no matter what it was.

Strangely, the feeling that was trying to enter seemed good. In fact, he thought, for a very brief second, that if he allowed it to enter his mind that he would feel better.

But he stopped it.

He wasn't ready to feel better. Now wasn't the time to feel better. His friend was dead, and he was harboring thoughts that his other friend had killed her. This wasn't the time to feel better.

He forced the thought away and it instantly began to subside. It was replaced by a thought that he simply wasn't strong enough to force away.

You didn't help her! How much of this is your fault?

Although he wasn't ready to take Sandy's death upon himself, he had to wonder how different things could have been if he had taken a more active role in helping her. At the very least, he should have confronted Marcus. But he didn't do that. He was weak. He could never stand up to Marcus. Why should now be any different?

Because maybe if you had, Sandy wouldn't be dead right now!

Those words ripped through him and cut much deeper than anything else he had heard all day long. If that was true, if he really could have stopped Sandy's death by taking an active role, by standing up to Marcus, then maybe he *was* at fault.

And then, just to confuse him a little bit more, Cam heard another voice.

You had nothing to do with it.

The voice was calm, not like the cutting blow he had felt before, but it had just as much conviction. Cam focused on these words. They soothed him, if only enough to take away some of the sting of the other possibility.

A doubt followed this thought—back to the sharp, cutting blow. *Yea, take the easy way out Cam. Don't take responsibility. Do you really think you can just decide you had nothing to do with this just because your mind concocts some false story explaining why it wasn't your fault?*

Why did he have to feel this way? Cam slumped down on the couch as if he were trying to sleep, even though he was sure that it would be some time before he actually closed his eyes and slept.

He pictured his friends—both Marcus and Sandy. This was not what he wanted to see right now, but it was likely to be what dominated his visions—both when he was awake and asleep—for a very long time. He gave in to that fact and allowed the pictures to take over.

Chapter Eleven

"I heard," Julie said. She asked what she could do to help just by looking at him.

They were sitting in Julie's living room. The lights were bright and burned Cam's eyes. He reluctantly turned away from Julie and squinted. "I just have to wonder if there's something else I could have done. I mean, I know she didn't want to hear it from me, but maybe if I would have taken a more active role or something instead of abandoning her like I did."

"You didn't abandon her, Cam," Julie retorted. "You have a lot to worry about in your own life. I guarantee you that if you'd have hung out with them you would have relapsed. You may not have made it. Besides, you offered. You can't force someone to accept your help."

Cam agreed, but the feelings of doubt refused to let him be. It was like the nagging his mind had given him when he stole his first candy bar. It had driven him absolutely insane until he finally told his dad what he had done—at one o'clock in the morning. This was nagging him even more, and talking to someone he loved didn't seem to be helping this time. Part of him wanted to go to bed. Maybe a little sleep would help, although the bad news of the day was still very fresh in his mind.

"They said she killed herself," Cam said blankly.

"I know. They even showed her picture. It felt weird. This kind of thing isn't supposed to happen to people in your own home town." She pulled nervously at the hem of her gray sweater.

"It doesn't fit." Cam felt dazed. "That's not the kind of person she was. I can't imagine her doing that. I know he was beating her up, but suicide wasn't something she ever talked about. I don't think she was even capable of it."

Julie thought about the right approach to take. He seemed as if he were on the verge of freaking out. She wasn't exactly sure what freaking out would entail, but she didn't want to see it. That thought brought back the memory of the look she had seen in his eyes the night they had met. It was the strangest, most scary look she had ever seen in anyone's eyes. Over time, she came to realize that it really wasn't something to fear. It was a jumbled up mind pleading for help. He had been hoping, in his own way, that someone would help him see the way out of the life he had been living. It also involved trust, or his lack of it towards everyone. In time, Julie figured he had gotten himself together, because she hadn't seen the look in a long time.

Cam shook his head. "Marcus had something to do with this. I have no doubt about that. I don't know if he actually killed her, but he had a hand in it."

"Why would he do that?"

"I don't know, but I guarantee you that he was so far into drugs that anything is possible. That's what drugs do to you. They mess up your mind so bad that you completely lose track of what is right and wrong. Nothing matters but getting high—and quite often, anger is the result.

Julie led Cam out of the large living room

151

and into the kitchen. Neither of them spoke as she lifted the pan off the stove and poured hot water into two cups. She added powdered chocolate mix to each cup and stirred them. When she finally set the cups on the table, one in front of Cam at the head of the table, and the other to his right, she knew where she wanted to take this conversation.

"What do you know about death?"

What kind of question was that, he wondered? Over the past few months she had tried to explain the plan of salvation to him. Death wasn't the end of it all. He understood that, and he even wanted to believe it. All of a sudden though, he was wondering just what he did believe. He felt as if he had been walking on a thin line all along. For a long time, he had felt like he had been learning to believe, but for some reason her question was pushing him the other way this time. Not away from her, just away from his belief, or was it only hope that he had been clinging too all along?

"I don't know what to believe. I mean, I know you believe that there's more to *us* after we die. I thought I believed that, but I am really having a hard time with it right now. In fact, I hate to say this to you, but I'm really having a hard time with the whole religious thing right this second. What kind of God would allow something like this to happen to someone he supposedly loved?"

It was a harsh reaction, one that she hadn't expected, but it wasn't all that hard to understand. Cam was teetering. She knew he had been close to finding his faith for a long time, but he wasn't quite ready to accept it all. Time had been helping, but this had happened way too early in the process. She said the only thing that she could think of, risking sounding like a cold hearted, spiteful woman.

"We all make our own choices, Cam. God will lead us in the right direction, but only if we choose to follow his lead. Sandy wasn't following God anywhere." Julie shifted in her seat. "I'm not trying to be rude. I know she was your friend, but she chose the life she was living. It could have happened to you if you would have stayed in that lifestyle. People who do drugs and drink tend to have a better chance of dying."

Cam wasn't sure how to take Julie's comment. She was probably right. It did make sense. At the same time, he didn't want it to make sense. Not right now anyway. "I doubt if she chose to be beaten by her boyfriend on a regular basis," he said

"She chose to stay. You tried to help her, Cam. You tried to get her to leave. She wouldn't. That was a choice she made. We both know it was a tough choice, but we all have to make tough choices in our life. Sandy just chose the path with the least change…the least resistance…even though it was painful."

Cam wanted to argue with her. It was just the mood he was in. But the more he thought about it, and the more he tried to come up with something to say, the more he realized that she was right, entirely.

He took a sip of the hot chocolate then set it down on the coaster. He slid his chair around the corner of the table until his knee was touching hers. He reached out, took her hand in his, and looked at her. After a second or two, he leaned over and kissed her. It was quick, but it helped a little.

"I'm sorry. I guess I do know this is what I want. I'm just not sure what to do right now. Things just seem really muddled up all of a sudden. I thought I was getting a handle on all of this."

Julie squeezed his hand, stood up, and picked up her cup. It was hot, and after drinking a little bit, she set it back down. "Come on. I want to show you something."

She led him through the laundry room, which also served as the storeroom for all the games and toys she had collected over the years. They turned right down two stairs and then right again. Surprisingly, Cam had never been this far in her house. It was a big place, considering only one person lived here, but he had often wondered why he had never seen this part of the place. It was almost like the basement had been off limits.

But they were going there now, and the anticipation built in his mind making him really wonder what was waiting at the bottom of the stairs.

The further down they went, the darker it became. He could still see, but not really well. At the bottom of the stairs, Julie reached above her and screwed the light in tight. It wasn't a bright light, and the room was suddenly filled with shadows, creepy shadows. It reminded him of something out of a horror novel. The only question was where the boogey man was going to come from.

Several old rickety shelves lined the wall to his right. They wrapped around and covered half of the wall in front of him as well. There was a darker area to his left. It was just light enough to see that it was nothing more than a storeroom with a dirt floor filled with old bikes, boxes, and empty jars. No wonder they hadn't been down here, he thought. It was almost scary.

Julie led him to the closed door directly in front of them. She opened it, reached in, and flipped on the light. She then stepped to the side and allowed Cam to enter first. "This is just a spare room. No one's ever down here. I planned on it, at first, but I started sleeping upstairs and just never bothered with this room."

The room was amazing. A queen sized bed took up most of the room, but it looked strangely perfect. It was pushed up against the left and back walls leaving just enough room to the right for a chest of drawers. It looked as if it were made in the eighteen hundreds but well-preserved. Cam could touch the ceiling without jumping.

To his right, beneath the tiny window that wouldn't have let in enough light if the sun was shining directly in, was a large chest. It resembled a pirates chest made out of dark stained oak. It was beautiful, also well taken care of, like most things she owned, and almost as old as the chest of drawers seemed to be.

In the three visible corners of the room, candles sat in pairs in glass candle holders, upon fancy oak platforms. Each candle was white and as far as Cam was concerned, it symbolized Julie's near-perfect state. She wasn't perfect, and he knew that, but he hadn't seen too much to prove otherwise.

Then something struck him. In all the time they had been together, they were always so concerned about his alcoholism or his many other bad choices, that they had never—actually *he* had never—taken the chance to find out enough about her, at least not on a very deep level. He only knew the basics. She hadn't ever offered more than that, and he had never questioned. He felt stupid. She

155

had taken all that time getting into his mind, and all he had done in return was let her help him.

Somehow, though, he had a feeling that whatever she was about to show him was going to change that. If not, he was going to make it a point to ask. He wanted to find out all the things that made her not so perfect. Cam watched as Julie moved slowly to the chest. He noticed the reluctance in her steps.

She was more than reluctant, but she trusted him. She felt safe revealing her secret, the one that she had shoved so far into the back reaches of her mind that she had almost dismissed it forever (not forgotten…that would never happen…just dismissed to the point of never thinking about it). This secret made her fear of living her life as a hermit seem like a good thing. Suddenly, she wasn't sure if she would be able to finish what she was starting.

She reached for the cold, metal latch, paused before actually touching it, and then took hold. A flood of memories rushed through her at the same time. She saw good times and she saw some horrible ones, as well. She saw happiness and sadness. Above all of that, she saw her past, the life and the loss.

As the door lifted, seemingly by itself as if a strong gust of wind was pushing it up for her (really, she just thought it would be heavier), Julie peered inside. On the left, there was a wedding dress, there were stacks of letters and trinkets in the middle, and there on the right was what she was really after. She reached in, shuffled things around for a few seconds, and then pulled out the large picture.

Cam could see it was a photograph even before she turned it around. What he didn't know was who it was or why Julie kept it hidden in a chest instead of on her bedroom wall with the pictures of her parents. It was obviously someone she cared for. Why else would she keep it?

It was a picture of a lady dressed in a beautiful white wedding gown—probably the dress in the chest. Her hair was pinned up glamorously. She was about nineteen or twenty, well developed, and quite stunning.

"This is my sister—Becky."

Cam looked away from the picture and saw tears rolling down Julie's face. His stomach hurt, no longer from the loss of his friend, but from the pain he was seeing in Julie's eyes, face, and throughout her entire body.

"She was twenty-one when she went away."

"And that was taken at her wedding?"

Julie bit her bottom lip sharply trying to force the tears away by adding physical pain. "Sort of. It was taken at the church, where she was supposed to have been married. But Richard never showed up. One of his friends called from the hospital to tell us that Richard had been hit by some lady in a car. She ran a stop sign. Richard's jeep rolled and he flipped out. They said he died instantly." She shrugged, as if the fact that he died without much pain didn't really help her, other than to know that he didn't suffer.

"So what happened to your sister?" He wondered if he should have kept his mouth shut. He quickly moved to her, took the picture out of her hand, and laid it on the bed. He put his right hand around the back of her neck just as another bout of tears forced their way out, and he held her.

157

She cried on his shoulder for several minutes, no longer trying to control it. She was sure they were both going to drown in her tears before she actually felt like she could answer his question. She lifted her head and wiped the last tears from her cheek. After a deep breath, she pulled away from him, but just enough to look at him, still wanting to feel his warm touch. She said the words that she had never allowed to be spoken before.

"Becky couldn't handle Richards death. She secluded herself from everyone--even from me." Julie stopped, composed herself once more, and continued. "There was no doubt in anyone's mind that Becky was going to commit suicide. She was that far gone…and believe me, she would have had to be long gone to think that. We did the only thing we could think of. My parents had her checked into a hospital so she could get better. The doctors realized just how mentally unstable she was. That was strange, because she had never shown this before. She was always easily agitated, but not mentally unstable. They had some word for it, but I don't remember what it was. All I know is that she wasn't right, and it changed my whole world."

Julie was letting out a lot of horrible information. Cam could tell she was struggling to release the burdens that were buried in her mind. He began to feel some of that weight himself, and he wished he could take it all. He couldn't though. In fact, there wasn't much he could do other than listen, so he made sure that she knew he was doing that as well as he could.

"How old were you?" he asked, slowly rubbing her arm now.

"I was fifteen. I was fifteen and losing my best friend. It hurt so bad, but I looked forward to the day when she would get better. Unfortunately, she only got worse. She freaked out on us one day and told us to never come back for her. We tried for a long time to talk to her, but she refused. The last thing she ever said—to any of us—was to me. She told me that if I had any sense I would never fall in love, and that I should forget about her because she was going to forget about me. She told me to leave forever and to take our *so-called* parents with me."

"I'm sorry," Cam said and stopped moving his hand.

"I never saw her again. My parents have tried to contact her several times, but she won't take their calls. All our plans about growing up together, and being each other's maids-of-honor was destroyed. My best friend was gone. That was what I always dreamed of—having my sister as my maid-of-honor." Julie paused, fought off another round of tears, and then finished her thought. "I learned a lot about loss that year."

Cam pondered what she had just said. He wasn't exactly sure what message she was trying to get through to him, but he ventured a guess anyway.

"So you're telling me that you know how I feel and that I'll get over Sandy's death."

"Sort of. I had to find out for myself what loss, and ultimately death, really meant. I found it in our Savior. We get to meet our loved ones in the after life. I will see Becky after we're dead. I really believe we'll have the chance to be sisters again, something that was taken away from us here. I know Richard will be there, too."

"But if you came to terms with all that, then why are you crying over it now?" He sounded very sympathetic. "And why have you bottled it up for so long?"

Julie knew she was going to have a difficult time answering his questions. At least, the last part would be tough. The first part of Cam's question was simple. "I understand how the plan works. I know that it works, but that doesn't mean that I don't miss her. I do. I've just pushed it away for so long, forced the pain away so much, that our time together became more like a fantasy than reality."

"That's not healthy." Cam suddenly felt as if he may be able to help her for a change.

"I know it's not," she said. "But that's how I handled it."

Cam thought of another question, one that seemed much more important. "Have you ever thought about finding her? I mean, it has been a long time. Would you want to?"

"No!"

Her answer was quick, without so much as a tiny hesitation, but not entirely full of conviction. Just in case he was stepping out of bounds, he made his next statement sound like a joke. "Well, maybe one day I'll call her for you."

"Good luck." That was all she said.

Cam decided to leave it at that. When he didn't respond, Julie changed the subject. "I guess what I want you to know is that I have felt the loss you're feeling. You can be sure, just like I'm sure, that you will be able to see Sandy again."

Of course that's what she was telling him. He knew that. With all of the talk over the past few months, he had gathered that. What hadn't sunk in, until the very moment she said those words to him, was the reality of it all. It was almost like he had seen all of this religious stuff as mythical. It was

160

something that you believed in, but it didn't really exist... like Greek Gods. They were mythical, but people of that time, and even still today, patterned their entire lives around them. But now he felt something different.

"Are you okay?"

Cam heard the words but it took him a moment to respond. When he did, the words that he said both shocked and amazed Julie. "God really does exist doesn't he? He is real."

He had questioned her about her religion many times, but never with the conviction that he was now feeling. It was enough to make her eyes water again. "Yes," she said. "He is real."

"I want to be a part of it."

She had been praying that Cam would say those words to her for a very long time. "You'd be a perfect addition to the church." She laid her head on his chest and for what felt like a very long time, they held each other.

Chapter Twelve

Two weeks later, Cam was poised and ready to take the next step in his journey to a better life. He was about to be interviewed by the missionaries. Although he was still nervous, the church service he and Julie had just attended together had helped keep him calm.

Still, he had a lot to be worried about. What if the missionaries told him he wasn't ready, or wasn't worthy? The answer was simple. If the missionaries deemed him to not be ready, then he would work harder to get himself ready.

Julie walked with Cam down the hall. They were to meet in the bishops office, which was next to the door leading out of the building. They arrived before the missionaries, and instead of waiting inside, Cam led her outside.

It was hot. The glare from the sun made Julie squint. Her eyes had gotten used to being inside. Cam did not notice the sun or the heat. He barely noticed the people shuffling by him heading to their cars.

"You nervous?" Julie asked.

He thought about telling her no, but decided that now wasn't the best time to lie—even a little white lie. "A little--yeah."

"Well, let me be the first one to tell you that I'm proud of you. You've come a long way, Cam. But I want you to know, that without you, I

162

wouldn't be where I am either. You have helped me a lot. You've made me very happy. I love looking to the future and seeing you in it. Maybe I'm going to make you even more nervous saying that, but I'm not really even talking about marriage. Somehow, my future, however it turns out, will be because of you."

"Thank you," Cam said. "I just hope that the missionaries have as much faith in me as you obviously do."

"You'll do fine."

Cam felt a hand on his shoulder. He turned slowly and looked into Elder Cumming's eyes. Cam knew that this man, as well as Elder Jacobson, had a lot to do with the major changes that had taken place, in his physical and mental well being, as well as in his spiritual well-being.

"Are you ready?" Elder Cummings asked.

Julie walked beside Cam until he entered the room. Before the door was closed, she turned to him and smiled. "I'll wait out here," Julie said before he could speak. She nodded and smiled. "Good luck."

Julie watched as Elder Cummings closed the door. She knew what was about to transpire. She wished she could be in there with him, holding his hand, but she would survive. Not for long, however, and she immediately began counting the minutes.

Inside, Cam sat down in the brown plush chair. Elder Jacobson took a seat directly in front of Cam, and Elder Cummings pulled the chair out from behind the desk and sat down next to his companion.

"You made it," Elder Cummings grinned. "We had high hopes."

"I made it, thanks to you two, and to Julie."

Elder Jacobson nodded his head. "No, Cam. You deserve all of the credit. You have come a long way."

Cam nodded his head. He looked around the room quickly, just enough to see the picture of Jesus on the wall, the bookcase with church books (Cam assumed they were church books considering they were in a church), and a picture of a temple by the window. He couldn't read the words underneath the picture to see which temple it was, but it was brightly lit and for some reason Cam's eyes fixed on it a little longer than they did on anything else in the room. Whichever temple it was, he had a strong urge to see the inside of it.

"Well, let me ask you a question." Elder Cummings slid to the edge of his chair. He was preparing his mind and trying to show Cam that as a missionary, this is where he really wanted to be. "Do you feel like you are ready to take this step—to be baptized?"

Cam did not hesitate. "Yes," he nodded several times. He was about to make that his only answer, but they wanted more and he knew it. "I don't know everything there is about the church, but I do know that I want to be a part of it. I've finally found something in my life that makes sense."

"Do you believe that the church is true, and that God, and Jesus Christ, truly exists and is helping us today?"

Again, Cam answered quickly. "You told me, the first day that we met, that my life has meaning, and that I could find that purpose if I listened to what you had to say. I have found that meaning, and that means more to me than anything else in life. Yes, I believe in the church and in

Christ and in Heavenly Father. I wish I knew more, though. I know there is a lot I don't know."

"None of us know everything, Cam,." Elder Jacobson interjected. "We all learn as we go. It's like a flight of stairs. We can't reach the top until we climb each stair. At times we fly up the stairs, and at other times, we dredge ourselves along, forcing everything we do. What is important is that we keep working towards the top."

Cam recognized the fact that Elder Jacobson was much more confident than he had ever been before. In such a short time, Cam had seen him change from a kid who was trying hard to do his job, into a man who had learned how to use his gifts to help others. Cam was impressed.

"I understand that," Cam said. "But it's frustrating sometimes. I wonder where I could be if I had chosen this path years ago."

"I wouldn't worry about that anymore," Elder Jacobson said. "You should look forward. That is the only thing you have control over. Make it count, Cam."

"I intend to, believe me."

Elder Cummings took over once again, getting back to the questioning. "What are your plans for the future?"

Cam considered the question for several moments before answering. He studied the faces of the Elders as he thought. They were both so involved in this conversation. It was as if they were watching an intense movie. Although he didn't see the reason that would hold them so engrossed, Cam was impressed with their ability to focus on the task at hand.

He finally gathered his thoughts. He first looked over at the picture of the temple on the wall.

"I want to go there," he said. He thought about pointing, but didn't. "I want to get the priesthood, and I want to get married in the temple."

Neither of the missionaries spoke. They listened to the silence, allowing the depth of what Cam had just said to sink in—both for them and for Cam. Finally, Elder Cummings addressed Cam.

"That's a very good goal to have, Cam. The temple, as I'm sure you will find out, is a special place. If you attain those goals, and we have no doubt that you will, then believe me, you will find even more purpose in your life."

Elder Jacobson agreed, and then added his own thoughts. "I—we, would like to challenge you to work very hard to reach that goal. You will be amazed at what success in that realm will bring you in your life."

"And another thing," Elder Cummings added, and then paused, waiting for the correct words to come to him. "Fill your life with charity to others. You will never find more meaning in your life than helping others. I know that from being here, in the mission field. Helping others is the greatest gift in the world. It will bring you more happiness to your life than anything else."

Cam nodded his head. He realized the truth behind Elder Cummings statement. Even when he had nothing to do with the church, Cam understood the concept of helping others. It always seemed to make him happy before. How much happier would it make him now?

There were a few more questions, each of which took Cam to a new level of understanding. Most of all, however, he came to realize one important fact. He truly had come a long way. It had been a struggle, and it had taken the help of a lot of people, but he had found a way to overcome his weaknesses, and just as Elder Cummings had said—he had made it.

"Well, Cam," Elder Cummings said. "I think you're ready to be baptized."

Those words sent shivers down Cam's spine. Throughout the interview, even though they hadn't given him any reason to doubt that he would hear those words, he had wondered what the outcome was going to be.

"Thank you." Getting the words out wasn't as easy as he had hoped. He had to fight back the tears that were swelling inside of him.

"No, thank you," Elder Jacobson said. "You're a good man, Cam. We believe you'll go far in life."

They discussed the date that the baptism would occur, and then both elders stood up. Cam did the same, and shook their hands, again thanking them for their help. He walked out of the room feeling as good as he ever had in his life. He was about to become a member of the Church of Jesus Christ of Latter Day Saints. This thought was very soothing.

When Cam walked through the door, the first thing he saw was Julie. She was the very same person she had been before the interview, but to Cam, she appeared different. She was still wearing her light green dress and black nylons. Her hair was still straight, and her bangs were curled just as they had been before.

It didn't take long for Cam to realize what was different. Her smile was far more radiant than it had ever been before. It was as if she had been hiding her joy deep inside her, and was now letting it show. "What," Cam asked as if this was an every day occurrence.

"So, when is it? When are you getting baptized?"

"How do you know if I am or not? Maybe they said no. Maybe they don't think I'm ready."

The glow did not leave her face. "Come on, Cam. When is it?"

"Three weeks from yesterday." Cam was proud of himself, and was happy to show it. "I actually made it."

"Of course you made it." Without so much as a pause, Julie added more. "Why don't we celebrate tomorrow?"

Cam agreed, but wished that she could stay with him for the rest of the day. He wanted to share this elated feeling with her. Unfortunately, she had to go visit some of the ladies in the ward.

"I'll pick you up after work," Cam said.

"Okay." Julie was suddenly unsure how to react. She didn't want to go, but promises were promises. "I'll see you." She almost turned to leave, then stopped. She leaned over and kissed Cam. It was a quick kiss, but it made her tingle inside, adding to her already overwhelming happiness. "Congratulations."

"Thanks," Cam said and watched as Julie walked down the hall and back into the heart of the church.

Cam left the building, grateful that he had planned on walking home. Whatever the outcome of the interview, he figured that he would need the fresh air and a few minutes of solitude. Unfortunately, it suddenly looked as if it had been the wrong choice to make.

Halfway home, he noticed someone approaching him. It was Marcus. Cam could tell by the strut in his walk and the way he never looked up (it was amazing how he never seemed to miss anything, though). Marcus' hair was longer than ever. He looked rough, but then again he had only lost Sandy a few weeks ago.

The last time he had seen Marcus had been at the funeral. Even then, Cam had hardly taken the time to talk to his one-time best friend. "Thanks for coming. She really missed you," was all Marcus had to say, and other than the typical "I'm sorry" from Cam, nothing else had been said.

The fact that they hadn't actually talked about the situation, and the wonder that Cam had been harboring about the strange circumstances of her death, was making this moment very uncomfortable. He found himself wishing he was still in the church answering questions.

Marcus must have been deep in thought, though, because it seemed as if he hardly even noticed anyone in his path. With the distance closing fast, Cam realized that he was going to have to initiate the conversation. "How's it goin', man?"

It felt strange talking that way. It sounded so gangster like…an image that he was trying to shed. Then again, it wasn't surprising. Marcus had a way of bringing out the worst in him. He always had, and right now, Cam was praying that he would just let him go on his way.

Marcus was startled at Cam's greeting and his first reaction was to double up his fists. He relaxed as soon as Marcus realized who had caught him off guard, but Cam took note of the jumpiness. There was something else that he noticed, however, which took precedence in his mind.

It was his eyes. They were lost. It was almost frightening.

"Cam...what's up? Where you been?" His words were bland and boring.

Cam wasn't sure how to answer. This question was more difficult that the ones he had been asked a few minutes earlier. He couldn't very well blurt out the truth right now. Marcus didn't care about the truth.

Still, he wasn't exactly in the mood to lie either. Maybe it was time to lay things on the table, he thought. Maybe Marcus could handle it, although they hadn't exactly been friends lately. In fact, Cam wondered if Marcus blamed him for the suicide—if it was a suicide. Marcus wasn't the type of person who would take responsibility himself. Cam had been the one who changed everything, and he would be the perfect excuse.

As that thought bounced around inside of Cam's mind, another feeling returned. *It wasn't a suicide. It doesn't add up.* If it wasn't suicide it, was murder. The only one capable of murder was the man in front of him right now.

"I've been around," Cam answered Marcus' questions and then moved on. "I want to ask you something," Cam started carefully, just in case. Marcus looked at him but didn't say anything. "What really happened to Sandy? Things just don't add up. I know her too well."

"Man...I've been a mess. I can't deal with all this. I feel like I'm going nuts or something."

He had avoided the actual question, which didn't go unnoticed, but the comparison between Marcus' situation and the one Julie had described to him about her sister was eerie. Marcus sounded like he was going insane like Julie's sister had. Cam couldn't help but wonder if Marcus had heard the story and was living it out now, just to mess with his head. It couldn't be true, but he thought it anyway.

"You look like crap!" Cam said.

It wasn't supposed to sound harsh, but it must have been because Marcus turned on Cam like a cornered snake.

"What do you know about it jerk! You're off in some freakin' la la land doing whatever you wacko religious freaks do! Don't tell me I look like crap. You'd look like crap to if you had to deal with what I'm dealing with. As if you care anyway. What? Are we not good enough for you anymore, cause if not, just leave me alone!"

It was a bit more than Cam expected, and he wasn't ready to defend himself. He instinctively took a step back, cocked his head a little, and waited for the right words to come to him. But they didn't come. In fact, he quickly realized that he was beginning to look like a fool. He had to say something, but what? The right words finally came just as he was about to blurt out something that would have sounded stupid (mostly because he still wasn't sure what they were going to be).

"Sorry," he said and shook his head. "You're right. I guess I just can't imagine what you're feeling."

It was Marcus' turn to be taken back, only he didn't show it. Instead, he decided to take a harder stance, just to show Cam who was still the boss. "Man, what's gotten into you. Why are you getting messed up in this religious crap anyway?" Marcus stared at the suit and tie that Cam was wearing and shook his head. "You look like a dork, man.

171

His words bit into Cam's heart. Cam felt the urge, if not the responsibility, to defend the faith that he was really beginning to love and understand. He wasn't exactly knowledgeable enough to do it— or so he assumed—but he really felt like it was the right thing to do.

"It's a good thing. It gives me the sense that everything's right with the world. I never felt like that before. Drinking and smoking dope never gave me that feeling."

"It makes me feel better," Marcus said and shoved his hand in his pocket. He pulled out a box of Camel cigarettes, picked two of the smokes out of the pack, and offered one to Cam. "Here. Smoke one. Maybe you'll get your head on straight."

It was tempting. In fact, after staring at Marcus for what felt like an eternity, Cam reached out and took the cigarette. He pulled it out of Marcus' hand, and a very strange sensation overcame him. *You shouldn't have taken it! Give it back!*

He immediately pushed his hand out to Marcus, but Marcus pulled his hand away.

"Smoke the stupid cigarette!" Marcus was almost yelling. He was trying to assert his dominance just like he always did.

"I don't want it. I don't smoke"

"Yeah. You smoke. You're an addict just like the rest of us. That's what makes you part of us. That's why we liked hangin' with you. It's time to get that back, man. I guarantee you'll enjoy it. Smoke that, then we'll go back to my place and smoke something a little harsher." Marcus nodded, waiting for Cam to comply.

Two distinct sides of Cam's brain were battling. It should have seemed very unreal, even spooky to have that good versus evil battle going on right there inside of his mind. But it wasn't spooky or unreal. If anything, it was a relief. For the first time in his life, he didn't feel like he was being controlled. He had help from deep within himself. He had heard about the powers of Jesus Christ, but until that very moment, he wondered what that still small voice would sound like. The only part that seemed confusing was that the voice didn't sound all that small. It was urging him in a very strong way, yet it felt guiding and gentle at the same time. It was really battling for him, and Cam instantly knew what to do.

"I don't smoke," he said and held the smoke out for a few more seconds. When Marcus didn't take it, Cam dropped the smoke on the ground and looked at Marcus defiantly. "And I don't do drugs or drink, either. Maybe you ought to think about adding a little religion to your life, too. Maybe you wouldn't feel so overwhelmed all the time…like everyone is out to get you or whatever."

Never before had Cam been able to stand up to Marcus with such force and strength. It felt good, but it saddened him as well. He didn't want to have to talk to anyone like that. It wasn't his nature, but then again, neither was turning Marcus down.

"Yeah, that's what I need," Marcus said. "To turn into some freakin' loser like you. You used to be cool man. That woman of yours has really put it to you hasn't she?"

Those words were meant to hurt, and Cam flinched. Why would he say that? Why did he insist on pushing things until he got his way?

Cam knew the answers. Marcus was whining. A lot of adults had a way of doing that. Cam recognized it because he had done it for a very long time as well. The tactic was embedded deep inside Marcus, just as it probably had been in Cam.

This realization meant two things. He was going to have to thank Julie for helping him grow up. The second thing was going to prove more difficult. No matter what Marcus did or said, he had to stay cool, despite his urge to punch Marcus in the face. He was going to have to walk away from him forever.

"Look, Marcus," Cam started. He backed off another step as if he were going to leave after saying what he had to say. "Do whatever you want. You have that right, but I would hope you wouldn't stand in my way of doing what I want either."

"You sound like an absolute idiot! I'll bet if your woman disappeared you'd start having fun again! Maybe you both need to just disappear."

Cam wasn't sure if that was something that Marcus would ever carry out, but he wouldn't put it past him. Not anymore anyway. He would have to be more careful for a while. As for sounding like an idiot, maybe he did, but he felt better than he had ever felt in his whole life after a conversation with Marcus. He had finally broken what felt like a huge chain that had been wrapped around him; one that had been binding him for a very long time. No longer was he in thrall to Marcus Layton. He was free and that thought made him feel good.

Chapter Thirteen

Although Cam was nervous, afraid that his toe would come up out of the water and he would have to start over—in front of everyone—he was happy with the progress he had made. This decision was going to lead him to bigger and better things; things he could only have dreamed of two years ago.

He felt the spirit in the room and could sense the importance of this moment just by the pure white clothes that he was wearing and the thoughts in his heart. The reverence of the entire room left a warmth flowing throughout his body.

In a few more minutes he was going to be part of the Church . It had been a hard road to climb, but he had finally made it. As one of the speakers made their remarks, Cam listened intently. As the time grew closer, however, he found it more and more difficult to concentrate. He only heard pieces of what Sister Straingarden was saying. His mind seemed to wander every time he looked into the font.

He thought about Marcus and how he had acted the last time they had actually talked. He wished that his parents were here, although even if they were alive, they probably wouldn't have attended the service anyway. They weren't exactly religious, and they never had been much a part of his life.

But Julie was here and that made up for all of the negatives. She was sitting beside him. Her hands were resting comfortably in her lap, hardly creasing her blue flowered dress. He had never seen the dress before and figured she had bought it just for the occasion. That was saying a lot, because Julie seldom purchased anything unnecessary, especially for herself.

Cam was almost the same way now. Instead of spending his money on booze, he was saving it. He had a plan. One that he had been putting together since talking to Bishop Tortelson after church two weeks ago. Actually, it had been this conversation that had started him thinking.

"What are your plans for the future, young man?" Bishop Tortelson had asked.

Cam had thought about it for a brief second. He wasn't sure if the Bishop was talking about his spiritual plans or his worldly plans. After getting baptized, he wanted to receive the priesthood. Beyond that, though, he wasn't sure if he had any plans.

As his mind quickly filtered through the possibilities, several things came to him. He should go back to school. He needed to get a job so that he could support a family, and he wanted...he wanted-.

He wanted Julie!

The words took control of his mind leaving him more aware of himself—and of the world around him—than ever before. Of course that's what he wanted! After thinking it, he had the strong urge to say it, to get it out in the open.

"I want to ask Julie to marry me!"

Before Bishop Tortelson could say anything, Cam's mind became a little confused. Was he really worthy of Julie's love? He had thought so a while ago, but now that he was closer to being able to do it, he really wondered? Could he love her as much as she deserved to be loved? Could he make that commitment? Would the bishop want them to wait?

All of these questions flashed by in seconds, as did the answers. Yes, he was worthy of Julie's love; at least he would be as soon as he was able to go through the temple. There was certainly no doubt that he could love and commit to her.

Bishop Tortelson answered the last question. "If that's what you want, then I couldn't be happier for the both of you. You complement each other well!"

Those words had given Cam the go-ahead to start planning his proposal, and now, sitting in front of the baptismal font, he was about to take one of the biggest steps that he needed to accomplish before he could ask her.

"And this step will change your entire life if you allow it to."

Sister Straingarden's words brought him out of the past completely. Her words sunk into Cam's heart. What she was saying was important. He felt it, and he focused on her words.

"I hope and pray, Brother Bird, that you will go home and write down the feelings and emotions that you feel today. They will be important to you throughout your life. You will be able to use your own words to help you in times of need. They will help see you through almost any situation you find yourself in." She closed with her own testimony and sat down.

Sister Straingarden was the last person to speak. It was time. The first emotion that Cam was going to have to write down was "apprehension". He was sure that what he was doing was the right thing to do, but he couldn't help but wonder what it would really mean for his future. Could he live up to the higher standards that were about to be placed on him? He hadn't been able to live up to the lesser ones before. Why did he feel like he could do this?

Because he had help! That was an easy answer. Instead of trudging through the world alone, he had help. Physical help, mental help, and most of all, he had spiritual help.

Yes! The answer was yes! He could succeed. He could, and he would. There was nothing that was going to stand in his way. He wouldn't allow it.

"Thank you, Sister Straingarden," Bishop Tortelson said. He then turned his attention to Cam. "Brother Bird, would you and Brother Emery please step into the font?"

Cam looked at Brother Emery first, and then stood up. He looked at Julie, and noticed that she was smiling, as usual. This bright confident smile calmed him down just when he needed it the most. His legs were a little shaky. They weren't out of control but it was enough to make things a little uncomfortable. The curve of Julie's lips and the love in her eyes reminded him of the words she had said as they drove to the Stake Center. *It's going to be worth it. I promise.*

He held her words in his heart as he smiled at her and looked away. As he turned, he noticed two more people entering the room adding to the already larger than expected crowd, at least larger than Cam had planned on. Again, he realized how much help he was going to have in his journey.

He looked into the eyes of the man and woman who had just come in. They looked vaguely familiar, as if he should know them, but he couldn't remember ever having met them before. The man was strong, clean shaven, and tall. The woman with him appeared to be very much a lady. She was pretty, with short black hair and a stern face that said 'I could be a good friend, but don't mess with me'.

Julie's words came again. *It's going to be worth it. I promise.*

Cam pulled his gaze away from the couple as they quickly found a seat in the back of the room. They faded from his memory as quickly as they had entered, and by the time he reached the door to the font, he was ready, both mentally and physically. His mind was clear. His heart was as pure as it would ever be. Yes! He was ready.

The water was perfect, and Cam figured that this had been done intentionally. He was supposed to be concentrating on the feelings, the mood, the promises, and the vows that he was about to enter into. The last thing he needed to be worrying about was the temperature of the water.

Cam moved towards Brother Emery who was waiting in the exact center of the font. The water swirled calmly around him as he moved. Cam wanted to look up into Julie's eyes for assurance one more time, but he fought off the urge. Instead, he remembered her words.

It will all be worth it. I promise.

Again, Cam was comforted by her words, and he continued to move. He stopped when he reached the middle of the font.

He knew what was going to happen. Julie, in her infinite wisdom, had taken him to two baptisms. They had been a little different. There were more people being baptized, and everyone had been eight years old, but the process was the same. Each one of the kids had made it through okay, which added to Cam's confidence—and to his apprehension. They made it without messing up, so Cam had to make it too.

As if it were the most natural thing in the world, Brother Emery moved into position, as did Cam.

Brother Emery had dark hair, slicked back and neat. Cam had first guessed him to be thirty five, but later found out that he was actually five years older than that. He was single, and as far as Cam knew, he had no family anywhere. He was a loner. At least that's how Cam had pictured him until Brother Emery became his home teacher. Now, he was probably the second biggest influence in Cam's life. He hardly ever joined in the ward outings, and other than attending church, and serving as a home teacher with Elder Fatheringham, no one ever seemed to see him much.

There was more to Brother Emery, things that really touched Cam. He was kind, almost to a fault. He would help anyone, but he didn't get out in the neighborhood enough to know what was going on. It wasn't because he didn't like people though. He cared for others more than almost anyone that Cam knew. It was this knowledge that made Cam realize that Brother Emery would be the only person Cam would want to have baptize him.

Cam listened to the short, rehearsed, simple prayer that Brother Emery offered. He realized, however, that the meaning behind the words was not simple at all. It was something that would take some real studying on his part to figure out. At the close of the prayer, Cam took a breath, trying to hide it from the onlookers (he wasn't going to give the impression that he needed to plug his nose), and steadied his feet.

Don't let your feet leave the ground.

Sound words, but could he do it!

If they come up—don't let the toes come out of the water.

If he failed the first part, there was little chance that he was going to be able to maintain enough control and balance to keep his toes under the water.

Cam felt the water rush over his body as Brother Emery lowered him in. He was about to remind himself—just one more time—to keep his feet on the ground, but Julie's words made it into his head first.

It will all be worth it. I promise.

His nerves steadied as his head went under the water. He forgot about his feet altogether. When he came up, many feelings rushed through his mind at once. He was delighted that he hadn't messed up. He was afraid of the future. At the same time, he knew it would *all be worth it.*

Beyond that, however, he felt a strong feeling deep down in the pit of his stomach. He recognized it immediately, even though he hadn't had the pleasure of feeling it for a very long time.

It was purity. He was pure and whole again.

He held on to that feeling until he and Brother Emery had rejoined their friends. In a ceremony just as important, also handled by Brother Emery, Cam was given the gift of the Holy Ghost. At the end of this prayer, that sense of purity grew inside of him. This time there was something else; something that was just as strong. He had a realization, one that he had never felt before, at least not on this level. He would never be alone again and that was important to him.

As he shook everyone's hand in the room, watching Julie stand back awaiting her turn, he allowed his mind to rewind the entire day's events. Yes! He concluded. This was the right thing to do—without a doubt!

Julie's presence forced his thoughts to the back of his mind. She finally stepped forward and lifted her hand. Cam shook it, but quickly took her in his arms and hugged her. It was then that he noticed the couple who had almost missed the baptism.

He suddenly recognized them. He was a little amazed that they were here, but it had to be Julie's parents. They didn't look exactly like the pictures on Julie's wall, but he could see that was who they were.

In response to his thoughts, Julie stepped back and introduced them. "This is my mom and dad." She extended her hand to Cam but addressed her parents, "This is Cam."

Mr. Haws wasted no time. He stepped right up, shook Cam's hand, and smiled. "Congratulations, Mr. Bird."

Mrs. Haws, on the other hand, seemed a little more reluctant; almost as if she were threatened by him. "Yes," she finally said in a dainty yet powerful way. "Congratulations." She didn't shake his hand. She just smiled. If there was any doubt that this was Julie's mother, it was erased after she smiled. Their smiles were absolutely identical in every way.

The encounter was cut short by a hand on Cam's back.

"Cam." It was the same voice that had just finished praying for him.

"Brother Emery," Cam said and turned around to face his friend. "Thank you for everything. I appreciate you're doing this for me."

Brother Emery took the compliment in his usual ho-hum way and nodded. It was only then that Cam realized that one of Brother Emery's hands were behind his back. Cam glanced in that direction, which persuaded Brother Emery to move his hand into view.

He held an angel made of rock. A hand carved, one foot tall angel. "This is for you. I'm glad you've made the changes in your life that you have. It's important to your well being. I guarantee that you'll feel more alive and far happier if you live the teachings of the gospel. I've been making this for you ever since you asked me to baptize you." He handed the statue to Cam. "Thanks for the opportunity…really."

"It's incredible," Cam said, wondering if he should really accept something this beautiful (and no doubt costly). But knowing it would be rude not to take it, he said nothing more than "thank you—I can't believe how incredible this is."

"That's what I do, Cam. That's why no one sees me too much. I spend most of my time in my basement, working. You should come see it some time." He turned to Julie. "You should both come."

"We will," Cam answered for both of them.

"I have to get going. I'm not really good in a crowd. Congratulations." With that, Brother Emery walked out of the room leaving Cam to absorb everything he had seen and felt, and to get better acquainted with what he hoped would be his future mother and father-in-law.

Chapter Fourteen

That evening, Cam began to wonder if having in-laws was going to be as good as it had sounded. His uneasiness was attributed mostly to an aura he felt emitting from Julie's mother. It didn't feel like she disapproved of him, at least not entirely, but something wasn't settling well with her. Before he actually popped the question to Julie that evening, Cam felt it was important to find out just what the problem was. He hoped he could do it subtly, not arousing suspicions about what he was going to do, but he knew that in the end he would just have to ask.

Getting Mr. Haws permission to marry his daughter would be easy. All Cam had to do was ask him when Julie's mom wasn't around. Mr. Haws had a strong mind, but he didn't have the final say in most things, so having him alone would be important.

"So Julie's pretty persuasive, huh?" Mr. Haws asked just to get the conversation going again.

"She turned my life around," Cam admitted without reservation. He also sensed his first chance to butter up Julie's mom. "I can see where she gets her persuasiveness from." He spoke directly to Mrs. Haws.

"There's no doubt where she gets it," Mr. Haws said and he too looked at his wife. "It's a woman thing. Every woman in her family, as far back as you can go, was just like that. They want something and they get it."

"And we're proud of it too—aren't we?" Julie said to her mom.

"We are," Mrs. Haws agreed, shooting a quick glance at her husband. Everyone but Cam picked up the meaning at once.

"Okay, Mom," Julie said. "What are you two hiding?"

Cam was instantly curious. He looked at Julie's mom and waited for an answer, but she offered nothing. Mrs. Haws looked at her daughter, her blue eyes suddenly cool and relaxed. That one subtle change in her appearance altered so much about her, especially her overall demeanor. She now appeared happy, and yet worried too. Her hair, which up close Cam could see was graying slightly, made her seem sophisticated instead of witchy, which is what he had been thinking for most of the night.

"Your mother has something she would like to tell you," Julie's dad said.

That cleared things up a little, at least it did for Julie, but it left Cam even more puzzled. How could someone that in charge, be shy about saying what was on her mind?

"What is it, mom?" Julie asked. She was smiling, but trying hard not to all out grin. She enjoyed watching her mother squirm a little.

Mrs. Haws sat perfectly still and stared straight at Julie. When she still didn't say anything, Mr. Haws prodded her a little more. "Come on, Geri. You promised."

This time the glance Mrs. Haws shot out of her eyes was a mixture of fear, anger, sadness, and quite possibly happiness. It was a strange combination, at least it seemed so to Cam. The silence was suddenly making him a little nervous, but he was forced to sit still and wait.

"Fine," Mrs. Haws said and turned to her daughter. She hesitated, but knew exactly what she had to say. She had rehearsed them for hours on the plane ride to Utah. Saying them to a real person—especially to her daughter—wasn't going to be as easy as it had been when no one could actually hear her. Apologizing was something she had never gotten used to doing.

"Julie—I owe you an apology." Again she stopped talking, but this time it was for a purpose. She turned to Cam and continued. "And I owe you one as well."

The thought of a stranger, someone he had only met a few hours ago, owing him anything, let alone an apology, seemed very odd. His mind quickly tried to remember the last time someone told him that they owed him anything…other than another beer when his was gone and it was their turn to fetch. He couldn't picture it ever happening. He'd never earned an apology, and he was fairly sure he hadn't earned one this time, either.

"I'm not quite sure what you mean ma'am, but I'm fairly sure you don't owe me anything." He shouldn't have said a word.

Shut up and listen or I won't say this.

Mrs. Haws didn't actually say the words. She didn't have to. Cam read it in her eyes. There was no mistaking her well-intended warning. After allowing the look to linger, Mrs. Haws smiled and politely disagreed with him.

"Actually, I do," she said. "For a long time I was angry with Julie—because of you. I told her

187

that she shouldn't be getting involved with a person who drank. I've let that argument lead me and my decisions for a long time now."

This time it was Julie who tried to ease her mother's mind. "It's not worth worrying about, Mom. I forgot about that a long time ago."

"No you haven't! You have too much of *me* in you to just let things drop like that. I know it's lingered. I wouldn't even be surprised if you used it as a springboard to keep your relationship going, and probably to keep your mission to help Cam going too."

Julie didn't like her mothers words. She hoped that Cam hadn't picked up on it, but by the look he gave her—quickly and almost undetectable by anyone who didn't love him—she knew he had heard it.

"Excuse me, mother!" Julie decided to be a little confrontational. "Our relationship hasn't stayed together because I was on a mission to save Cam!"

Cam's chances for family approval had gone from bleak to positive to traumatized in a matter of two minutes. A real fight was about to break out, and he wasn't sure what to do. He glanced at Mr. Haws. He was frowning but looking off into space. This obviously hadn't gone as planned. Cam decided that as long as Mr. Haws didn't say anything, he would keep quiet too.

"That came out wrong," Mrs. Haws said.

It didn't. Cam was fairly sure of that. It was like in a court of law when an attorney let important information out of the bag—which he wasn't supposed to let the jury hear. They hear it and they absorb it, even when the judge orders them to disregard the statement.

"All I really mean is that I was wrong. I admit it. I'm sorry." She sat straight, but turned her head to Cam. "You have done a marvelous thing, Cam. I commend you for it. And I apologize for doubting your motives and your sincerity."

Cam could handle that. He still didn't feel as if the apology was necessary, or if it was all that sincere. It sounded more like the patriarch of the family was actually taking a stand and making her say it. Still, he could live with it. It was far more than he felt like he deserved.

"Thank you," Julie said. She wanted the conversation to end now, before anything else was said. "Would anyone like something to drink?"

Cam nodded. "Please. Anything."

"I'll help you," Mrs. Haws said. The two ladies left the room, and Cam realized that this was his chance. If everything was going to go as planned, then now was the time to ask Julie's father for his daughter's hand.

Knowing there wasn't much time, Cam got right to the point. "Mr. Haws."

"Please, call me Tom," the tall, stocky man interrupted but then fell silent again.

"Okay—Tom—I was wondering if I could ask you something?" Cam's mouth dried up and the sweat began to bead on his forehead. What was he going to do if *Tom* said no?

"Sure," Mr. Haws said and stared at him.

Cam swallowed and decided to just blurt out the question. The room began spinning and everything went a little blurry.

"Sir, I was wondering if I could marry your daughter?" There was a moment of silence, and just for good measure, Cam added a little more. "In the temple of course. I want to marry her in the temple."

The questions began, and the spinning in Cam's head got worse. If he would have been standing up, he wondered if he would have fallen over.

"Do you think you're ready—I mean really ready to marry her?"

"Yes." The word shot out of Cam's mouth without any effort or thought. As it expelled, as if by magic, the dizziness inside his head began to subside. Was it because he had been able to answer the question or because the hard part was now behind him? He began to plead silently for a 'yes' answer from Julie's dad.

"Getting married in the temple has always been important to Julie," Mr. Haws went on. "Marrying the perfect man has driven her for…well, for as long as I can remember."

"I'm sure it has, sir." Cam thought about changing that to Tom, but out of respect, both for him and for the solemn subject, he didn't. "And I only hope that she will view me as that person. But I won't ask her without your blessing."

"You have it!"

Those words topped off what felt like the best day in Cam's life. He had joined the church, added a lot of new friends, and now he had permission to ask Julie to marry him. All of this jumbled together and caused Cam's mind and body to float—quite a contrast to the fear he had been feeling.

But he wasn't allowed to drift mentally for long. Julie and her mother re-entered the room, each were carrying two cups. Mrs. Haws handed one to her husband and sat down. Julie handed her extra cup to Cam, and then sat next to him on the sofa.

What was left of the elated feeling that he had been having was gone at the onset of one thought. What do I do about Julie's mother? Was it imperative to ask her? Wasn't permission from Mr. Haws enough?

Looking for help, Cam looked at Julie's father. When Tom finally looked at him, Cam looked at Mrs. Haws and then quickly back to Tom again. Cam clenched his jaw and looked puzzled. He managed to keep this look from Mrs. Haws and Julie.

Mr. Haws knew the look. He also understood Cam's concern. He returned his own subtle 'you have both of our permission, now go do it' look. He then turned to his wife and set up the rest of the night for Cam. "Let's go," he said. "I think it's time that these lovebirds get on with what they had planned before we interrupted."

"You didn't interrupt, daddy," Julie said. "You can stay. You just got your juice."

With everything else on his mind, Cam hadn't even bothered to take a drink. It didn't matter though. He probably wouldn't have even noticed what kind it was anyway. His mind was focused elsewhere.

"That's all right, hon'. I'd like to go to the hotel and get some sleep." The only nice hotel was near Salt Lake, but only about fifteen minutes away. You two better do whatever you're going to do and then get some sleep. I need to go sight seeing in the morning. I'd like to see what's up in them mountains I've been hearing so much about."

Mrs. Haws didn't object. She stood up, congratulated Cam and thanked Julie for the drinks.

Cam could see that Mrs. Haws still wasn't comfortable, even when they left. He refused to dwell on this, however, because it was time to carry out his plan. Everything was perfect now, but he couldn't help but think that they needed to leave right away. He didn't want to give Mrs. Haws the chance to make Tom turn around so she could stop what was about to happen.

"Let's go for a drive," Cam said, sounding anxious—or was it hysterical?

Julie looked at him and nodded. Her face was lit up and she looked even more beautiful than ever. Cam wondered how she continued to grow more and more gorgeous with the passing of every moment. It was obviously a "love" thing.

"We need to go get something before we go," Cam said. "We just have to run to my house. It'll only take a few minutes."

"Okay," Julie said, but changed her mind suddenly. "Wait," she said. "I have something for you."

"What?"

"I have to give you something!" She started walking down the hall but stopped when Cam didn't follow. "Come on!"

Julie led him down the hall and into her bedroom. He had been in her room only twice. This was her sanctuary; the place where she could disappear from the world. She had told him this and he had respected it ever since.

It was a simple room: a bed, a chest of drawers, a closet, two oak nightstands on either side of the bed, and a chair. The curtains were light-blue, as was the carpet. The bedspread, pulled up neatly and tucked under the pillows, was covered with romantic flowers and coincided perfectly with everything.

Julie walked around the foot of the bed, opened the drawer on the nightstand, and pulled out Cam's book—Pet Cematary (the only thing inside). She handed it to Cam. "I finally finished it," she said. "It wasn't too bad."

"Oh, come on. It's one of the best books ever written." Cam stared at the cover surprised that he had completely forgotten that he had even lent it to her. "You really read it?"

"It took a while. I don't read fast, especially scary books, but I read every word."

"I'm surprised you got through it."

"Why?" Julie said. "I told you. I wanted to read it. I'll probably never read another horror novel in my life, but I wanted to read at least one."

"Thanks," he said and patted the book against his left hand. "I shouldn't have let you read it, though. It's going to haunt you for the rest of your life."

"It wasn't that scary," she lied. The book had frightened her enough that she could only read during the daylight hours.

Julie shrugged. "Okay, lets go," she said and stood to the side. Cam kissed Julie on the cheek before actually walking out of the bedroom.

It was almost dark by the time they stepped out into the woods. The half-moon added quite a bit more light than he had expected, which only made things better. Everything was working out exactly how he had hoped.

"I'm surprised you even remember this place," Julie said as soon as he stopped the truck. She climbed out and shut the door behind her.

Cam reached in the back of the truck, pulled out a back pack, and strapped it on his back. Julie wondered what was in the pack, but she figured she would find out soon enough.

"I don't forget places that have such a deep impact on my life."

"This place had a deep impact on your life?" Julie remembered almost every word that had taken place that day. This was, after all, where they had gone the first time they went out together. They were only friends then, but it was an important day.

"Some of the things you told me the day you brought me here have stuck with me forever. It was the first time I had ever heard about faith. It was the first time you really told me about the LDS church. But the most important thing about that night was when you showed me how to pray. You also challenged me to pray—do you remember?"

She did now. She remembered that her prayer, or something that he had felt shortly after her prayer, had affected him strongly. "Yes," she answered.

"I prayed silently, right after that. You seemed to be off in another world for a few seconds and I prayed. You must not have even known I had done it. If you did know, you never asked me what I prayed about. We never talked about it, and until recently, I was glad it never came up. It felt so strange and awkward praying to someone I couldn't see. But I wanted to believe it—even then. I really did, and by the time I said 'amen', I felt like maybe I could believe. It was the beginning for me. It— and you—helped me through some pretty tough times. I owe you a lot. I probably owe you my whole life."

As they talked, Cam led Julie deeper into the woods towards the water fall. Thousands of tiny creatures serenaded them as they walked adding a hypnotizing feel to the already electric evening.

Figuring that it was okay now, she asked what she hadn't dared ask that night. "What did you pray about?"

He answered without hesitation. "I admitted my weaknesses. I asked him to help me overcome them, and I prayed for you."

Julie stopped. Her legs grew weak, and as if on clue the night went completely silent...at least it did for her. A warm feeling of true love swept through her body leaving her both stunned and amazed.

"You prayed for me?"

Cam wasn't sure why she had stopped, but he turned around and placed his hands on her waist. "Yes—I prayed for you. I prayed that you would have the strength to really help me no matter how hard it got."

Why would he pray for me...especially on his first try at praying? Julie wondered. Why would he even think to pray for someone else? That was something that she figured was a learned response.

She knew why, and her stomach fluttered and her legs felt even less secure. She gripped Cam's arms just in case. He loved you even then, she thought. He really loved you, and he loves you now.

It was hard to understand, but that really would explain why he would pray for someone else. He truly cared for her—and not in a self-serving way. Suddenly Julie wished she had been more observant. Things could have been much easier for her if she would have known how he really felt.

"Come on," Cam said, interrupting her daydream.

After forcing her legs to work, Cam and Julie continued. Just before rounding the last bend, and just before darkness really settled in, Cam stopped in front of a large rock. "Wait here," Cam said. "I have something to do real quick." Cam noticed the questions in her eyes. "Just two minutes. That's all. I promise!"

He walked away leaving Julie to her own thoughts. She had no idea what he was up to. This wasn't right. She should be throwing him a party. He had just gotten baptized. She shouldn't have listened to his request for a quiet evening together. She should have planned a surprise party. She let go of these thoughts and tuned in to the sound of the crashing water from the not-too-distant falls.

She looked around for a few seconds and then climbed up onto the rock. Two sharp points poked at her as she sat down and she quickly moved around until she found a more comfortable spot. She then tried to figure out what he was doing. Before he came back, she had arrived at the only logical solution. Cam had bought her something. He wanted to thank her, and this was the most romantic place to do it. The only thing wrong with her explanation was that she owed him, not the other way around. He had done the work. All she had done was show him an option that he hadn't seen before. All she had really done was fall madly in love with him along the way. After that, it was just two lovers allowing life to bring them closer together.

Besides, he had helped her more than he would ever realize. She had grown in ways that he would never be able to see. He had reminded her that she deserved to be loved. It was difficult, especially at first. She really believed that she was destined to be alone. Not only had she been afraid of being alone, she was afraid of the mental pain that loving someone could cause. Her heart had broken when Becky disappeared. It had taken a long time, and a lot of love and understanding from Cam, before she realized that love was worth the risk. Cam had broken the wall she had built. He had seen through the pain and fear and had toughed it out, all while dealing with his own problems.

"Okay, let's go!"

Cam's words startled her. She jumped off the rock, and as far as Cam could see, she was ready to run the other way. That was a bad thought. He figured that she would at least wait until he asked the question before leaving him standing in the mountains all alone.

"Sorry," he apologized. "I thought you heard me coming."

Julie shook her head. "My fault. I was— you know—just drifting."

Cam took Julie's hand and because he was walking too fast, he half-pulled her towards their final destination. They rounded the bend, but she still couldn't see anything. He wasn't wearing the backpack. She looked for it lying on the ground somewhere, but it was too dark.

And then she saw a flicker. Almost immediately after that, she saw what Cam had set up for them. It was between one of the largest rocks and the water at the base of the cascading falls. The flicker was coming from three candles which sat atop the white blanket he had laid out on the ground. There were two champagne glasses sitting in the center of the blanket and a bottle standing up in front of them: sparkling apple juice.

Cam led her to what he hoped would be forever known as 'their spot'. He even showed her where he would like her to sit. From there, she could see the cascading water in the background as she focused on him. At least that's how it was supposed to work, and why wouldn't it?

He sat down, leaned over, and opened the non-drinkers wine. He filled the two glasses half full, replaced the screw-off cap, and handed Julie her drink. "I have a toast to make," he said. "I want to toast us! We've been together for a long time now. I am very much in love with you. This toast is to our future. The future I want to share with you."

When he lifted the glass into the air, Julie met him at the peak. Of course she would drink to that!

They drank, and as soon as they finished, Julie took her turn. "And a toast to the riddance of the past. It was a difficult road, but we have both overcome obstacles that were keeping us from growing."

He hadn't really thought about it much, but of course she had grown along the way. It would be impossible to help a man overcome addictions and not learn something in the process. He held his glass out to her and after the soft clanking sound that seemed to echo through the trees around them, they sipped a little more of the apple juice.

Wasting no time, Cam reached over and took her glass. His fingers brushed against her soft hands and he longed to hold them. But he had work to do, and he had to do it before the nerves took over and made this more difficult.

He sat her empty glass down, just as he had practiced, and filled his own glass with a little juice. He smelled it and sat it down in front of him. He made sure that her eyes followed his hand by pretending like the glass was about to tip. With his other hand, he reached behind him, felt for the ring case under the lip of the blanket, and slipped the ring into the palm of his hand. He casually brought his hand around in front of him. He picked up her glass and poured two fingers worth of juice into her glass and sat the bottle on the blanket.

Again, he used the unstable glass routine to distract her, which allowed him to slip the ring into her champagne glass. The soft clink was very subtle. She couldn't know what had caused it. He handed her the glass, picked up his own drink, and lifted it into the air.

"I've found someone—finally—who really brings out the best in me. I want to thank you for everything, Julie. I have found that meeting people is the best thing in the world. Finding things, inanimate objects, is a very distant second. I only hope that the next thing you find makes you as happy as it will make me."

Julie looked at him a little puzzled, but more in awe of Cam than ever. He was even showing his romantic side, and that was something to admire. She remembered seeing him sitting on the bench the first time they met. He had looked so alone, so sad, and more than a little depressed. Now he was full of life. He was actually happy and that made her happy.

She lifted her glass, leaned forward so that she could reach his glass, and sealed the toast. Cam drank, but watched her carefully. He prayed that she wouldn't swallow the ring when she took the drink. He could see it sitting in the bottom of the glass thanks to the candle light. When she tipped the glass, the ring slid towards her lips. Cam stifled a gasp and held his breath for what felt like an eternity.

The ring hit her lips. At first her mind said "it's an ice cube," but there were no ice cubes in the drink. She pulled the glass away from her lips, swallowed the cool liquid that remained in her mouth, and she did it just in time. She gasped as she looked into the glass. She knew what it was immediately, and then shock took over. She maintained enough control, however, to reach in and pull the ring out of the apple juice.

"Julie—will you marry me?"

Cam was on one knee, smiling and praying for the millionth time that she would say yes. His entire future hinged on her answer. How could he live without her? She had succeeded. He was finally cured and converted. What if that was the end? What if she walked away thinking it was a job well done? What if she moved on to some other lost soul in need of the best help anyone could dream of. She was an angel, and she looked even more like one now. But all he could do was kneel perfectly still and hope.

Twice, Julie opened her mouth as if to answer but said nothing. Was she debating? Was she trying to find the easiest way to let him down? Again, the questions bombarded him.

Finally, on the third try, she succeeded in getting the words out. "I have no doubt in the world that you are the most incredible man that I will ever meet. We are perfect together. I have no doubt as to my feelings for you…"

Cam's head almost exploded as she paused. It was the typical way of ending a relationship. *We are perfect...you are perfect...but--.*

"And I have never been happier than I am right now. Yes! I will marry you, Cam. I will definitely marry you."

Tears began streaming from her eyes. "Yes," she said again, this time leaning towards him while she nodded her head. Cam quickly moved the champagne glass to the side, this time not caring where it sat or even if it tipped over. He took her in his arms, and held her for the first time as an engaged couple.

They stared at each other, as if their minds and their souls were one. They leaned in closer together and kissed. Their lips touched lightly, and for the first time, Julie allowed the feelings to linger. She was in love, and she really enjoyed how love felt...especially knowing that the feeling was mutual.

Chapter Fifteen

Julie's fingers were warm, small, and comforting. They fit into Cam's hand as if they had been made to match. Of course, that was what Cam now thought about their entire lives. Julie had been sent to Earth for him. He would always believe that. Why else would things have worked out the way they did. Everything in his life was perfect, and he owed this to Julie—to his soon to be wife. Where would he be had she not taken the time to speak to him in the theatre?

"What are you thinking?" Julie asked.

Cam subconsciously held on to the feeling Julie's skin was having on him. This was something he would never grow tired of. Her touch was magical and the lingering effect left him wanting to feel that forever. He could hold hands with her, and feel the softness of her touch, forever.

The sky was cloudy, threatening to rain, but they hardly noticed—other than it was certainly cooler than it had been over the past few days. The park was crowded, full of families and friends playing, talking, and having a good time. None of them were having as good a time as Julie, however; at least, not according to her.

"Just wondering--," Cam said. "About the past, and about the future—our future."

"I know what you see in your past," she said and moved closer until her shoulder brushed against his. "What do you see in the future?"

Cam smiled, considered stopping his slow pace, and then changed his mind. They were moving around the perimeter of the park, which was where they had set out to go. They had just passed the baseball diamonds, where they had half-watched the game being played—a bunch of ten-year-olds just learning. They were now heading towards the two tennis courts.

"Do we really know enough about each other to know what our futures will hold?"

Julie thought about that question. She was unsure how to answer. Finally, after careful contemplation, she waded in. "It's just one more chance to prove how much faith we have—part of the test, I suppose."

"Maybe. I just hope we have the same dreams. I mean, when you think about it, we are quite different."

"We're not all that different." Julie stopped and turned towards him, but she did not pull her hand away from his. In fact, she stared into his eyes and casually searched for his other hand. "We have a lot in common."

"Like what."

"We both love the gospel. That's important." She hesitated before going on, but only for a moment. "We both are in love with each other, and we both see a future with each other in it."

"And there's something else," Cam said, and once again they began to walk.

Of course there was. She had taken mental notes of a great many traits that they shared, all of which added up to her saying "I will" at the prospect of marriage. The intrigue of hearing his perspective fascinated her. Did guys actually think like that? Not according to people she talked to…mostly women in the office.

She didn't respond fast enough, and instead of waiting for a response, he blurted out his answer. "Kids."

Julie's heart rose. Even her fingers seemed to go numb, and for a moment, she wondered if she would be able to hang on to Cam's hand. "Kids?" Her eyebrows rose and her smile enlarged. She could feel the sides of her face stretching. It had to look a bit strange, but she didn't care. Right then, she was as happy as she could ever be. He knew that she wanted kids. In fact, he knew that she had to have a family to feel whole, although they had barely touched on the subject. She had a good idea that he wanted kids as well, and thus it never really came up. His character wouldn't have allowed him to marry her if he wasn't of the same mind. Hearing the words come directly from his cute little mouth was powerful.

"We both want a family," Cam reiterated. He had wanted to say those words for a long time, but he had to wait. He wanted to make sure that everything was right between them before they spoke too much of the future. This was the right time. She had now heard the one thing that she needed to hear from him. This would finally show her how serious he was, both about her and about his commitment to her. "I know that having kids with you would bring me more happiness than I could have ever hoped for."

Julie's stomach ached, forcing her to stop walking. She stared up at him with adoration and a lasting sense of peace. It was a longing feeling that she had often wondered if she would ever get to feel. She was truly in love. There was no doubt in her mind. Not that there ever was, but this just added proof.

A quick buzzing sound moved towards them, followed by a loud crash. From the corner of their eyes, they each saw a yellow tennis ball rolling away from the fence beside them. But they did not take their eyes off one another. Instead, they embraced, their eyes piercing each others souls. Soon they would be married, and they would be together forever. For now, they shared time, happiness, and a short but intense kiss. They allowed their lips to convey the meaningful love that they truly felt for each other.

Chapter Sixteen

Julie moved briskly along Vine Street. She was heading towards Cam's house, taking in the beauty of the back roads. As she walked, she thought about her wedding. The date was creeping closer; less than two months to go. May twenty fifth was destined to be the most incredible day in Julie's life. It would be incredible if she could ever get ready, that is. She hadn't picked out the perfect dress (she couldn't bring herself to wear her sisters, although she had thought about it). She hadn't even decided on the style of cake or finalized the guest list. Actually, until a week ago, she and Cam hadn't even agreed fully on the size of the wedding.

Her maid-of-honor had been chosen though. She didn't have that many friends; at least not ones that she would like to share this honor with. At least that step was complete. That was what was important. It was one thing she wouldn't have to worry about any more. That was one of the main reasons for the smile on her face now.

Her happiness, however, didn't last long. Someone was coming towards her and she knew who it was as soon as he rounded the corner and came into view. She had only seen Marcus once, outside the grocery store with his arms full of beer. Cam had sheltered her from Marcus very well, to which she would always be grateful. Seeing him that once had been enough to embed his image in her mind. This was definitely him. She also knew enough about him to know that she needed to steer clear of him if possible, but it didn't look like there was much chance of that—not this time.

The glare, and the evilness in Marcus' eyes had grown more intense since the last time she had seen him. He was sick. He looked possessed. Julie hated to even think of that. His eyes never wavered from hers. She wanted to turn or to cross the street, but it probably wouldn't help. He would follow her. Marcus wasn't just passing by. There was a reason for his being here.

Fear swelled in her chest as Marcus moved to the center of the small dirt road blocking her path almost entirely. Why had she gone this way? There were three ways to Cam's from the center of town. Why had she chosen this old road? It wasn't even the shortest way. It was the prettiest way, which was the only reason she had chosen the route. The trees stood tall and green, and the road was usually deserted and peaceful.

It wasn't deserted today!

Those words echoed in Julie's head just as they would if she were yelling into a deep canyon; slow but repetitive and somehow deeper each time they came back around.

Julie's muscles tightened as Marcus moved within twenty five yards; certainly speaking distance—but he didn't say a word. He just stared at her, trying hard to put the fear of the devil into her.

It was working!

She was afraid; especially if what Cam had told her about Sandy's death was true. If Marcus could kill someone who cared for him, what was he capable of doing to someone who didn't like him much?

You're blowing this way out of proportion. He's going to walk by, probably not say a word, and it'll all be over.

No chance! Something wasn't right. He wasn't just going to walk by.

Whatever he does, don't show your fear! Don't let the beast know the truth."

Julie focused on her muscles, quickly willing them to relax. It worked, but not enough. She forced a smile and even decided to address him.

"Hi—Marcus?" It sounded very contrived and false.

Marcus didn't say a word. He didn't even blink. He just continued to move closer, slowing his pace a little more as if trying to add suspense to the situation. He was dressed in black Levi's, a black T-shirt, and high top Nike look-a-likes. He looked as if he were intentionally trying to reveal his mood—and Julie read the look correctly. She couldn't help but notice that he looked—*dead*!

Julie wished she hadn't thought that word. She swallowed hard and stopped walking. She was in trouble. Her mind shifted from 'what if' to 'what do I do'? Simply stepping to the side wasn't enough; not now. She had to run!

She bolted to the right—towards the line of trees closest to her—hoping that she would be able to outrun him. If not, she would head into the trees and hope he stumbled and hurt himself before she did.

But he was ready for her. Just as she began to run, he too veered towards the trees. He cut her off easily and reached out for her. His hands slipped off her arm, but his momentum carried him even closer to her. When he reached out the second time, the race was over.

Julie screamed with all the strength she had, but it was no use. There was no one within several blocks. Still, she continued to scream, over and over, until she felt his hand reach around her and slam against her mouth leaving her silent and breathless.

She stopped, mostly out of necessity. She couldn't suck in any air and the grip he had on her left shoulder stung as if a vampire's sharp claws were sinking into her flesh. The pain lessened slightly as she came to a complete stop. She struggled against his strength trying desperately to fight for air, and for the opportunity to get away.

As if sensing her close to the point of passing out, and not wanting to have to carry her, Marcus lowered his hand below her nose. He kept her mouth clamped tightly shut, however, and Julie was forced to inhale slowly and deeply in order to supply herself with enough oxygen to remain conscious.

"You've got two choices right now, girl!" Marcus eased the grip he had on both of his hands, almost to the point of allowing her to inhale through her mouth but not quite. "You can be real quiet and breath, or I can clamp down so hard that you never breath again."

Marcus took his hand away from Julie's mouth moving very slowly just in case. He stuck his finger up warning her again. She didn't scream or struggle so he loosened his other hand slightly, but not enough that he couldn't re-apply the pressure if necessary. The pain in her shoulder subsided a bit more.

"Let's go," Marcus said and pushed her towards the trees. "And don't say a word or it very well may be the last one you ever speak. You got that?" He looked to see if she would agree with the nod of her head, but when she didn't, he laughed out loud. "I'll cure your defiance. I guarantee you that"

She knew he would try. She also knew—without a doubt—that Cam had been right. Marcus had killed Sandy, and now he had nothing to lose. He was desperate—or was he just overly cocky at having gotten away with murder? Whatever it was, she was afraid that she was going to be the next victim.

She was not going to give in to his violence and torments. Whatever he was going to do, she was going to remain defiant. She would attack if necessary, run if she could, and die with her head up if that's what it came down to.

Marcus walked slightly behind Julie pushing her into the trees and away from any possibility of being seen. Although she had never been off the road here, she was quite sure that the trees went in so deep that if he killed her, it would be a long time before her body was found...if it ever was.

They moved through a large clearing and into a second grove of trees. The darkness here was eerie. The sun had a hard time breaking through. The entire area smelled like rotten dust and decaying animals. The air and dirt couldn't escape the cavern of trees and had sat dormant for a very long time. She felt sick to her stomach. She had to get away from him. She had to get out of these trees and back on the main road. Why had she left the road? Only women in stupid horror movies headed into the woods when the boogey-man was after them.

Using the only weapons available to her— her hands and the element of surprise—she swung around and landed a blow across the bridge of her assailant's nose. It was a perfect shot, square and full of purpose. She couldn't have done it better if she had time to line it up. She felt his nose squish against the back of her hand.

She could have asked for better results, however. Marcus locked his claws into her arm tearing what felt like giant holes deep into her skin. When he backed away from her blow, the nails dug deeper, and she screamed again.

His right hand went to his nose. He covered it for a few seconds and then pulled his hand away to check for blood. It wasn't broken, at least he didn't think so, and he immediately turned his attention back to Julie. He spun her around and let go of her arm. As she turned, he let his right hand fly. Her cheekbone and his fist met somewhere in the middle. Julie fell to the ground. A sharp pain stabbed at her left arm and shoulder. She figured that she had caught something sharp. But this time the screams of pain did not come out. She was stunned—too stunned to even scream.

Marcus was standing above her in an instant. Before she even had the chance to see it coming, he followed his crushing right hand blow with a sharp kick to her stomach. She doubled over, rolling across the dirt like a dying animal. The sickness she had been feeling was replaced with sheer pain. She covered her stomach with both arms and tried to scoot away from whatever he was going to deal out next, but her back hit a tree and she stopped.

Marcus watched her with a morbid sense of satisfaction. Seeing a woman writhing on the ground, trying to get away, reminded him of Sandy, only this time it was better; this time it was someone he actually despised. This was the woman who had changed his life. She had messed with what was "real". He was determined to make sure that she knew it had been the stupidest thing she had ever done in her life.

"Get up!" Marcus said, no longer worried that anyone would hear them. He was standing directly over her again.

Julie did as she was told. It hurt to move, but she knew it would be worse if she didn't comply. Besides, lying down she had no chance of escape. As she pulled herself into a standing position, she wondered if she had any chance of escape anyway.

Instead of pushing her, Marcus decided to pull this time, which hurt her left arm even worse. She could see large amounts of blood soaking through her shirt. Marcus moved through the trees like a seasoned hunter. He had been practicing for years. He used to chase his friends through these trees. It was an art now.

Julie, on the other hand, was not as good. She was glad she had worn tennis shoes and jeans and not a dress and high heels, but she still felt like a child in the middle of a professional football game. She was being run over and stung with pain with almost every step she took.

Finally, Marcus stopped. Julie stopped too, but only after almost running into his back. Marcus fell a little off balance, but not enough to allow her to get away. It was demoralizing, because the scene she saw made her eyes water and her body to lose control. She had to escape—right now.

She tried to pull away from him. She jumped up, came down right on top of his foot, and pulled away again, but nothing worked. He held tight and all her effort managed to do was to cause more pain in her rapidly weakening body.

He grabbed her with both hands and dragged her to the spot that had obviously been set up for this moment. He was obviously prepared to carry out whatever he had in mind. She had just made it easier by going this way. It didn't matter though. She realized that he had probably been waiting for the right moment to attack her. He had probably watched her for a long time. Today, she had finally made her mistake.

A hammock was stretched out between two trees. He dragged her to it, forced her on top of the thick mesh rope, and held her down using his body weight and a tight grip. Four ropes dangled from each corner, and he carefully pulled each one up and tied her, first her arms and then her legs. She struggled to get away, but with each knot, she knew she was falling more and more into his complete control.

After securing all four knots, Marcus disappeared behind her. She struggled to turn so she could see him, but for the moment, he was gone. Her mind began to work double time. She knew what she needed to do. She had forgotten the most important thing she could do in this situation. She needed to pray. She began pouring all of her energy into a prayer, and although it was short and to the point, when she finished, she was crying.

"Yeah! I like seeing tears coming from you."

Marcus' words were almost inaudible, but the mere sound of his voice tore her heart out. She only hoped that he wasn't going to tear it out literally.

"Please, Marcus—don't do this! Don't!"

She had no idea what he was going to do. She couldn't even imagine what he was capable of, but pleading with him was all she had left. It proved to be the wrong move.

Marcus slapped her so hard that the stinging sensations didn't register until he had lifted his hand for a second blow. She screamed, closed her eyes, and felt the second slap as soon as it landed.

"You were told not to speak, girl!" This time he yelled out in complete hatred and then took two steps back

Julie opened her eyes just in time to see him pull his other hand into plain view. It was a needle, and she had no doubt that it was filled with drugs— illegal drugs. Drugs that would kill!

She began to cry again but quickly forced the tears away. If he liked tears then she wouldn't cry.

"This isn't going to hurt unless you try to pull away. You move, and I swear to you I will jab this into your body until you stop moving. Just relax and it'll all be over soon."

What would be over? The pain, this experience, or her life? She had no idea. All she could do now was close her eyes and hope that her Heavenly Father would take care of her. It was time to really test her faith.

She didn't doubt God or her Savior. She definitely had faith. If this is how her life was going to end, and it appeared as if it was, then testing her faith was a challenge that she was going to pass. She would never lose her faith.

Time slowed down considerably. Between the time Julie closed her eyes, prayed for a second time, and then felt the prick of the needle as it slid into the vein in her arm, she had time to re-evaluate her entire life…or so it seemed.

Julie focused on her life. It was all she had left. There were so many more good times in her life than bad, and what more could a person want. She had what she considered a very good relationship with her Father in Heaven. That alone made her life worthwhile.

Also important, she pictured the people she had helped convert into the Mormon religion. Dying would be worth it if only one of those people ended up in Heaven.

And she thought of Cam. She wanted to see him. She wanted to be with him one more time before she died—if that was what was going to happen to her. It wasn't going to happen in a physical way, but she could hold on to him mentally. She focused on his struggles, but more importantly, she thought of his many victories, which had been capped off last Sunday, just after church, when he was given the gift of the priesthood.

Those thoughts, the good times and good memories she had, were interrupted suddenly when her arm clenched. She could feel the poison beginning to work its way through her body. As it did, the good thoughts were replaced with a strange feeling. She was losing control of her mind.

Her physical body grew more and more tense, but did not seem to lose its function. She began pulling on the chords that held her down. As she did, the tiny fibers of rope bit into her hands.

The pain of the rope burns, and the cuts and bruises she already had, forced her to stop struggling. This left her with one option. She was a prisoner. Nothing she could do was going to change that fact. She would wait and watch. If an opportunity arose, she would take it. Until then, she would do her best to hold on to what sanity she had.

That sanity was tested immediately.

She opened her eyes, having been praying that Marcus would be gone, but he wasn't. He was standing over her, his arms folded, and he was scowling at her. There was so much hate in his eyes that Julie's body flinched.

"How's that?" Marcus asked and shook his head. He loved being in control. It was something that he had thrived on from early on in life. His parents were wimps. They cared, he wouldn't say they didn't, but they were far too easy to manipulate, and Marcus had taken full advantage of that.

Julie did not answer him. She even thought about shutting her eyes, but decided that she wanted to appear defiant, not afraid. She stared back at him, expressionlessly.

Marcus began to rock back and forth, and after ten seconds, Julie realized that he knew exactly what he was doing. Her head began to rock to the same rhythm as Marcus' body. She didn't feel as if he were hypnotizing her with his movements. If anything, it felt more like she was a puppet and she was attached to him. He was controlling her.

Out of the clear blue, Marcus stopped rocking and screamed. Julie jumped. Her body tensed even more, and her lips closed tightly. She wished he had screamed because something had gone wrong, but she knew she would not get that lucky. Nothing was wrong here. Not from his point of view anyway. He was just messing with her head.

Although Marcus was no longer rocking, Julie's head did not stop. It grew worse. She was spinning now, as if on a carnival ride that was stuck on full-speed. The outside world disappeared more and more. The smells of the trees and the forest faded as if it had never existed.

She tried to fight off the effects of the drugs, but she couldn't. It was too strong. The more she fought, the more the drugs were reacting inside her. It was at that point where she finally decided that there was no use fighting it at all.

As she closed her eyes and relaxed, she felt as if she had slowed things down. While it may not prove to make much of a difference, at least she felt as if she had won one little battle. Marcus may ultimately win, but she had fought it off, at least a little.

She began to pray again, placing her hands in her Heavenly Father's once more. It did her heart good to know that she had her faith, her Father in Heaven, and her Savior, to always lean on. Whatever happened now was out of her hands.

Suddenly, the thought of Cam popped back into her mind. Where was he? He would find her. He had to. Those were the last words she remembered before her entire body grew warm and heavy. The world went black around her and she felt dizzy just before blacking out completely.

Chapter Seventeen

There was no physical evidence, but Julie was definitely missing—or at least not where she was supposed to be—and that meant missing. The police refused to get involved—except to "keep a look out." Until the twenty-four-hour period was up, there was nothing they could do, unless there was at least a little proof that something illegal had taken place. It was up to Cam.

Even in Pine Hills, a missing person could be hard to locate—especially if they didn't want to be found, which was one thought that kept invading his mind. Maybe she had gotten cold feet and skipped town. It didn't make sense, though. Even if she changed her mind, she wouldn't leave without telling him. One of Julie's most appealing attributes was the way she conducted herself. She wouldn't leave like that.

There had to be another reason for her not showing up. The idea that Marcus had something to do with her disappearance forced its way into his head over and over, but he refused to consider that. Cam relived the threats that Marcus had spewed, but that simply couldn't be what had happened.

After two hours of sitting around wondering, his fidgety brain had had enough. He had put a 'went looking for you, stick around' note on the kitchen table, and left the house.

Now, after an hour of looking, circling the entire city, and covering just about every side road Julie could possibly be on without finding even the slightest clue as to where she went, he was confused.

Maybe she really did leave town! There were few other explanations to fall back on—at least that he was willing to consider.

Wait a minute! he thought. He followed his urge to slow down and then pulled to the side and came to a complete stop. What am I doing? If there was a problem she would call. The idea of marriage was just causing him to worry more than necessary.

Cam turned the truck around and headed towards his apartment. She was going to be there, probably waiting for him. She was home worried about him. He wished he had a cellular telephone and promised himself that he would get both of them one as soon as they were married.

As he slowed for the red light, then sped up as it turned green before he reached the white line, he began thinking about the future—or his desires for the future. He wanted kids. Two of them…maybe three. He wanted to get a house. He wanted to grow rhubarb and fresh green peas in the back yard so he didn't have to pay the high prices at the grocery store.

He focused his mind on children—his children—his and Julie's children. They would definitely be cute, especially if they took after their mom. Of course they would take after her. They had to!

Cam focused on the road in front of him. Around each corner, he expected to see Julie sitting on the curb waiting for him. He covered every road he could think of. He checked her house—twice—and even called the hospital from her house. He didn't believe that anything was wrong, but it was precautionary. He was relieved to find out that no one had been admitted who fit her description.

Reality was beginning to break through by now, and suddenly he was forced to believe that something really was wrong. He had no idea what, but he knew he had to look in places that he had thus far ignored.

He hit the roads once more. He went into the grocery store, the convenience store, and even stopped to talk to two of her friends a second time.

When he turned off Main Street and headed towards the river, he saw the one place that he hadn't checked, and it was now calling to him. There was no reason for her to be inside the old, abandoned warehouse. No one had been in it for years, at least no one sober. If she were in there, she was really in trouble.

Cam searched for a vehicle in the parking lot but saw nothing. Why would there be? If someone—if Marcus (he finally admitted it) had attacked her—he would have dragged her here through the back field. He could have gotten into the building unnoticed by using the rear door.

The dirt and rocks shot out behind the truck as he pulled into the parking lot. Some of the dust filtered into the cab of the truck through the open window. Cam felt as if he were about to choke. He coughed, but did not roll up the window.

He skidded to a stop five feet away from the front door. Not bothering to remove the keys, Cam jumped out of the vehicle, slammed the door behind him, and began shouting.

"Julie! Julie!"

For a moment, he wondered if he should have kept quiet. If Julie was here, there was a chance that her assailant was still here, and wouldn't it be better to keep silent?

Too late.

"Julie!"

Did his voice actually reach into the house, or did the words just bounce off the hot silver metal and dissipate in the hot sun? "Julie!" he screamed a little louder just in case.

No one answered.

He reached out for the front door, realized that the metal handle had been bathing in the sun all day, and stopped. Using his shirt as a hot pad, he tried the latch. Although the place had been abandoned for years, he expected the door to be open.

It wasn't. It was locked tight. He backed away from the building and surveyed the front. None of the bottom row of windows was broken enough to climb through. Most of the glass in the upper windows was completely missing, but you couldn't get up that high.

If she was in here, she had to have entered through the back.

He ran as fast as he could around the large building, slowing as he rounded both corners just in case someone was waiting for him on the other side. But just as he had seen in the front, the yard was empty.

The back of the building had no windows at all. It was nothing more than metal, rusty rivets, and a metal door. As he approached this door, he saw instantly that it wasn't locked. Not only wasn't it locked, it was open at least six inches.

221

Cam pushed on the door. It creaked slightly then swung open on its own. From the small platform he was standing on, the warehouse appeared pitch black. The only light came from the windows on the distant wall. Nervously, he entered the darkness not quite knowing what to expect. The heat almost made him sick.

With the sunlight behind him now, the room grew lighter as the seconds passed. The windows across from him were letting in light, and by the time he had crossed the first ten feet of the wooden floor, which was old and splintered, he could see most of what was inside.

The warehouse was approximately forty yards across and more than a football field long. Before closing down three years ago, it had served as an auction block and a storage facility, mostly for restaurant equipment. Hundreds of antique, well worn booths, chairs, and tables lined the floor to Cam's left. To his right, the floor was empty, except for the three stairs that led to a small platform where the auctioneer would conduct business.

Cam moved slowly towards the stairs. The other half of the room would be much more difficult to search. A flashlight would be nice, Cam thought, but he would have to make do without one.

His eyes adjusted fully now and he could see that the floor was covered with dust. He could also see footsteps. In fact, there were hundreds of footsteps. His body shuddered at the thought of being here alone. At the same time, that was exactly what he was praying for.

The first stair creaked, and the second one almost fully cracked. Cam quickly stepped up onto the platform and looked around. Shadows cast suspicion, but there was nothing here.

This is ridiculous, Cam thought and turned around. "Julie—hello—anyone here?"

A bird, or was it a bat, flew from one side of the building to the other, using the shadows on the ceiling to keep hidden. Besides that, nothing moved or made a sound. He stood perfectly still for a few more seconds and then realized that he was wasting time. The dust was beginning to get to him as well, causing his nose to feel plugged and scratchy at the same time.

Cam left the platform, intentionally missing the second stair entirely. He didn't even bother to check the rest of the building. Julie wasn't here. There was no way. He was absolutely convinced of that.

The sunlight hurt his eyes, but he wasted no time. He quickly made his way to the truck and climbed in. Why had he wasted so much time? More importantly, how was he going to find Julie?

He sped out of the parking lot throwing rocks onto the metal building. Where to, he wondered. There was no way of knowing, so he did the first thing that came to him.

He drove to his house, flipped off the engine, and ran into the house. Unfortunately, his hopes were dashed immediately. She wasn't there. Why? Why is this happening?

Frustration had come and gone. Now he was battling anger. At first, he was mad at Julie for not calling. That being a ridiculous thought, he quickly turned his anger on himself.

Think! Think you idiot!

But clear thinking was not his strong suit when he was angry. Instead, he jumped to one more conclusion. Go ask Marcus where she is!

Just the idea of Marcus threatening Julie increased Cam's anger. He slammed the front door and headed for his ex-friends house. "You better pray you had nothing to do with this, man." He was talking to the windshield of his truck, but hoping that Marcus could read his mind. "You better hope."

He was past the point of worrying about speeding, tickets, or even being arrested—if that was what it came to. The only thing that mattered was finding Julie. Admitting to himself that Marcus just might have a hand in this made him cringe and lose any control he once had.

The drive that usually took five minutes took less than three. He slammed on his brakes at the last second and stopped just behind Marcus' Ford Thunderbird. He opened the door and ran to the front door. He thought about barging in, but decided against it. If he was wrong, and Marcus had something going on inside, rushing in could get him killed.

He knocked and listened, but didn't hear anything inside. "Marcus!" Cam yelled at the top of his lungs. "Open up, Marcus."

Still, he heard nothing.

After a second knock, and yelling once more, he tried the door. It was locked. That was very strange. Marcus never locked the door. Even when Sandy had begged him to, for their own safety, he wouldn't do it. Then again, Cam thought, maybe he didn't do it just to spite her.

That reason was gone now. Cam shook his head and felt his heart break again. Sandy's death was something he didn't want to dredge up right now. He didn't have time to worry about that.

He shook off the bad thoughts, and when they finally disappeared, the space was filled with another evil thought.

Marcus has gone off the deep end. He has Julie and you better find them fast.

"No!" Cam refused to see what may be happening if that were true. By the time he returned to his truck, however, he found that keeping those thoughts away was becoming more and more impossible.

He pulled out of Harrington Circle and turned right onto Wilmont Street. His jumbled up thoughts were adding to his anger, making him feel very mixed up and confused. This was not making sense. He had lost complete control, and the idea scared him.

Even his head grew heavy. Afraid that he may crash, he pulled to the side of the road and stopped. He put his head on the steering wheel and squeezed it tightly, trying to fight off what was happening.

Everything around him seemed to go blurry. It did not take long before Cam realized what was going on. He was being attacked. The devil was doing his best to keep him from finding Julie.

That was it. That was exactly what was going on.

Cam fell deeper into what felt like a trance. Strangely enough, he did not feel as if he were out of control. He could still think. He believed he could even drive if he would just fight off the impaired vision.

He had to fight back—and he knew exactly what to do.

It was not easy, because the force fighting against him was strong—much stronger then he had ever felt before, even at the height of his drinking problem. With all of the force he could muster, he battled the feelings and bowed his head. He actually laid down on the steering wheel.

After a short prayer, asking only to help him help Julie, a partial calmness came over him. The terrible feeling that had been plaguing him swept away like a thick fog blown out by a strong wind. Suddenly his head was clear.

He did not move, however. The steering wheel held him up while he allowed a peacefulness to enter his body and mind.

The more Cam listened, the more the spirit came to him. At first it comforted him, and Cam accepted the relief. From there, he just sat completely still, focusing on the powerful feelings, and listened.

Just before opening his eyes, he was stopped by a sharp image. It darted in and left just as quickly, but it left an image that sunk deep into Cam's heart.

He saw Julie. She was in the woods. It appeared as if she had been beaten up, or had taken a spill down a very large, rocky hill—something.

Cam clamped his eyes tighter, making sure they would not open. He hated the idea, but he needed to see more. It was the only way he would ever know where Julie was.

Wherever it was, she was hurt. He believed that now. Julie was laying somewhere and she wasn't going to get up. What was worse, he didn't know if she was dead or alive. There was a reason for what he had seen. Someone was telling him something. Either Julie was calling out to him mentally or the Holy Ghost was trying to tell him something. Whichever it was, he had to find her…and now!

And then it appeared again. This time, however, the image didn't immediately go away. He saw a glimpse of Julie again, and then the scene grew larger, as if the camera had been zoomed in and was now zooming back out. As it did, Cam was able to see the landscape surrounding Julie.

It must have been a very long zoom lens, because the picture just grew larger and larger until Cam felt like he was looking down on the world.

And from that vantage, Cam knew about where Julie was. What he was seeing was amazing, but not unbelievable. This was happening, and Cam would not disbelieve. He didn't have time for that. Julie had to be helped—if she wasn't gone already.

That thought forced Cam to bolt up into a sitting position. "Find her!" he yelled at himself.

He pulled the truck onto the road, squealing the tires much further than he believed possible. "Hurry up!" he said and pushed himself faster.

Chapter Eighteen

The thick underbrush cut at his legs as he ran through the woods. His sense of concern had grown into complete desperation. There was no doubt in his mind that he was on the right track. There had even been signs of a struggle where he had entered the woods. He just wished that he had more information. If he didn't have a little luck on his side, it was possible that he could get lost—but he didn't care.

He followed the path for a short distance, then cut off through the timber, hoping that it would save him time. Besides, he didn't see the trail when he seen Julie. She was somewhere else—somewhere far more difficult to find.

A steep hill lay ahead of him. Instead of going around it, which again would be easier, Cam began to climb. From the top, he hoped to be able to see the layout of the land better. With any luck, he would see Julie—but he doubted if he would get that lucky.

He reached the top of the hill and stopped for the first time. His heart was pounding, and he realized just how out of shape he really was. As if it would help, he pushed at his chest with the palm of his hand.

As he rested, he debated whether or not to shout out Julie's name. He almost did it, and even took a deep breath, which wasn't anywhere near as deep as it should have been, and then stopped.

If she were out here, and could call out, she would be doing so already. Calling out her name could only jeopardize her safety—especially if Marcus had her.

Just the thought of Marcus being any where near Julie got Cam moving again. He moved slower now, fighting his way around the three large pine trees that distinguished this hill from all of the others around.

As he moved, he scanned the land below. He didn't see anything, but felt as if he were closer now. At least he was still heading in the right direction.

The trees served one more purpose. They provided him with cover, just in case anyone was looking from below. It would serve him better if he spotted anyone else before they spotted him. The element of surprise may come in handy.

After circling the top of the hill, taking about fifteen minutes, his heart sunk. Julie wasn't down there. If she was, she was well hidden.

Still, he did not doubt that this was where he needed to be. As if to help his faith a bit, he saw the snapshot vision of Julie once again. It lasted only a second and then vanished, but it was enough to keep his confidence level up.

He started down the other side of the hill, sensing the right direction to go. Actually, he knew that it wasn't merely a sensation that he was feeling. He was being led. There was no doubt about it. The spirit was helping him, telling him where to go. It was enough to make his heart pound a little harder.

"Help me," Cam said, barely loud enough that he heard the words, but no one standing twenty yards away would have heard. "Please, help me."

He slowed his pace as he neared the bottom of the hill. He crossed a path, probably the same one he would have been on had he stuck to the trail. Then again, maybe not. It was just as possible that he would have ended up taking the wrong fork, or the trail could have ended and he would be on the other side of the mountain altogether.

Just then, a deer bolted out from behind a tree. It startled Cam so badly that he stopped and was barely able to stifle a scream of surprise. His eyes watched the doe bound fearfully away. She disappeared before Cam even caught his breath.

Cam continued to make his way through the brush and timber until he came to a small clearing. A small stream gurgled as it wound lazily around the trees, through the rocks and on downhill towards town. Eventually, Cam figured it would spill into the main river just before the big power plant and help feed Pine Hills with electricity. What it was doing now, was disguising the sound of his footsteps and making the walking a bit easier— although he was still unsure why he really believed he needed to be silent.

He moved upstream for a few minutes, crossing the tiny creek with short leaps as needed. The third time he jumped, however, his foot slid on the bank where he landed. His feet slipped out from under him and he fell backwards.

There was no way to avoid what was coming. His back hit a rock in the center of the stream and his body bent in directions that it was never meant to. Fortunately, he was able to keep his head up before it too crashed onto the rocks.

He screamed. His voice echoed around the trees, bouncing off the walls of the surrounding hills.

So much for the element of surprise.

A small hawk took to flight, a squirrel darted through the dry leaves, and all around, the mountainous wildlife grew restless.

Cam forced himself up. He stood in the pooling water for a second feeling dazed. His conviction to find Julie stood out strong in his mind however, and after cupping his hands and splashing water on his face, he stepped onto dry land once again. This movement sent pain shooting down his back. He took a deep breath, but began walking—despite the strong need to rest.

Almost as if his mishap had never happened, everything around him returned to normal. Even the hawk returned to its tree, not fifty yards away. It landed, spread its wings, and nestled down. It watched Cam, and Cam watched it.

The drugs were working full strength now, and Julie's head felt like it would explode. Besides a headache, which had only started a few minutes ago, she had to fight off multiple attacks of both shear panic and a spinning sensation that seemed to come and go at will.

Even more disturbing, was the fact that her eyes were closed and yet she knew that Marcus was standing over her, staring at her as if she were dinner for a mountain lion. She refused to open her eyes, because actually seeing him would cause her panic level to rise even more.

Though it was difficult, and made her head pound worse, she forced herself to think. She had passed out—there was no doubt about that, but for how long? Had a day passed, a week, or had it only been a few minutes? If it had been days, how much drugs had Marcus injected into her system.

She had another thought, one that nearly made her entire body jerk. Had Marcus raped her? It was quite possible, although she figured that she would feel the pain if he had, but she didn't feel anything abnormal.

No. She was fairly sure that he hadn't touched her—yet, which probably meant that it had only been a few moments.

As she focused on her own thoughts, she began to hear a faint buzzing sound. It lasted a few seconds, then stopped, and then continued again. Unsure what it was, she tried to dismiss it. Unfortunately, it didn't work. The sound grew more and more audible, and she soon realized what it was. A fly was circling around her head. The annoying sound stopped when the insect landed.

Go away!

The last thing in the world that she really wanted to do was shoo away a fly. It would only have horrible consequences. But could she really lie perfectly still as a dirty, disgusting fly pranced around on her face. Until now, it hadn't landed on her skin, but it was only a matter of time.

Again the buzzing began, this time sounding as if it were dive bombing her. Ordinarily, she would be near the screaming point; jumping around, throwing her hands around the air frantically until the fly found something better to do. It took a great amount of mental control to be still. She wondered if the drugs were helping this, or making it worse.

The sound continued, but muted. It took Julie two seconds to realize what had happened. The fly was trying its best to fly through her hair. Just the idea made her body shiver with fear and disgust. Why? Why was this happening?

She caught a break when the fly took to flight once again, but the luck ran out all too fast. When the noise stopped this time, Julie knew that she would not be able to hold off any longer. It landed on her upper lip, and immediately moved up. Julie prayed that it would stop there, but it didn't. It entered her nose, tickling her beyond comprehension, and almost making her throw up at the same time.

Her head moved involuntarily, shaking vigorously—anything to get that thing out of her nose. It worked, but only momentarily. It lifted into the air, buzzed, and then landed right back where it had the first time.

She had already blown it. Whatever happened next, was going to happen despite her next actions. It was time to get rid of that fly. She pulled her hand up to swat at it, but was suddenly reminded that this was not going to be possible. The little movement was enough to get the fly to move, but for how long?

It really didn't matter. She had bigger things to worry about all of a sudden. Her right arm stopped in mid flight. She had been moving so fast, that the force of stopping pulled something inside her wrist.

Only then did she fully realize that she was still tied to the hammock. She had known all along, subconsciously, but now the truth had made it to reality. Although the pain in her wrist was excruciating, she could now feel the ropes that held her arms and legs. And with this knowledge came another sensation. The ropes itched. Unfortunately, there was nothing she could do about it.

She began tugging softly with her left hand, and pulling—almost desperately—with her legs.

She no longer cared if Marcus was standing overhead. He was. She could still see his shadow above her, but she couldn't care.

In fact, it was time to face him. She couldn't think of anything worse than facing him, but it was inevitable, and it may as well be now. Maybe, just maybe, he would untie her and let her rub the itching spots.

She opened her eyes slowly, praying that the dark spots above her would be nothing more than trees waving overhead.

Unfortunately, she was wrong. He was standing with his arms folded, staring down at her. She pictured a vulture, waiting for the right moment to dart in and start pecking at the flesh of its dinner. The fact that he was so calm, so in control, made Julie mad.

"Well, you decided to rejoin me," Marcus said.

His voice made her as sick as the fly had done. How anyone could seem this repulsive to her was strange, but he did. Just the thought of him touching her with his disgusting hands was enough to make her want to throw up.

Still, she said nothing. It would do her no good. Besides, she had nothing to say to him. She definitely didn't want to respond to his stupid comment.

Although he was slightly blurry at first, her eyes focused rapidly. Her head continued to spin, but being able to see added a little hope. If she could get away from the ropes, there was a chance of escape. She had her eyes, and apparently she still controlled her arms and legs. Hopefully, they would hold her if she got the opportunity.

"You like drugs," Marcus insisted. "I can tell. Just think about it. Now you're an addict like the rest of us—just like your pitiful boyfriend."

Yes, Julie thought. What about Cam? Where was he? Was he looking for her? Of course he was, but would he ever find her out here?

"Still not talking, huh," Marcus shook his head. "You'd think you'd learn that defiance will only get you in more trouble. I guess you're not as smart as I thought you were. Then again, how smart do you have to be to get Cam eating out of your hands?"

Again, she didn't respond.

To punish her for her defiance, Marcus took off his shirt, and began rubbing it across Julie's face. She turned her head and closed her eyes until he stopped. She opened them in time to see him flexing his muscles. Again, he repulsed her.

"You like that, baby? This is what a real man looks like. Not like Cam. I'll show you something else."

Julie closed her eyes for good. She figured he would get to this. Why else would he drag her out here in the middle of nowhere? If he wanted to kill her, he would have done it a long time ago. Her body shivered, and she began to cry—silently at first, and then out loud.

Through the whispering trees, Cam heard something. He wasn't exactly sure what it was, but it definitely didn't belong. Nothing that lived out here would make that noise.

He picked up his pace once again, moving towards where he thought he heard the sound. The fast walk became a trot, after he heard it again. It sounded like a voice. Was someone talking? For a moment, he wondered if he was hearing things. Impossible, he thought, and then began an all out run.

By the time he saw what had made the noise, it was too late to stop. Not that he would want to.

Julie was laying in a hammock, tied up, while Marcus was undressing. The idea of what could have happened, or what might have already happened, forced him to move faster.

The sound of him barreling out of the woods, crashing through trees, caught Marcus off guard. He spun around, expecting to see a bear or a mountain lion. At the last second, he knew who it was.

Cam plowed into Marcus like a semi hitting a moped. The two men fell to the ground in a pile, rolling in the dirt, hitting a tree, and then stopping. Cam's back twisted, and the damage that had already been done by the rock earlier intensified. He screamed, but stood up anyway.

Marcus scrambled up as well and faced his enemy. He was ready for this. Part of him wanted Julie to never be seen again. It would be easier to get away with murder. Deep down inside, however, he almost wanted Cam to show up. Now he could take care of both of them—first Cam, and then his woman.

"Nice of you to make it, jerk weed," Marcus scowled.

"What are you doing?" Cam asked. He felt a strange sense of doubt surge through his body. Was he capable of standing up to Marcus? He didn't have time to think about it. He had to be capable. If he wasn't, Julie wasn't going to survive—and neither was he. Not that he would want to if she didn't.

"What does it look like I'm doing, Cam?" Marcus relaxed his doubled up fists, but stood ready just in case. "I wanted to show your woman the joys of drugs—and sex." He smiled at this, knowing it would cut Cam deep down where it hurt the most.

It did hurt, and it threw Cam off balance, mentally, just enough to give Marcus the advantage he needed.

Marcus lunged at Cam, throwing his shoulder, and his thirty extra pounds of weight, against Cam as hard as he could. Again, they went backwards. Cam fell, but Marcus was able to regain control of his body before hitting the dirt.

Without hesitating, Marcus kicked dirt into Cam's face. It missed his eyes, the intended target, but it forced Cam to shake his head.

Figuring that he had the upper hand now, Marcus grew bolder—and meaner. "You know, Cam. I gave her more drugs than either of us has ever taken at one time. It's quite the combination too—coke and heroin. She has no prayer, and you're next."

Marcus left Cam laying in the dirt and walked back towards Julie, who was now struggling with what little energy she had left. It was no use, and she knew it, but she refused to sit still and let Cam think she had given up.

Although it hurt, she turned her head and saw Marcus approaching. She pulled her feet harder, as well as her left arm. Her right arm was throbbing. Drugs were supposed to dull the pain, she thought. If that was true, she was glad she couldn't feel the full effects.

"Leave her alone," Cam screamed.

Hearing Cam's words was enough to make Julie stop struggling. There was nothing she could do anyway. She was just going to have to wait and hope that Cam could fight off Marcus.

Marcus turned, knowing that Cam would be coming for him again, and was ready when Cam made his move. Marcus punched at just the right moment and caught Cam square in the mouth.

Cam continued, despite feeling a stream of blood running out of his mouth. He too connected with the blow he had planned. His right hand plastered Marcus' face, sending him flailing backwards.

Knowing that momentum was all he had going for him, Cam lunged again. Marcus regained his balance, but caught a second blow to the back of the head. What was happening? He refused to lose.

Marcus fell to the ground but bounced back up and sprung like a tiger. He was on top of Cam before his ex-friend knew what was coming. Wasting no time, Marcus began pounding on Cam's face, chest, and body. He stood above him like a giant bear and swung wildly. He finally stopped, and laughed. "It's really going to feel good killing you, man."

With little else he could do, Cam tried a verbal onslaught. "Yeah, like you killed Sandy, you jerk."

Marcus saw no reason to hide the truth now. No one was going to survive to talk. "You got it, Cam. Just like that. She was going to warn you that I was going to take care of you and your woman. She had to go. She was in the way."

It was time to end it. Marcus punched Cam once more, landing the strong blow directly across his face. He quickly walked away from Cam, wanting to take care of things before the almost dead body decided to stir again. Although he was sure that Cam wasn't out cold, it gave him the chance to take care of Julie first.

In less than fifteen seconds, he made his way to the small pack he had stashed behind one of the trees. He quickly pulled out a second needle, one with more than enough cocaine and heroine to end this charade for Julie.

The smile that had dominated his face for most of the day was gone. His final plan was going to work, but he wasn't going to get the pleasure of teaching her much of a lesson first. Oh well, he thought as he moved into position above Julie.

Julie screamed. It forced Cam to react, but slowly. His back felt as if he had been stabbed, or shot, and maybe that would have been better. He tried to stand up, fell to the ground again, and screamed.

Hearing this helped Marcus feel like smiling once again. He looked at Cam quickly, saw him wincing with pain, and returned to Julie. She was tearing at the ropes with all she had, but that only made him laugh maniacally.

Cam was getting up again, and Marcus knew he had to hurry. He grabbed Julie's arm, the hurt one. She squealed with pain, but he didn't let up. He laid the arm out straight, and immediately plunged the needle into her arm. He squeezed the entire contents of the syringe into her arm and quickly stood up.

"That'll take care of you," he said and turned to Cam. "You're too late, my man. She's dying, and you're next." He threw the syringe into the trees behind him and moved to Cam. "But just think," he laughed again. "At least you get to die with her. You can be dying buddies."

"You're getting good at murder," Cam said as he struggled to his feet before Marcus caught him. "You're going to die for this."

"I doubt it."

The shear madness in Marcus' eyes frightened Cam. He was gone—insane, possessed, and totally whacked. Again, Cam wondered if he had a chance against someone like that.

From deep down inside of him, something rose. It was a strength. With all of the desperation occurring, he had forgotten one thing. He had help. He didn't have to do this on his own.

Remembering this brought knowledge. That knowledge brought more strength, and the courage to pray. It was quick, almost happening in the blink of an eye, but when he finished, he felt something very different. He knew what was going to happen.

Marcus took another step towards Cam, planning to land another punch. This time, however, he wouldn't stop until Cam was dead.

He did not get the chance to throw that punch.

Cam swung his arm at Marcus' face. With the force of his entire body, and the help from above, the punch plowed into Marcus' nose. Cam saw a blankness appear in Marcus' eyes before he fell hard to the ground. He was out, and would be for quite a while.

Wasting no time, Cam raced to Julie. He untied her, hoping that it wouldn't be too late. He picked her up, and still using the extra help and strength, no longer even concerned about his back, he carried her out of the woods.

Chapter Nineteen

Although Cam's entire life felt like a roller-coaster, the emotional ride he was on now was far worse. He sat in Julie's private room in a very uncomfortable chair. At least it was next to Julie, which is where he needed to be. The beige hospital walls tried to offset the somber mood. A clock (which now read 10:30) hung on the wall next to a television set that jutted out from the corner. They had been in the hospital for over twelve hours already.

But Julie was alive, and at this point, what more could he ask for. *A lot! He could ask for a whole lot more—and he had asked.* Unfortunately, nothing more had come. In fact, things had grown worse as the evening turned into early morning and now into late morning—now 10:31.

He had been in plenty of hospitals but never under these circumstances. This was more stress than he could handle. The door opened to his left, and Cam looked up but did not move. It was the doctor. Hopefully it was time to find out what was going on. No one was tell him anything. Not even the nurses. Everyone kept deferring to the doctor— who only told him that he wanted to wait and watch.

Any news was better than no news at all, he had thought all night long. The words haunted him now, seeing the doctor look into his eyes. Another thought popped in again. This entire situation was wrong. It wasn't fair! He should be the one in the hospital on the verge of death. Julie was innocent.

Still, he couldn't change the way things were. No amount of sulking or anger was going to fix this situation. This left his mind feeling twisted and tormented.

Two new nurses followed the doctor into the room. They headed straight towards Cam, and he couldn't help but notice that they looked like they had done this a million times.

The nurses were dressed in white dresses; one was blond and the other had red hair. The blonde lady was three inches taller and much cuter. The doctor, young for having completed that much school, had dark hair and a slight limp. He walked very relaxed, however, and Cam figured that the limp was permanent, something that he had gotten used to years ago. He was also dressed in white.

Cam tried to foretell what the doctor was going to say, but he couldn't. He was too experienced or to wrapped up in his work, to show any emotion at all. That was his job—to break it to you gently.

"Mr.--?" The doctor wasn't sure of his name, nor did he seem too concerned that Cam wasn't exactly family.

Cam stood up, never taking his eyes off of the doctor. He braced himself mentally against whatever he was about to be told. *Please let her live*, he begged. *Please let her be okay*!

"Can we go out in the hall for a moment," the doctor asked and turned around.

Cam followed the doctor outside. He continued to pray, and to hope, but his mind wandered and only proved to confuse him more.

"Ms. Haws has had a rough go of it," the doctor said as soon as the door slammed shut. "She has several broken bones. We put thirteen stitches in her, six in her left arm and seven in her shoulder."

"Is she--?" Cam started to question, but the doctor shook his head and Cam stopped mid-sentence.

"Ms. Haws' is having a tough time handling this, as would anyone with that much drugs in her system. She's in a coma!"

Although the doctors words were spoken very calmly, they shattered inside Cam's head. A coma! Why! What had she ever done to deserve that? He screamed these words to himself. He also begged, again, to be in her shoes instead. It was in vain, of course, but he didn't know what else to do.

It wasn't as if he hadn't expected this, however. Of course she was in a coma, but until now, he had been able to justify telling himself that she was just sleeping very deeply. Hearing the actual words were damaging.

"How long until she comes out of it?" Cam finally asked, knowing full well that no doctor could answer that question. It depended on too many things.

"If she shows improvement within the next twenty-four hours, she'll have a better than fifty percent chance of everything being fine. If there's no improvement--," he paused as if wishing he hadn't started that line. "We'll just have to wait. Hopefully she's able to fight this off." The doctor and the nurses walked away leaving Cam to his own thoughts.

Up and down. Up and down.

The roller coaster was soon to continue. Mr. and Mrs. Haws were on their way. What pain and trouble was that going to bring? Julie's mother had already freaked out. While her husband was on the telephone, listening to Cam explain what had happened, she had all out blamed Cam for this—probably with good reason. If Julie hadn't taken the time to help a loser, she wouldn't be on the verge of--.

He couldn't finish the thought. Actually, he refused to finish it. Instead, he opened the door, re-entered the room, and walked to Julie's bed.

"Come on, hon. Wake up." His pleas went unnoticed (or at least without fruition).

His blood-shot eyes burned almost as much as they did when campfire smoke worked its way around the circle and attacked his face. What he needed was a good muscle relaxant and a lot of sleep. He was stressed, but probably not as much as Julie was. Then again, maybe she was at peace? Was she oblivious to the world or completely aware of everything that was going on? Cam wondered which option would really be better. He had heard of people waking up from a coma and claiming to have heard everything—but he wasn't sure if it happened all the time.

Fifteen more minutes past. The four walls around him were closing in. Then the door opened behind him. Cam didn't turn around. He didn't dare. His breath shortened, his pulse raced, and his eyes fixed on the wall in front of him. It was going to be Julie's parents.

"Hi."

The female voice was kind, high pitched, and whoever it was seemed very sure of herself. It was definitely not someone who had just found out her daughter had overdosed on drugs and may never wake up.

He was saved, at least for now. Cam's vital signs regulated almost immediately and he turned around. It must have been time for shift change because it wasn't Magdaline. Cam was a little disappointed. Magdaline had been a good nurse. The new nurse was cuter than Magdaline, however. In fact, she reminded him a little of Sandy. She had blond mid-length hair, not too skinny but certainly curvy, confident, and perky. Her looks weren't going to help Julie though, and that was what mattered. She was going to have to prove her nursing skills before Cam would be impressed.

Cam stepped back to the chair and sat down as the nurse went to work. She was professional and quick. She finished her checks, rechecks, filled in the chart, and only then did she turn to Cam.

"Do I know you?" she asked.

It was a horrible question to ask. After so much professionalism, she had to blow it like that. What if Julie heard her? What would she be thinking now? She didn't need to think that her nurse was someone Cam had been with in the past. He quickly dispelled the idea. "No, I don't think so."

But was it the truth? Certainly he would remember her, but he really had no idea. It was possible…maybe at some drunken party somewhere? He didn't remember, and until he did, he wouldn't feel like he was lying.

She must have realized her mistake. "I'm sorry. You just look a little like someone I knew, but you're not him. Sorry!" Embarrassed, the nurse walked out.

Eleven O'clock came and went and Cam began watching the black hands of the clock even more. It got so bad that he had to leave the room fifteen minutes later. He told Julie he would be back in a minute and left the room for the first time since she had been admitted to this private room.

A small sign on the side of the wall directed him towards the cafeteria and gift shop. As he passed the desk, he noticed the nurse again. She was looking at him, obviously still wondering if she knew him. This time, however, she wisely chose not to say anything.

Cam walked past her and down the wide hall that was dominated by a pure white color. His feet fell hard against the tile and the sound seemed to echo against the walls. Halfway down the corridor, he turned right into what looked more like a large walk-in closet than a cafeteria. Two small tables sat against the right wall. It was big enough for two people if both ordered a very small meal. The counter in front of him took up most of the room, leaving just enough space for three small shelves against the left wall. They were stacked on top of each other to preserve precious space. The top shelf housed stuffed animals. The middle shelf was for general knick-knacks, and a bottom shelf displayed a few books and magazines.

He walked straight up to the counter, ordered a cheeseburger, and began looking over the small, worthless, high-priced items on the middle shelf: coffee cups (a matching set), a hand carved mountain lion, fake cigars, and a few other uninteresting objects.

Something against the back wall, however, did catch his attention. He turned and only then realized that they were balloons. They were taped to the wall for display. *Get Well Soon*, one said. *It's A Boy* and *It's A Girl*. In all, five balloons had been stuck to the wall. There were probably others to choose from, somewhere, but one had already called to him. He knew he needed it. Julie needed it.

I Love You With All My Heart.

Plain, simple, yet so full of truth. That is exactly how he felt about Julie. It wrapped up all of his emotions—the special ones he reserved just for her—all in one short sentence.

He also believed that this was how Julie felt for him. No matter what happened, he would always hang on to that. That was a bad thought and he wiped it away. He quickly ordered one of the balloons from the old lady behind the counter and sat down at one of the tables.

After being served, Cam ate his burger so fast that he hardly tasted it. He barely noticed that he had forgotten to ask if she could remove the pickles. He didn't hate pickles, but if he had the choice, he preferred most anything without pickles, especially hamburgers. This time, because his mind was drifting far too much, they didn't bother him.

Timed perfectly, and no doubt planned that way, his balloon was delivered to his table by the same gray-haired lady who had taken his money and served him his food. She wore a half-smile that said *I haven't got the energy to be too chipper, but you should have seen me in my glory days.*

Cam smiled, respected the look, and stuffed the last bite of lunch into his mouth. He took the now fully inflated balloon from the lady, nodded goodbye, and left.

He had only been gone for twenty minutes, but it was long enough. There was a good chance that Julie's parents would be in her room now. Not ready to face them yet, he slowed his pace. He even thought about waiting outside for a few minutes, but the nurse was staring again so he went straight in to Julie's room. He half-heartedly pulled the door shut behind him, but when it didn't close, he didn't make a second effort.

He was relieved to see that Julie's parents still hadn't shown up. Cam wondered if their plane was late or if they couldn't find the hospital. Either was possible. Salt Lake City wasn't gigantic, but none of the hospitals were easy to find. It would be easy to get lost in Salt Lake, especially if they were looking for Hickory Heights Hospital. This was the smallest hospital in the valley. It wouldn't be long before Julie would have to be transferred to one of the larger hospitals—especially if she didn't improve. Hickory Heights didn't have the facilities necessary to take care of coma patients long term.

"I got you something, hon!" Cam said after taking Julie's hand. He rubbed the balloon against her fingers. "It's a balloon. One of those real cool ones that say things. It says 'I Love You With All My Heart'." He paused. "I really do love you, Julie. I can't wait to get married." He thought about telling her to hurry up and get better so they could finish making plans, but it sounded negative and she didn't need anything but absolutely positive thoughts right now.

Cam carefully laid Julie's hand across her stomach. "I'll tie it to your bed okay?" He tied it so that when Julie woke up she would be able to see it.

Just like earlier, another female voice interrupted his thoughts. It came from out in the hall. This time, there was no mistaking the voice.

248

It was Julie's mother. "I'm looking for Julie Haws," the voice said.

Cam couldn't judge her tone. Was she mad? Had the long plane trip dulled her anger or heightened it? It was time to find out. He was glad he had left the door open. At least he had a few seconds to steady himself.

The door opened slowly, and after enough time to make Cam wonder (and almost hope) that it had been the wind, Mrs. Haws peaked in. It was obvious to Cam, that she had been crying for a very long time.

So many emotions ran through Mrs. Haws body and Cam seemed to be able to read every one as if each had been written on her red cheeks. Much to his surprise, anger wasn't one of the emotions. He saw a troubled mind, overworked and hardened from concern. She had been crying, and why not? Mrs. Haws had already lost one daughter—or so it would seem. She was not going to do well if she lost the other.

The strongest emotion she was emitting, however, was fear. It was a fear that seemed to be rooted very deeply. This was true fear felt for someone you loved; a mothers true, unrestricted love. It was a feeling that went much deeper than anything Cam had ever felt and had only occasionally ever seen. This was the kind of love he aspired to have.

Mr. Haws followed his wife into the room. While obviously struck just as hard as his wife was at the sight of his daughter lying in a hospital bed, he was able to curtail (or was it hide?) his emotions enough to speak. "Hello, Cam. How are you?"

It was direct, and it meant a lot to Cam. He had expected to be torn in two, but those two simple

249

sentences, and the look in Mrs. Haws eyes was enough to show him that he was safe.

"Sir." Cam nodded and looked at Julie. He felt like crying all of a sudden but fought it off. "I'm okay." He almost asked how the flight was but why would he want to bring that up? How could it have been anything but horrible?

Mrs. Haws moved to the left side of the bed opposite Cam. "Daddy and I are here, Sweetie." She brushed back the hair on her daughter's sleeping face and looked at her. Again, Cam could read the heavy torment in her eyes.

A single tear rolled out each of Mrs. Haws' eyes. Cam wanted to look away but he couldn't. The soft rolling liquid against her flushed warm skin was hypnotizing. He continued to watch as the tears raced towards the bottom of her cheeks, each curving with her worry lines and amazingly meeting in the center of her chin. A dead heat, Cam thought.

That word again! Why did he have to think of death? Why was his faith so low and unrefined that he had to even think that? He knew Heavenly Father had the power to heal her. That wasn't where his faith was lacking. The problem was deeper than that. He wasn't sure how to know if that was what Heavenly Father had planned. How could he know that?

There was no time for an answer. His mind had drifted far enough that he hadn't noticed that Mrs. Haws was crying now, full-fledged and uncontrollably. Mr. Haws moved to his wife's side, held her, and cradled her when she placed her head on his shoulder. While her sobs became muffled, they intensified.

"How long has she been in a private room?" Mr. Haws asked Cam.

It was a question that probably didn't matter, at least as far as Cam could see, other than to break the period of silence.

"Not long. I just got to see her a few hours ago."

Mrs. Haws began to cry again, and this forced Cam to fight to keep back his own tears. If there was a more depressing, scary moment ever depicted in life, Cam had never seen it.

Finally, her tears abated and Mrs. Haws turned her attention outward. She began to clean. This was her way of controlling her sadness—the same way she controlled her fear, her anger, and her pain. Cam had seen his own mother do the very same thing; cleaning and working; anything to keep busy.

Mrs. Haws began with the blankets on Julie's bed. She pulled them down a little and straightened them. She picked up two small papers from the floor and put them in the wastebasket. She moved around the room methodically, straightening and picking up where needed—and even where it wasn't needed. She untied the balloon Cam had bought and moved it to what she felt was a better spot.

Cam didn't say a word. He just watched her. Most of what she accomplished was a waste of time, at least on a purely physical level. In a more cerebral way, it served its purpose. It calmed her nerves. Actually, it seemed to calm everyone.

It also solved one more problem, one that Cam was quite glad to see. Mrs. Haws began to act differently towards him. She began looking at him without animosity and without blame. She seemed to be accepting him…and it all added one more climb up on the roller coaster he was on.

Chapter Twenty

"Have you given her a blessing yet," Mr. Haws asked.

Cam had thought about it several times during the night, but he hadn't had the chance. "No sir, there really hasn't been any time. We need to, though."

Mr. Haws looked at Cam and nodded. "I'm glad I made it in time to take part."

Cam really liked Julie's father. He was sure that there were a lot of people who liked him. He just seemed to have that God-granted ability to make—and to keep—friends.

"Why don't you call someone and have them bring what we'll need," Mr. Haws said and turned away.

Cam remembered seeing a telephone on the counter at the nurses station and quickly exited the room.

Inside Julie's room, Mrs. Haws finally sat down. She was exhausted in every aspect of the word. The plane ride, the not knowing what was really happening to her daughter, and the relapses into the past—thinking both of Julie and of Becky—had drained her. The only way she had managed to get through it so far was the reconciliation she had done between her and her Savior.

She had been wrong in her anger towards Cam. She felt guilty from the moment she had spoken bad about him. She knew he had heard her comments. She had wanted him to hear them…at least she had at the time.

Sitting in the plane before lift off, after noticing all the people heading in so many different directions, each to take care of one thing or another, she felt the pains of guilt grow even stronger.

Why had she said that? Cam was sitting in a waiting room not knowing what was happening to his soon-to-be wife, and now, because of her, he had one more thing to worry about. She hadn't been fair to him, and now she was feeling the effects of her words deep inside her own stomach.

By the time they were in the air, four hours from touching back down, the torment had eaten what felt like a grapefruit sized hole in her stomach. She felt sick.

"I hurt him!" Mrs. Haws said as she shifted her weight in the small airplane seat. She figured her husband knew exactly what she was talking about.

"You sure did," Mr. Haws spoke blandly, very matter-of-factly, and yet full of love and understanding.

That was all he said. Mrs. Haws could tell that her husband believed—and had believed all along—that she would eventually set things right. And she would. She started taking care of business while still in the airplane. She said a silent prayer asking for forgiveness, and she instantly began to feel that grapefruit begin to shrink.

They landed at the Salt Lake City Airport and although the guilt had been nearly eroded away, enough of it remained to remind her that she still had work to do. She still needed to make amends with Cam.

That reminder burned inside of her when they first arrived at the hospital, but the fear and hurt she felt for her daughter had forced the thought of healing Cam's mind further down the chain of importance.

Now that Cam had walked out of the room, the hole in her stomach began to grow again. The worry and sadness wasn't as strong as it had been on the plane, but it was growing. *As soon as he comes in I'll tell him I'm sorry.* She thought the words, but it didn't make her feel any better. She had the chance and failed to take it.

No! If she wanted to feel better, she needed to take care of it now. She had just gotten settled in the chair, but she stood back up forcing her mind and body into action. "I'll be right back," she said and looked at her husband, who understood perfectly. He took over the seat in the chair before his wife even left the room, almost as if silently saying, *see…your rude comment is even costing you your seat.*

She shook off her husband's actions and swallowed hard, trying to force her pride away. Besides, what did she have to be proud of? She had berated a man—one who had done his very best to change his entire life's course and who was now ready to take her daughter through the temple. That was what she had always wanted for Julie, and now that it was happening, she was hurting the man who was making that dream come true.

Mrs. Haws prayed as she walked. *Please help me to overcome my stubbornness. Please help me to do what I need to do.* For some reason, praying felt strange. Did she really have the right to ask for help while still in the process of making up for her mistake? She definitely needed help, however, and what better help could she receive than from her Savior.

She thought of Christ being nailed to the cross; dying so that people like herself could repent of their wrong doings. At the same time, she would be setting her life—and the life of her son-in-law-to-be—on the right track.

Cam finished his conversation with Bishop Tortelson just as Mrs. Haws was approaching him. He figured she would veer off towards the nurse—who truly must have just mistaken him for someone she knew because she hadn't even looked at him since giving him permission to use the telephone—but Mrs. Haws continued to walk towards him. By the time he hung up, she was within three feet.

No one was close enough to hear their conversation, and Mrs. Haws was grateful. "Did you get a hold of someone?" she asked, not as much to avoid the inevitable as it was to check on Julie.

"The bishop will be here in a few minutes."

"I'm sorry, Cam!" Mrs. Haws blurted out as if it were now or never.

Her words, obviously full of pain, came very unexpectedly. Cam was taken back, but only for a few seconds. He knew she was speaking from the heart. She had apologized to him before, but it hadn't seemed all that contrite. Right now, he could tell that she truly felt sorry.

"You know, Mrs. Haws. You don't need to apologize to me. I had nothing to do with this—directly—but maybe in an indirect way I did." He didn't bother to tell her the whole truth. Maybe he had more to do with this than they needed to know. Maybe he even could have stopped it altogether if he had taken Marcus serious. It was a guilt that he would have to live with forever…deservedly.

"Don't even think that, Cam. My daughter is a much better person today because of you."

"And I'm a better person because of your daughter." Cam smiled and Mrs. Haws responded by placing her hand on his arm. This touch—a touch that reminded him so much of the way Julie touched him the first time they had met, so gentle and kind—prompted him to say a little more. "I truly want to marry your daughter, Mrs. Haws. No one in this world could ever make me feel like Julie does."

"I know how you feel. I was wrong about you. I really am sorry. I've been so skeptical about you, but I see what you are and I feel ashamed that I judged you."

"Don't worry about it ma'am. Let's just let all that go. It's in the past. Right now, we need to pull our strength together…for Julie."

Mrs. Haws pulled her hand away from Cam's arm, turned around, and then stopped. Cam watched as she stood perfectly still, as if pondering deeply, and then turned back to him. "Would you give Julie the blessing, Cam?"

Mrs. Haws certainly knew what to say to cause Cam to panic. Her question was possibly the worst, and yet the best, words she had ever said. No! He wanted to say it but he couldn't. He was worthy, and had been for two months, but could he actually do it? He had no practice using the priesthood. Julie needed someone more experienced—someone more knowledgeable— didn't she?

But there was no way he could turn Mrs. Haws down. No matter what he wanted to do, or what his level of fear, there was absolutely no way he was going to tell her no.

The medicinal smell of the hospital, which had bothered him from the moment he and Julie had arrived, was completely overtaken now by the pure sense of fear. He fought this off enough to answer her.

"If it's the best thing for Julie, I'll do it," Cam said. His hands were trembling, and they continued to shake as they made their way back to Julie's room.

A short while later, there was a soft knock on the door. Mrs. Haws opened the door. "Come in," she invited. She didn't know exactly who the man was, but she had a pretty good idea.

Cam introduced everyone, and then stepped aside while Bishop Tortelson moved closer to Julie. He held her hand and said his own silent prayer.

Cam began to feel a deep level of concern. A few hours ago he had been doubting his own faith. In a few minutes, he was going to be taking Julie's life into his own hands and praying for her. Without faith, that wouldn't work.

His brain began concocting excuses as to why he shouldn't be the one to give her the blessing. The best excuse, the one he decided he would use if he really felt like he couldn't do it, was the experience factor. He just wasn't sure if he was ready. Surely they would all understand that. Wouldn't they?

At the same time, another part of him was telling him he would do just fine. The Holy Ghost was speaking to him now, just as he had done so many times in the recent past. He also knew that if he would only listen—closely and attentively—that he would know what to do, and what to say. He focused, tuning in more and more to the voice, and he did listen. The surrounding noises and distractions drifted away.

Over the next few minutes, he fully accepted his responsibility. He did so based on faith, and on a deal (or a miracle as Cam would forever know it).

You do your part, and Julie will wake up.

The words were repeated over and over until Cam finally understood them. Even more importantly, they didn't stop until all doubt had eroded from inside Cam's mind.

If he did his part, Julie would wake up. That was all he ever wanted. Since he had found Julie, and even while he was battling Marcus, he had been pleading with the Lord to let him take Julie's place. He was the one who deserved this, not Julie. This didn't make a bit of difference, however. It was time to prove his love for her—and to prove that he really would do whatever it took to help Julie. He couldn't take her place, but he wasn't expected to. While it felt like death may be easier to handle, at least until he actually completed it, all he really had to do was overcome his fear.

Mrs. Haws had overcome her fear and apologized to him. That couldn't have been easy. Julie had overcome her fear the day she approached him at the theater. She had eventually admitted to having been afraid. She had approached a complete stranger; one who was obviously drunk and lost to the world. She had overcome that fear and saved his life. But she hadn't stopped there. She helped him find eternal life as well. The least he could do to repay her was to overcome his fear and give her a priesthood blessing.

"Shall we get started?" the bishop asked.

Bishop Tortelson moved towards the head of the bed. Mr. Haws moved in closer stopping right beside the bishop; close enough to reach his daughter's head.

Cam still had to fight off the urge to give way to Bishop Tortelson. He stepped to the other side of the bed. All three elders looked at each other. The situation certainly had the makings of being a little uncomfortable at first. Cam dispelled the problem without hesitating.

"Mr. Haws, will you anoint her? I'd like to give the blessing if that is okay."

Everyone stared at Cam, and a brief silence overtook the room. The time passed quickly though. It wasn't a strange silence, which it could have been. Actually, it was a pleasant, thought provoking moment of silence for everyone in the room.

Julie's parents prayed that this blessing would bring their daughter back to the full, rich life that they believed she fully deserved. For Bishop Tortelson, it was a time of remembrance. He thought of his own first blessing. He had been filled with such doubt and such fear, but he got through it using everything he had inside of him (and with a lot of help from above). It pleased him to see Cam—someone who had come so far—so willing to fulfil the duties he had just recently been given, and apparently so sure of himself. Maybe he was hiding it well, but he definitely appeared calm and sure.

Surety was not what Cam was feeling. What was pushing him further was a sense of determination. Instead of hoping, or looking to the past as the other adults were doing, he took the time to look forward.

Everyone has milestones in their lives; crossroads they come to that define their very purpose on earth. For Cam, this was one of those moments. If he could overcome this obstacle, what greater things could he aspire to? Not that there is much that could be considered greater than the priesthood and the power to help others, but how much more of a man could he become if he could truly use this gift.

It was time to overcome his doubts and fears, and he was determined to do it; for himself, for Julie, for her parents, and for his future children—if there were to be any.

The moment of silence was broken by Mr. Haws, first with a smile, and then with words. "I'd be honored Elder Bird."

The bishop's mind wandered as Julie's father prepared the oil. He remembered seeing Cam—about four years ago—outside Mr. Jenken's coffee shop. Cam and his friends had obviously been drinking. All four of the kids (and that was exactly what they were then—kids) were stumbling around, laughing, cussing, and smacking each other around.

What a waste! Bishop Tortelson thought as he slowly drove by. So much potential going down the tubes thanks to Satan's vices. What could these kids be if they only chose the path of righteousness? Doctors? Bishops? Missionaries? Upstanding citizens of Pine Hills.

Four years later, he had the answer to those questions. He knew what one of those kids could become, and the truth was far better than he had even imagined. Cam was a child of God—one who was about to bless the woman he loved—and he did truly love her. Bishop Tortelson knew this without a doubt.

The Bishop looked at Cam. "The first time I did this, I was afraid…scared to death that I would do it wrong." He hesitated and then threw in a few encouraging words, words that he hoped would ease Cam's mind. "You are worthy of this responsibility, Cam. You have earned the right to act on behalf of your Heavenly Father. Listen to the prompting you'll feel and just say what comes to your heart. You'll do just fine."

There were other formalities and Bishop Tortelson filled Cam in…a crash course that only took a minute. He told him what he had to say, and when he had to say it. Cam absorbed his instructions, hoping that he would get them right when the time came.

The room fell silent as Mr. Haws anointed Julie's head. After he finished, not a sound could be heard. Cam wondered if anyone was even breathing. He especially wondered if he were still breathing. Every eye in the room closed and each ear focused on the words that Cam was about to speak.

Whatever his level of fear had grown to, it subsided as Cam closed his eyes and silently prayed for the ability to perform his responsibility to the best of his ability. His mind fell silent, and the entire world seemed to blink out of existence. Everything disappeared but Julie and his own hands. He felt other hands touching his, but they barely had form or substance. It felt more like having his hands in warm, soothing water.

The first few lines of the blessing were learned, carefully administered word for word just as Bishop Tortelson had instructed. It went smoothly, as if he had been doing it for years.

In fact, the entire blessing went smoother than anyone in the room expected. Everyone understood the moments of silence. Cam was listening to the words that were being spoken to him. The words that came out of Cam's mouth seemed to be his own, yet not his at all. To Cam, it felt like he was being told what to say and when to say it.

When the chorus of "Amen's" followed his own, Cam was overcome with a strong sense of happiness. He had done it. He had trusted in the spirit and it had pulled him through. Deep down inside, he knew that each word he had spoken had been true, from the part of "many people love you" to the part of "getting better very soon." There was absolutely no doubt in his mind that Julie would get better. He had faith.

"That was perfect, Elder Bird." Bishop Tortelson extended his hand to Cam. "Very good."

Cam wasn't sure what to say. "Thank you," was all he could think of and all that he offered. It must have been sufficient because, after shaking Julie's parents hands and offering his sympathies and great hope, Bishop Tortelson left the room.

The hours passed slowly. It felt a little like those days leading up to the vacation that you have been planning for months. It's almost time, but the anticipation seems to bring your entire world into slow motion.

Emily, the nurse who hadn't been able to keep her comments to herself, was replaced by Jonathan. Right away, Cam noticed a very big, and a very impressive, difference in the quality of care.

Jonathan was not as professional in the fundamental nursing duties. He fumbled around for things; although he seemed just as sure about his abilities as Emily had been. He came in more often. His dress was more informal. His blue hospital shirt was unbuttoned a little, revealing the white shirt he had on underneath.

Despite his looks and laid-back attitude, Jonathan obviously had a gift for nursing. Cam was impressed with the way Jonathan was willing to speak to Mr. and Mrs. Haws. He was able to ease their worries, if only a little. More importantly, Jonathan really cared for Julie. It was his job to make her as comfortable as possible, and he took that job seriously. Cam understood that the only way he could do this, was if he genuinely cared. To Jonathan, Julie was just another patient, one of many that he was currently dealing with, but she was important to someone and he made sure he treated her that way.

At ten thirty that evening, Mr. and Mrs. Haws left the hospital. They had arranged for a hotel—despite Cam's insistence that they stay at his apartment or at Julie's house. They had already decided to stay at the hotel. Although they were a little reluctant to go, a promise from Cam to call if there was the slightest change, helped them feel comfortable. Julie was in good hands. Jonathan and Cam would take care of her, and the doctor had just left. Her situation was "the same", and there was no telling how long it would be before there would be any change.

With Julie's parents gone, the room suddenly felt quiet and lonely. Cam paced slowly between the foot of the bed, and the head. He stuck to one side for several minutes and then switched just to change the scenery a little.

He dimmed the lights and continued to walk as he prayed, sometimes silently, and sometimes out loud. He was so wrapped up in his own thoughts and prayers, that he failed to hear the monitors when they changed. He didn't miss the opening of the door, however, and when Jonathan rushed in, Cam instantly turned to Julie.

Her eyes were open. She was awake.

Or was she dead!

Cam almost fainted at the mere thought of her being dead. No! he screamed inwardly. She's not dead!

She wasn't dead. Her eye twitched. It was the first real sign of life Cam had seen in Julie for many hours.

She was trying to focus, her entire world was blurry and she felt sick. Each time she tried to make the picture in front of her clear, her stomach turned over. She knew where she was, but the idea of not being able to see, confused her dazed head that much more.

She also remembered what had happened. She remembered the beatings, the needles, and the strange feelings that the drugs had produced. She remembered hearing voices, calm and soothing; some male and some female. Most of all, however, she remembered hearing Cam's voice.

Cam was here now. She could sense his presence, and she assumed he was the moving object to her left. She only wished she could talk so that she could tell him to be still. It was hard enough to focus without having things around her moving. Besides, she had had enough of moving objects while she had been drugged. Right now she wanted stability.

Instead of stopping, Cam's movements grew almost frantic and out of control. She was also sure that someone else had joined him in the room. Another thought crossed her mind. Maybe the moving thing wasn't Cam. Maybe it was Marcus! Maybe she was dreaming and instead of being in the hospital she was in the woods still—drugged and waiting to be abused again.

The thought made her head hurt even worse, and she shut her eyes. The pain dissipated slightly, just enough to allow her to think more clearly. It wasn't possible. Well, it was possible, but unlikely. She had heard Cam's voice, and the voices of many others who loved her including her parents. No! She was safe and in the hospital.

She risked opening her eyes again, and this time the world seemed much clearer. A man was leaning over her. She couldn't see what he was doing, but when he touched her with something metal, she assumed he was a doctor.

Shortly after, two more people entered her room. She could now see clearly. Cam was standing beside her, arms folded and with a look of complete horror on his face. She wanted to tell him she was okay. She wanted to, but she couldn't speak. She was fairly sure the doctor wouldn't allow her to even if she could.

What felt like a million things were going on at the same time. Thermometers, oxygen masks, needles, and who knew what else probed, prodded, and pricked at Julie's body. Each sensation seemed to bring her back to reality just a little bit more.

Still, she tried hard to forget about what they were doing. It was unpleasant, and she had had enough unpleasant things happen to her over the last—the last—. She realized she had no idea what day, month, or even what year it was. It was possible that she had been gone for a very long time.

Her eyes caught something else now, and she focused on it. She knew what it was and what it said without reading it. It was something that she was going to treasure forever. It was a balloon. She read the words, although she knew what it said. *I Love You With All My Heart.*

Cam was smiling now, and Julie smiled back at him. Whatever he had been afraid of was fading. She was fine now, and feeling better with each passing moment. Then again, she knew she would be fine for a while—ever since she had heard her life-long partner giving her a priesthood blessing.

Chapter Twenty One

Julie left the hospital just over one week later. It took a long time for the side effects of the drugs to wear off. Just as Marcus had said, the tests revealed a mixture of cocaine and heroin. The combination would have killed most people. Julie knew she was lucky—in many ways. She had the Lord. She had her family, and she had Cam. This made the bumps, bruises, and cuts, which hurt for several weeks, livable.

On their wedding day, all of the struggles and the pain that they had overcome all seemed to fade into the far reaches of their minds. Both Cam and Julie were looking forward to a wonderful life together. There would be troubled times ahead, but they also knew that they could overcome them. They would have each other for time and all eternity, and that was all that really mattered.

The wedding ceremony had gone well. The Salt Lake Temple, the same one Cam had seen in the Bishop's office during his first interview, was incredible. The beauty and the peacefulness blended itself with the pure knowledge of what they were doing and made everything perfect. Now it was time to worry. Julie had prayed for a long time that everything would go as smoothly at the reception.

Cam watched from the middle of the church, seated in a hard, uncomfortable chair, as Julie scurried around like a cute raccoon—too busy for her own good. She had help, lots of it, and everything had already been set up. Just to be herself, however, Julie kept busy touching up here, fixing this, and rearranging that.

It was the break that Cam needed. Cam's present to Julie was going to take a few extra minutes to get all set up. It had taken a long time to arrange for the surprise, almost as long as it had to plan the entire wedding, but it would all be worth it. Just a few more minutes and he could reveal the present.

"Cam?"

Cam turned and looked at his wife. Her white dress was pinned up in the back and she hadn't put on her veil. She was by far the most stunning lady he had ever seen. Her hair flowed, her face glowed, and her entire body seemed to scream "Hey, I'm married!" As Cam looked at her, his happiness grew even more. He still wondered how he had ended up with someone so incredibly beautiful, but he wasn't going to complain.

"Cam?" Julie repeated and walked towards him. She stopped when Cam stood up. "I think we better get set up. People are going to show up soon."

"I need a minute—maybe five minutes."

"Why? Okay, hurry." Her heart rate rose even more.

Julie looked worried and Cam assured her that he wouldn't be long. It helped, but not enough to erase the lines in her face. "Just get everyone lined up and I'll be back in a minute," Cam said and turned towards the stage. Then he stopped, turned back to her, and caught her looking at him. He paused before saying anything just to show her that he had caught her, and then spoke.

"Okay, I have something for you, but I have to give it to you right now."

The lines in her face grew larger and much deeper. "We don't have time, Cam. I really want to know what the surprise is, but can we wait until nine. I promise I'll make it worth the wait."

"No! It has to be now," he said matter-of-factly.

Her head dropped and her face turned white. This, combined with her worry lines, only made her better-looking. "It has to be done right now. I'm sorry." He smiled, and for a moment, Julie wondered if he were doing this just to make her worry.

Cam scrambled to the stage and picked up the box. Hopefully everything was ready. Julie half followed but didn't say anything. She looked around every ten seconds just to make sure no guests were coming. When Cam turned around, she stopped and watched.

Cam approached her, but out of the corner of his eye he could see Mrs. Haws closing in on them as well. She beat him to Julie and waited for Cam to join them. "I just want you two to know that I'm very proud of you. What you have done today is right. I know I didn't exactly like the idea of you two dating at first, but I am very glad you didn't let me to get in your way."

"Thank you," Cam said and smiled. He reached out and took Julie's hand. "I've never blamed you for not trusting me Mrs. Haws. I just want you to know that I will spend the rest of my life making up for my past and ensuring your daughter's happiness and safety."

That was a bold statement after what had happened to Julie at the hands of Marcus, but he felt confident in saying it. Besides, Marcus was heading for prison. He was now being charged with attempted murder and a myriad of other charges after what he had done to Julie. He was also being charged for first degree murder. Under the circumstances, the police decided it would be prudent to check into Sandy's death. They found more than enough evidence to send Marcus to prison for a very long time.

"I know you two will be happy," Mrs. Haws said. "I can see it in you just like I could see it in my husband's face the day we got married…and the way I felt that day, too. People who are truly in love have a look about them, and you two definitely have it."

The words of confidence strengthened Cam. It felt good to have the approval of Julie's parents. He had worried for a long time that he would never have that.

"We better get set up," Mrs. Haws said. She turned around and walked away leaving Cam and Julie alone.

"Here," Cam said and held the box out to Julie.

She took it from him and held it in her arms. She began to tremble. Her hands shook and her knees threatened to fail her. But why? What was it? Why was she acting like this? The box was large enough that it could be almost anything. It was light, but this didn't register.

"Open it," Cam said. "We have to hurry up don't we?"

Julie looked for the tape on the sides but there wasn't any. She hesitated for a second and

270

then placed her hands on the sides. Cam quickly placed his hands under the box and held it as Julie lifted off the top.

She stood holding the top of the box in one hand as she stared into the box. There was white tissue, but nothing more. She looked up at Cam with glassy, dazed eyes. The box was big enough for an entire outfit, but it was empty. She didn't understand and she looked at Cam for help.

"If you could put anything you wanted in this box and could give it to yourself as the perfect wedding gift, what would you put in it?"

Julie was more puzzled than ever. Did she have to buy her own gift? Was there money inside, hidden in the tissue? She tried hard to come up with the answer that she knew he was looking for, but nothing came to her. "Nothing. I have you and that's all I need."

He began to probe. "Come on, Julie. You told me once what you really wanted on your wedding day. What would fit in that box that would give you the most pleasure."

Julie shook her head.

"What kind of box is it?" Cam hinted.

Julie looked at the box more carefully. It was white with small gold accenting lines making it look fancy and delicate. There was no writing on it. In fact, there was nothing to give her even the slightest clue. But she took a shot at answering the questioning.

"I guess it could be for a new winter coat. I definitely need one." She almost laughed at her own answer. Why would he have to give that to her now? Winter wasn't going to be for a while.

"A coat--?" Cam asked, "or maybe a dress?"

Of course! It was a dress box. It was almost exactly the same size of box that Tina's dress, her maid of honor, had come in. "A dress? You got me a dress? She was obviously still confused. "Did you leave it home so it wouldn't get wrinkled or what?"

Cam was surprised how well everything was going. She even said the very words he thought she would say. "No," he said and turned around. "It's in the bathroom down the hall. Do you want me to go get it or do you want to get it?"

He knew the answer to this question too. Julie wasn't going anywhere. She had to be here just in case someone came in, which is exactly why he had planned to wait until the last minute to reveal his secret.

"You get it," she said and once again looked at the entry door. No one was signing the guest book yet. She gave him a worried look, begging him to hurry.

"Get everyone lined up then stand in the middle of the floor facing the line. Don't turn around though. It's a surprise, and I really want you to get the full effect."

Julie agreed, but time was running short. Any other time this game might be fun, but not now. At least everyone would be set up just in case. If they had to, she and Cam could join the line before the guests made it that far.

Cam was gone for only a couple of minutes. In that time, Julie had arranged the line, with her mother's help, and was standing with her back to the door that her husband was about to enter. She wanted him to hurry, even silently begged him to hurry, but when she heard the door shut behind her, and the entire line grew instantly silent, she wished he had taken a little longer.

Was this whole thing staged? Was everyone in on this surprise? That was the only way it could have been so perfectly orchestrated. Everyone stopped talking at the same time. Every eye turned to her, which made her even more nervous. Why were they looking at her? Why weren't they looking at Cam?

A shocking realization rushed through her mind. She had absolutely no clue what was going on. That thought was unnerving. She didn't like the idea of being the only one in the room with no clue as to what was happening. It left so many possibilities. Whatever it was, it had all been set up by Cam and her mother. That was just something they would do. But why now? Was it even a dress he was giving her, or was this some sort of practical joke. Having fun was fine, but not at the expense of your wife. Not at her wedding reception anyway.

Still, she didn't turn around. She looked at the line in front of her, staring at everyone: her parents, the brides maids, Tina Orwell—her best friend and maid-of-honor, Mike Statton, the best man--, and their friends John and Andrea Call. She stared at each one trying to get some hint as to what was going on...and praying that one of them would just blurt out the truth.

She had to take his word for it. He did have a dress. She tried to picture what the dress would look like, but the image wouldn't form. It just didn't fit. None of this fit. Why would he give her a dress right now? She was already wearing a dress. She wasn't going to change that now. It wasn't possible.

This image was snatched from her mind, thankfully, by the line. Again, as if on cue—probably initiated by a signal from Cam—the entire line began walking towards her. She wanted to turn around. She couldn't take this anymore. She felt like screaming from the sheer torture.

But she did nothing.

If there was any doubt that this scenario had been rehearsed, it all faded when the entire line stopped at the same time, five feet in front of her. Tina continued moving and took her place directly in front of Julie.

"I have something to tell you," Tina said. "Sort of a good news—bad news kind of thing." Tina closed her eyes and for a moment, Julie figured she was holding back her tears. And why shouldn't she be crying? She was about to tell her best friend that behind her was her man dressed in drag. Julie couldn't exactly see the good news part of it. When Tina reopened her eyes, however, there were no tears, just pale blue color and an unmistakable happiness. "I can't be your maid-of-honor anymore. I ask that you demote me. I still want to be part of your line, but I want to be one of your brides-maids."

The pressure of what she had just been told caused many emotions to run through Julie's head. She was confused, sad, hurt, and afraid. She wasn't sure if this whole thing was supposed to make her feel good or bad. She simply didn't know what to do—or what to think.

Julie took a deep breath and spoke. As she did, she finally pictured Cam in a dress. It was shocking and almost caused her to forget what she was going to say. She just did get the words out. "I have no idea what's going on here. I don't think I like it, but if that's what you feel is the best thing to do, then fine. But I have to have a maid-of-honor. She looked through the line, wondering what to do. Why was she having to go through this right now. What did this all have to do with her surprise?

Tina stepped back and Julie heard Cam moving behind her. This time, Julie looked directly at her mother. Why are you letting this happen? She wanted to scream the question at her.

She wouldn't have had time. She caught a glimpse of white on her right and knew it was Cam. Figuring he would stop, just to add to her torment a little more, she took a deep breath. By the time she had let it out, however, Cam was in full view.

He was not holding a dress. Where was the dress? What was going on? She exhaled almost too fast and too loud. It sounded like a gasp. Her nerves were quite frazzled. Her sigh showed this to everyone. Again, she had to fight off the urge to turn around. She decided just to stare at her husband.

Cam took over the spot that Tina had just been in. He didn't hesitate before speaking. "Hon, I love you with all of my heart. I want to do everything I can in this lifetime to make you happy. And it is my pleasure to give you this as one of your wedding presents."

He extended his hand towards her, and for a moment she expected him to hand her something, but he didn't. His arm continued away from her his palm up in a, *look behind you,* way.

She turned slowly, feeling more confused than ever. When she saw her present, she stopped moving altogether.

It took her a moment to realize what she was looking at. By the time she did, Cam had moved in and slipped his hand around her waist. It felt good to Julie, but after seeing who was in front of her, she knew that he had done it just in case she wasn't able to stand on her own.

It was a dress. Exactly like the one her "former" brides-maid was wearing. Only it was on someone. It was her sister.

Tears fell from both Julie's eyes and the woman standing in front of her. Neither could control their emotions, and neither was expected to.

Cam let go of Julie, realizing that the surprise had the opposite effect that he had expected. She hadn't wobbled. She hadn't come close to fainting, which her mother had promised would happen. She had gained strength and now Cam understood why. She had just had a very heavy burden lifted from her shoulders. He couldn't pretend to know what kind of weight that was, but he hoped to find out soon enough.

"Becky?" Julie's words were almost inaudible through the tears. "Oh—how--.!" She had no idea what to say.

Becky stood completely still, tears flowing down her face. She was smiling, but that was all that her emotions would allow. Finally, Becky said the one thing that came to her mind. "Looking for a brides-maid?"

Julie cried harder. Her makeup was ruined and she no longer cared if the guests had began filing in or not. They would just have to wait.

Finally, Julie moved. She raised her arms, took three steps, and fell into her older sister's arms. It was a feeling that she would never have allowed herself to dream of. It would have hurt too much to think this could happen, but the happiness and pleasure she was feeling now was extraordinary.

The entire line backed up and gave the two sisters their space. Everyone in the room was overcome with what they were seeing and not one person said a word. Even Mrs. Haws had had been part of this plan, and had even had a chance to talk to Becky earlier, though briefly. Right now, she too just stood still and cried.

For what seemed like an eternity, Julie and Becky remained embraced together. As the time passed, however, Julie realized that they still had a wedding reception waiting. She reluctantly pulled away, and after staring at her sister, she smiled.

"Will you please be my bride's-maid?"

Becky smiled, pulled her sister close once again, and whispered to Julie. "I always said I'd never miss this. I came close, but I would be so honored to stand next to you right now."

When Julie finally turned around, she stared at the friends and family surrounding her. Most of them were crying—especially her mother (Julie knew that her mother had something to do with this, or at least had known it was coming. Otherwise, she would be a frantic mess right now).

What more could she ask for? Julie thought. What better group of people could she ever hope to know? "Thank you—everyone." She continued to look around and then stopped when her eyes met Cam's. "You will never know what this means to me," she said.

She was right. He didn't know exactly what this meant to her, but more than anything at that moment, he was glad he had been able to find Becky. It had taken a very long time, and a lot of telephone calls. Becky had been reluctant for awhile, but she finally spoke to him. It didn't matter what it took, however. He was just glad he had been able to do this for her.

Cam hugged Julie, and it felt absolutely perfect. "I look forward to doing a lot more for you over the next...forever. I love you!"

Through her tears, Julie responded. "I love you."

Hand in hand, Julie, Cam, and Becky joined the line. Julie found it difficult to concentrate. She no longer had a burning desire to make everything perfect. Cam had already taken care of that. All she had to do now was look forward to a wonderful life.

Don't miss the exciting sequel!

With new hopes and dreams, Cam and Julie begin their lives as a happily married couple. They look forward to starting a family, and they pray that they will be able to forget the horrible things which have plagued them in the past. They intend to build a strong relationship based on love and on Gospel principles, which will enable them to overcome the problems that will surely come.

Unfortunately, the obstacles bombard them sooner than they had expected. Julie's dream of becoming reacquainted with her sister is threatened, an old enemy plots revenge, and then the unspeakable happens:

"No!" Julie screamed. "It's not going to be all right. It's never going to be all right. Never!"

About the Author

In addition to writing, Alan J. Brown works in the accounts receivable division of a local business. He is also a delivery driver for this company. He enjoys camping, hunting, fishing, basketball, golf, and reading.

His goals in life include; becoming the best family man possible, being a successful full-time author, traveling, and helping the church missionary program.

Alan lives in Pleasant Grove with his wife, Bonnie, and his son, Josh.